WHO
a novel of the near future

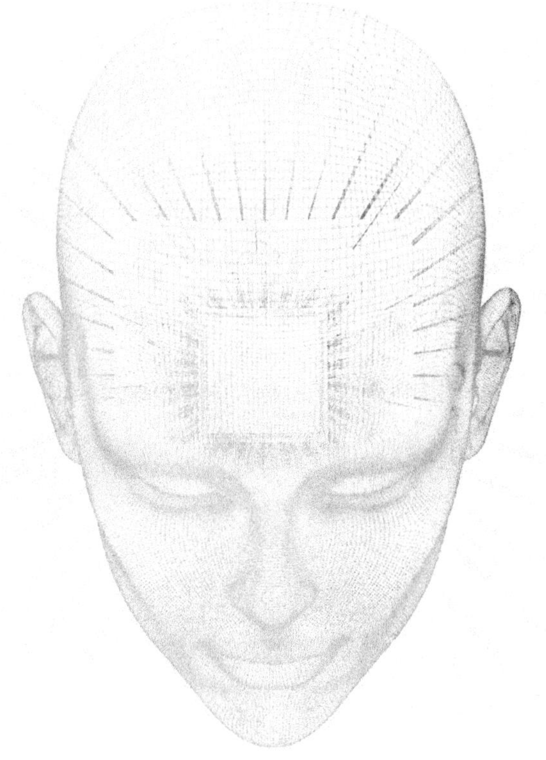

Karen A. Wyle

ISBN 978-0-9905641-9-5
Published in the United States of America
Oblique Angles Press

Cover design by David Leek and Karen A. Wyle

Author photo by Alissa Lise Wyle

Dedication

To all of us
who have not yet allowed ourselves
to despair.

Prologue

THE ULTIMATE sweepstakes, or an elaborate prank? A monumental research project, or a diabolical temptation, or both at once? Opinions differed greatly; but millions of people were willing, for whatever combination of reasons, to take part.

After all, one need only choke down an unpleasant quantity of colorless viscous liquid, and then submit to a series of scans (if indeed any scanning took place) over an eight hour period, in order to receive one's initial payment. The sum, always in the local currency, would more than cover a dinner and a show, or a bowl of hashish, or a prostitute. And supposedly the nanoparticles (if there were any) would exit the body within a day or two.

Those who believed, or did not entirely discount, the asserted goals of the research would then enter their contact information in the growing database. If they wished, they could return for new scanning sessions once a month, to keep the recorded information current, and receive another (smaller) payment each time.

After that, it was just a matter of which lucky participants would die first.

The first few to be successfully revived in virtual form would achieve both historical and digital immortality, while their conventionally surviving families would become wealthy overnight—wealthy enough to join their pioneering loved ones, whenever their own time came. For of course, once testing was complete, those who sought digital revival after death would be paying, not paid.

CHAPTER 1

THE AD agency had little in common with the hierarchical organizations of past centuries. Team members were expected to attend meetings of this importance in person rather than by projection, but inducements in the form of sandwiches and pastry littered the room, along with those mind-altering substances likely to boost creativity rather than suppress it. The sofas and chairs appeared casual, but provided more lumbar support than the hand-me-downs they resembled; and for those who disliked actually sitting, stationary bicycles with well-oiled mechanisms, as well as a few ball chairs, provided an alternative. Most wore wristbands with the latest holoscreen tech, supplied by a client with the proviso that they be used as publicly and conspicuously as possible. A few, too set in their ways to use the latest tech or too busy to transfer old files, carried tablets instead.

Their oldest member, who had allowed her hair to become a free-form tapestry of copper and silver, stood up to attract the group's attention. "Thanks for coming in, everyone! Let's get started."

The young man reclining on the love seat stretched and yawned. "Whose baby is this?"

"Partly mine. LiveAfter figured I might understand their customers' perspective a bit better than you babes in arms." She stopped to allow a chorus of raspberries to subside. "But we also needed someone younger, a lot younger, to make the LiveAfter tech folks feel comfortable." She waved toward a tall thin girl in colorfully and erratically patched denim overalls, balancing on a ball chair. "I'll let her tell you about the curve they threw at us last week."

The girl stood up. "Okay! Some of you know what we first proposed. We focused on the virtual environments available to the digitally stored customer. We were going to sell wish fulfillment: the customer could go places and perform feats they'd never have managed during their lifetime. We had a series ready to go, from the athletic to the physically adventurous to the erotic, depending on where the spots would run." She tapped her wristband in the appropriate places to display a large three-dimensional holo facing in five directions. "Maybe these were a waste of work, but we might be able to use them later."

This first series of images showed Alpine skiers, hang gliders riding the thermals over an erupting volcano, and astronauts floating; then came indoor images, lit with a golden glow, with beckoning dancers in diaphanous costumes and naked men and women intertwined. The girl froze and dimmed the final image and went on.

"Last week, we *finally* got a straightforward update about the technical progress on, or rather, the technical problems plaguing, the environmental features. Turns out that early adopters — any customers stored within the next few years or longer -- aren't going to have a whole lot in the way of entertainment options. No wilderness adventures, no space travel, no species transformations, only basic erotica . . . . So we've had to change direction."

Next on the holoscreens, a split image, sketches rather than the hyper-realistic images already shown: an archetypal grandmother holding an oversized old-fashioned picture book on the right and a cluster of adorable little tykes on the left. "Since we don't know when the client can actually provide the more escapist and fantasy elements of the customer's virtual experience, we've switched to emphasizing the customer's interaction with loved ones left behind. That interface is pretty much ready to go. . . . Half a sec."

She slipped the small speaker button off her earlobe and placed it in on a nearby table, then started the video, with a succession of sketches fitted to the audio. Almost immediately she paused it to say, "These aren't the final actors. We used local talent for the voices." She restarted the video, the audio track fading in on a warm and elderly voice in the middle of reading a classic tale, the sketches moving from the reader to the page to the rapt audience. Every so often, one or more of the children interjected some exclamation or excited noise. The reader finished and closed the book; the accompanying sketch captured remarkably well the woman's look of fondness and satisfaction, suggestive of barely-restrained sentimental tears.

The next sketch showed the same woman facing the camera. "I'm so glad I can read to my grandchildren again. And I'll be able to watch them grow. What a wonderful gift!"

The final sketch showed a younger couple, presumably parents, with two of the children. The accompanying audio exchange started with a young voice: "I missed Grandma so much! But now she can read to us, and we can tell her about school and everything."

A slightly older voice chimed in. "What about Christmas? Can she be there when we open our presents? Can she, pleeease?"

The response came from the mother. "Of course she can. It wouldn't be Christmas without Grandma, would it?"

The girl paused and looked around. "Who's DA on this one?" The abbreviation had originally come from the old Catholic custom of having a Devil's Advocate argue the case against beatifying a potential saint; in company parlance, it stood for Designated Asshole.

A man as round as the girl was thin raised his hand. "First comment: 'Grandma'? I'd say great-grandmother at least."

The girl shrugged. "People still have at least a subconscious idea that grandmothers should be gray-haired and round-shouldered, not to mention padded enough for cozy hugs. And let's not forget the potential customers. *Their* grandparents may have looked like that."

The DA cocked his head. "That doesn't mean the customers want to think of themselves that way. But go on."

The girl turned off the screens. "That's just the first spot, but the rest have the same throwback quality our DA flagged. We've got father-daughter talks about boyfriends, and a mom admiring the daughter's prom dress, and parents coaching their teenagers for job interviews. And for the late night audience, we could have some intimate talk between spouses or other partners. The actors for those will be somewhat younger." She glanced once again at her notes. "Well, that's the idea." She stretched out a long arm for an oversized chocolate cupcake, then sat down on a rug with her legs stretched out in front of her.

The DA turned to the man who would have probably become a lawyer if the obstacles were less annoying and expensive. "What jumps out at you, if anything?"

The law buff stroked the stubble on his chin. "The more we emphasize interaction with the living, the more it matters that these uploaded versions of people—"

The tall girl interrupted. "LiveAfter calls them permanents—in public, anyway. At least, that's what they're calling them this week. And they haven't bothered to consult us about it."

The law buff rolled his eyes and continued. "—that these digital facsimiles are functionally indistinguishable from the deceased originals." He looked across the room toward their main IT guru. "Have the client's tech people been keeping you in the loop?"

The young woman beamed back at him. "It's fascinating! There's a very consistent relationship between the neural patterns recorded in the subject's lifetime and the digital signature. And the underlying science is full of lovely mind-twisting equations."

A chuckle ran through the group. The DA waved it down. "I'm not through grilling our legal expert here! What, if any, laws and regs might trip us up?"

The law buff started counting on his fingers. "There's the possibility of fraud liability. That's where I was going with my earlier question. We can't tell people they'll get their relatives back, and to keep, if we can't support the claim. Next: the child welfare folks could start imagining the nightmares kids might have about Zombie Grandma."

The DA held out a palm toward him and looked around the room. "Anyone have a good response to concerns about scared kids?"

"Maybe," said the tall girl. "We could have a spot early on where a child asks the grandmother, 'Is it really you?' The grandma could respond along the lines of: 'Of course, dear. I'm here, just like I was when you climbed up the steps of the school bus on your first day of kindergarten, and I waved goodbye; and like I was when the bus brought you home again.' That should have the audience, especially parents, tearing up and feeling mellow."

One of the visual artists held up her knitting, a fuzzy pile of light orange and cyan. "We could use warm tones and light pastels in the spot—as far from zombie colors as you can get. And for the viewers with odor capacity, fresh air and cookie smells for Grandma, and new-cut grass in sunshine for Dad. That sort of thing."

The DA looked back at the law buff. "Anything else?"

"Depends. I need more details. Such as, what else are we encouraging these stored, mmm, 'people' —" He inserted air quotes; the tall girl stuck out her tongue at him, and he laughed, then continued. "What else will the ads encourage them to do?"

The tall girl looked toward the older woman, who glanced at her tablet before responding. "As we've already said, the theme is continued involvement in the lives of the living. So they could be giving advice, in all sorts of areas, and sharing helpful hints."

A copy editor with tangled and unwashed hair let out a snort. "*That'*ll go over well with the relatives. If the client needs cooperation from relatives, you might want to stay away from that notion."

"Good point." The DA gave him a thumbs-up.

The older woman nodded. "The customers don't

need to be always focusing on the past. They should be able to attend lectures and other events, in universities and in the community — any that have the setup for long-distance participation. 'You never need to stop learning' is one of the angles we're working up."

The copy editor smirked. "Maybe they could tune into political rallies and ask tough questions." Several people chuckled again. But a quiet older man sitting off by himself, whose role in long-range planning was not widely publicized, looked thoughtful and, pulling his tablet toward him, started tapping away.

* * * * *

The session started as work, the best kind of work.

Max and Thea had started composing the piece by themselves, as they usually did. Most of the time, they needed no one else, from start to finish, even if they were producing the final tracks instead of handing their composition over for others to record. But this client wanted Max and Thea to record with all live instruments, nothing synthesized, and not just Thea's flute and Max's guitar.

Time to bring in friends!

They could have just asked their friends to play parts handed to them, but as Thea put it, "Let's get their ideas, not just their skills. And it'll give us a chance to spread some credit and cash around if it all comes together well."

So Max mixed the punch, with just a splash of vodka, while Thea rolled joints from her own blend of leaves; and by midafternoon, their small back deck was crowded with musicians playing lute, hammered dulcimer, hornpipe, bassoon, and the Welsh violin-like instrument called a crwth.

They started by showing everyone what they had written so far, and declaring the jam session open. Every once in a while, Thea or (less often) Max would ask everyone to stop while one or another of them repeated what they had just played. After this happened a few times, Max suggested that they go around the circle once with everyone playing solo. Then they all plunged back into a mad medley, finally coming to a chaotic crescendo, with several musicians helpless with laughter.

As everyone caught their breath, Thea, her white-blond hair backlit and tinted gold by the setting sun, picked up a stack of menus from nearby restaurants and waved them in the air. "Takeout time! Our treat."

The zany creativity of the session carried over to the choice of food. The bench around the deck soon held zucchini pizza, grilled cheese sandwiches stuffed with macaroni and cheese, almond-stuffed dates, spicy Thai noodles, and foot-long veggie dogs.

Then people picked up their instruments again, playing folk songs, jazz riffs, classical adagios; joining each other or kicking back to listen; eagerly intent or relaxing with eyes closed, breathing in the salty tang of the breeze from the sea.

As the stars came out, the collaborators started drifting away, one couple leaving together who had each come alone. As Thea closed the front door on the last of them, Max collapsed on the couch, beaming. "That was great! I'm sure we've got good stuff to work with. And it was great even if we didn't. But we did."

Thea, still energized, bounced around the apartment picking up trash. She swooped down on her way by the couch and kissed Max on the forehead. "It was, and we did." She flitted out to the deck, where she had left her flute, and brought it inside, closing the door. Then she perched on the back of the couch and started playing, then varying, a theme their clarinet-playing friend had come up with.

Max managed to stretch enough to reach his guitar, then hauled himself to sitting position so he could play along, improvising a counterpoint. They played together, moving through different ideas their friends had contributed, until Max stopped, laughed, and collapsed back down on the couch. "No more! I'm beat."

Thea put down her flute and reached down to stroke his hair. Then she headed to the fridge and hauled out a few cartons, assembling a late leftover supper for them both.

Then they headed to bed, Thea leading Max but both half asleep, and made drowsy love before letting the day end.

Another day, another project. And this one, if they could land it, could lead to more. They'd never pitched to this large an ad agency.

It was Thea's turn to work on their proposal, so Max was sketching. Thea's voice roused Max from something of a trance. "Max! Come listen to this and tell me what you think."

Max closed his sketchbook. The motion stirred a short black hair on the cover. Not quite the first hair he'd lost lately. His father had been mostly bald by forty, and Max would be thirty in a year or so. Thea wouldn't care, so neither did he.

Thea craned toward the sketchbook with her "there's a treat coming!" smile. "My birthday tattoo? When do I get to see it?"

Max hugged the sketchbook, hunching over as if hoarding it, earning a laugh from Thea before tossing the sketchbook on the couch. "Not for a while. I'm still playing around with ideas I'm not ready to show. But you have something to show me?"

Thea beckoned, and Max followed her into their cramped recording and production studio. Thea sat at her console and hit Play. Flute music, two intertwined tracks, flowed forth, instantly setting a nostalgic mood. Despite the room's lack of windows and stuffy atmosphere, Max found himself imagining autumn leaves fluttering down in the breeze, the distant calls of children at play, and the smell of apples from tree branches hanging overhead. He stood rapt until the passage ended, then swooped down to hug Thea where she sat. "It's wonderful! We're a shoo-in for that grandmother spot. The others shouldn't even bother to send in their bids. . . . But I don't know what you've left for me to add."

"It could use a bass line, quiet but supporting the flutes. And celesta, after the first twenty measures or so. . . . But what do you think of the flute lines?"

Max frowned in thought. "They were lovely, but they didn't sound like your playing. Where'd you find the musician? Or did you sample your way there? It sounded too fluid for sampling."

Thea's face lit up with mirth, even without smiling. "Before I answer that, let me play you something else by the same flutist." She hit a button, and the strains of a Shaker hymn filled the little room. She let Max listen for a moment, then shut it off again. "Good choice, no?"

Max cocked his head. "You'd have done just as well playing it yourself."

Thea's expression transformed in a moment from

mischievous to stern. "Don't try to snow me. Or to kid yourself. That was the three-time first place winner of the Kobe International Flute Competition."

Max lifted his chin and folded his arms in ostentatious defiance. "You could have done damn well in one of those competitions, if you'd cared to enter. But—wait a minute. Didn't the guy get some sort of weird infection and die in about a week, last year? If you can sample that well, we should talk about a whole new business model."

"I wish. No, I didn't use sampling. Guess again— and remember what the campaign is all about."

Max looked at Thea, smiling now, bouncing her knees up and down as if too tickled to sit still. The campaign. Digitally stored personality and memory. Immortality in circuitry. He felt his eyes go wide. "No way."

"The man himself! One of LiveAfter's first customers, or test subjects, or whatever. I didn't even realize it until the ad agency sent out a revised RFP that asked bidders to include flute music." Thea's smile dimmed a bit. "I suppose he probably recorded for all the bidders, not just us."

Max swooped down and picked Thea up out of her chair, then twirled around in a waltzing motion, holding her to his chest and humming the lyric line from her composition. But he couldn't carry her for long: they were almost of a height, and he was the skinny one. He plopped her back down in the chair, panting just a little. "They'll hear your piece and not even bother with the others. And I wouldn't be surprised if the flutist flat-out refused to play any of the other submissions once he'd had a chance to play yours."

Thea threw back her head and laughed, curls

bouncing, her arms and legs relaxed and flopping over the edges of the chair. Then Max saw a new thought run through her like a wave, tensing her muscles, wrinkling her forehead. "I hope he could refuse to do something and make that refusal stick. The people in charge have a lot of power over anyone they've stored. I wonder if they abide by any limits on how they use it."

Max headed back over and started massaging her shoulders, relishing how quickly she relaxed again. "Borrowing trouble, aren't you?"

Thea looked stubborn for a moment, then smiled up at him. You're right. Again. . . . If you're ready, you could start on the bass line. I can't wait to hear it."

* * * * *

A memo from Sales had circulated among LiveAfter's technical employees, reminding them of their employee discount and hinting vaguely that the amount of that discount would diminish over time. A few juicy rumors soon started circulating as well, muttered from one cubicle to another, or over vending machine sandwiches in the break room.

"Did you hear about that guy who got stored and ended up as a girl? And that wasn't his thing, at all!"

"No, the way I heard it was, someone who identified as female got reverted to her genetic starting point as male, and the company wouldn't fix it."

"Yes, they did! But only after the family threatened to sue."

"I don't know about that. But when they first started testing, some lady ended up speaking French instead of English. And playing the piano!"

"Are you sure she didn't *ask* to be able to play piano, or speak more languages?"

"Can they *do* that?"

"Who knows what they can do?"

* * * * *

Max squeezed orange juice for Thea while Thea spread apple butter on Max's toast, then poured a heaping mixture of three cereals into a bowl for herself. Thea opened the sliding door to let the morning breeze into the kitchen, and they sat down to eat.

"I'm still kind of blown away that we got that contract," mumbled Max around a mouthful of toast.

Thea blew Max a kiss across the breakfast table. Her shoulder twitched, a familiar tic that always reminded him of a horse (a young, graceful filly) trying to shake off a fly. "They had good taste. It happens!" She paused for a spoonful of cereal. "It's been happening more lately. Pretty sweet."

Max grinned, then could not maintain the expression as an unwelcome thought struck him. "I'm glad we're dealing with the ad agency and not LiveAfter itself. That outfit makes me a little nervous."

Thea looked at him with sudden intensity. What was behind it? "Hon? What gives?"

"The storage company, LiveAfter. We shouldn't have to think about this for a long time yet—but would you ever contemplate signing up with them? Or are you dead set against it?" She stopped short, then chuckled. "Dead set. That's an appropriate turn of phrase."

"Whoa. You'd want to turn into some sort of computer program?"

"Whoa, yourself." Thea got up and headed for the

coffee pot. She had already had two cups. She almost never drank three. Max got up as well and caught up with her, resting his hands on her shoulders, pulling her gently back against his chest. She let him, but her body did not melt back into his as he had hoped. "Think about that flutist for a moment. He'd be dead, and he's alive! Alive and playing music! Does it matter so much how he's doing it?" She turned her head to look at him. "Would it matter so much to you, if it were me?"

Max massaged her shoulders, and sighed in relief when she began to relax; she heard it, or felt it, and turned to face him, putting her hands on his upper arms. She looked as serious as he had ever seen her. "Max, lover, I would want to keep *you*, any way I could. It would be terrible not to be able to touch you." She squeezed his arms. "Not to be able to kiss you." She kissed him, a soft swift kiss, then stepped back again. "But it would be worse, much worse, to lose you completely. If something happens, if you go first, do I really have to let you go?"

"Wow. I need to think about that. Which means *I* need more coffee." He pivoted the pair of them so that he was nearer the coffee pot, then reached for a mug resting on the dish drainer and poured a full cup, taking a moment to relish its aroma. Thea stretched with him to allow his movements, then led the way back to the table. She sat down first and pulled him toward her lap. He chuckled and settled down carefully, so as neither to pinch her anywhere nor spill coffee on her.

He sipped the coffee, resisting the urge to gulp it down. "I guess you've been thinking about this a lot."

Thea nodded, even that slight movement sloshing the coffee in his mug. He took a bigger sip to lower the level of the liquid.

"Which means you've been reading all sorts of technical updates. So maybe you can tell me. Just what is there for these stored people to do all day? Do they even have days and nights? Do they sleep? Do they dream? Do they feel like they're moving around? How do they feel things, have emotions, without all the chemicals slopping around in us when we feel?"

Thea had been counting his questions on her fingers. She lowered one finger at a time as she answered him. "The techies know how the chemicals work, and they've synthesized the effects and made it part of the programming."

"Programming. There's a word I just love to hear applied to how I might be living someday."

"Programming is still one of the more useful metaphors for how our brains and even our bodies work. Where was I?"

Max tried to remember. "I guess you're working backwards, so next is whether they feel like they're moving a body around."

Thea shrugged, her shoulder jostling his hand, but fortunately not the one holding the coffee. "No one's published a first-person account. But we both know the people can do things. Those flute tracks, they were genuine. What's next? Dreams. I did see an article about that. They didn't dare leave dreams out, with all the evidence that people go crazy if they can't dream for too long. But it turned out they didn't have to do anything special. Digitally recreate a human brain, and it dreams."

Max had another chilling thought. There seemed to be a steady supply of them, the longer he dwelt on this subject. "And those dreams are happening on someone's computer or server or whatever, so they can be recorded."

Thea patted his coffee-free hand indulgently. "Computer or server or whatever. I shouldn't find that cute, I suppose. . . . Anyway. I read something about how you can pay more for a privacy contract that puts you in charge of what gets saved and what gets wiped."

"If you trust them to honor it."

Thea bit her lip. "That's what it comes down to, doesn't it? You have to trust them; or at least, you have to decide that staying alive is worth the risk of what they might do."

She looked as if she might cry if they kept talking. To hell with the rest of the questions. It wouldn't matter for years, and the answers would mostly be different by then anyhow. "I propose a change of subject." He put down the coffee mug, brushed her hair aside, and laid his lips on her neck, humming in the way that could almost always get her going. Her face lit up at once, and she arched her back, thrusting her neck toward him. Then, when he paused to take a breath, she grabbed his waist, thrust him off her lap, stood up, and towed him toward the bedroom.

CHAPTER 2

THE AD agency didn't throw a party every time a campaign launched, but when they did, they had plenty of local connections to help stretch their budget. Even the introverts showed up for the lavish spread; and the workaholics trickled in before even half of it had been consumed.

Once the party hit its likely peak attendance, the senior member of the team gave a dramatic recital of all the team had endured in reaching this day of celebration: the obstacles overcome, the regulatory red tape, the client's inconsistencies and resistance to serving its own interests. Those who had drifted away on their private thoughts, or had resumed contemplating work left undone, pulled their attention back to her when she raised her voice to herald an announcement.

"Just as this has been a groundbreaking campaign, it comes with groundbreaking benefits for those who made it happen—in fact, for everyone in the agency. The client is offering accounts at substantially reduced cost. Sign up before they change their minds! Then you can make appointments for the various baseline readings and examinations at your leisure."

A buzz of conversation arose. Anyone looking around the room would have seen a wide range of expressions: confusion, among those who had not taken part in the campaign and were hazy about its details; from those better informed, emotions from excitement to nervousness to pensive absorption; and from the busier and more cynical, amusement about the supposed availability of leisure.

By the time the last to leave pitched in to clean up the mess, all the bottles and platters were empty, and the livelier folks had moved on to a favorite local dive. The tall girl who had shaped the campaign and the round gentleman who had served as DA had neither stayed to clean nor followed the crowd, and were instead tangled in the sheets of a nearby motel.

Among the first societal sectors to grapple with the new storage technology: hospitals and lawyers. Not to mention hospital lawyers.

Hospital administrators and legal departments worried at first that patients they were unable to save would carry the grudge into their digital "lives," and be more likely to sue for malpractice as a result. It would take time for the data to show whether that was happening. Something else happened first. Grieving families started suing because no one had offered their loved ones the option to be digitized.

The hospitals settled the cases they could and, when they couldn't, prepared for the long haul through the courts. Ethicists struggled over issues of informed consent. Was such consent necessary before an ailing patient could sign the contract? Or was it necessary before the patient's medical decline? And who should inform patients of the possibility, and at what stage of treatment, and in what terms?

Financial planners and probate lawyers were inundated with requests for wills, trusts, and savings plans that would ensure the availability of funds for the process. The lawyers prepared for the inevitable disputes between executors and the deceased parties whose estates they were supposed to be administering.

Religious leaders tended to disapprove. The intensity of that disapproval, and the willingness to take direct action against those who recommended or provided digitization, varied considerably. The adherents of "singularity" ideas, on the other hand, were enthusiastic boosters of the new technology. A few sects, such as the Unitarians, left the matter to the conscience of the individual congregant. An entirely new religion, invented, publicized, and monetized by a software engineer with indirect ties to the technology's proprietors, posited that the digital state constituted a modern purgatory, essential for eventual salvation.

The funeral industry dithered: should they oppose the technology as making funerals less important? Should they attempt to co-opt it, restructuring services to include the participation of the deceased, providing weather-resistant interaction stations beside the grave?

And then there were the political implications. These did not immediately become apparent.

* * * * *

"Did you take your sun pill? I hate it when you get burned and I can't touch you for days." Thea bustled about, packing up her kits for the sand art competition and the surfing afterward. Max watched her with amusement and some admiration. She could not exactly be called efficient in her movements, but her energy and speed got the job done in record time. And she had energy to spare.

"Is it OK with you if I under-dose a bit? I'd like to get a bit darker. Give the ladies that smoldering-Italian thrill."

Thea blew him a kiss and tossed him a beach towel. "It's your sweet body, love. Smolder away— metaphorically speaking. Where's my mix tape?"

"The chip's on our dresser next to your lucky sand dollar." Max swallowed a lump in his throat. That his artist lover allowed him to choose her inspiration music for every competition, and even to surprise her with it when they got to the beach, never ceased to move and amaze him.

"Race you to the van!" While he'd been woolgathering, Thea had bundled everything together except the surfboard waiting in the garage. She slipped by him, her lithe figure disappearing through the doorway and her hoot of laughter ringing in the hall. He dashed after her, bumping the doorway and rattling the door in his haste.

Of course she got there first. She almost always did. He didn't mind.

They were early enough that Max was able to get a spot looking down at Thea's assigned area, with enough room for the surfboard and all Thea's gear, and high enough up that he could also turn and watch the waves. Thea ran off to find out the competition's theme; Max sat cross-legged on the blanket, his head back to let the sun warm his face, the view behind his closed eyes a deep red-orange. The waves rumbled and hissed, breaking and receding, and the breeze brought him the smell of salt and sun-heated sand, and the squawking cries of the gulls.

Soon he heard Thea's footsteps pattering closer. He

opened his eyes and looked up at her, beaming, the sun behind her lighting her hair in a halo. "It's perfect! The theme today, it's dragons! Like the tattoo you designed for me last year! This is going to be *my* day!"

Max worked to control his expression. It always made him nervous when people, even Thea, said things like that. But while she would be indulgent about his superstitious pangs, she was far too logical to feel the same, and he had no desire to distract her or dampen her glow. He focused on her shining eyes and was able to smile back at her. "It's your kind of day, baby. Now go make it yours."

She dropped down on the blanket beside him, threw her arms around him in a quick firm hug, kissed his cheek hard enough to almost knock him over, then sprang back up again and ran to start her sculpture. Max watched her, relishing the pumping of her legs and buttocks. . . . His pill! He hadn't taken it yet. He scrambled in his bag for the bottle and dry-swallowed the capsule. No way did he want to be too sore for them to tumble and grapple and roll when he finally got her to bed tonight.

He glanced at the waves again, tumbling and rolling into shore, and took a few deep breaths before he turned to watch Thea haul buckets full of damp sand up the beach to her site.

* * * * *

Thea paused to dribble more water on her growing sculpture, then stood, stretched, and looked up the hill to where Max was sitting. He saw her movement and waved, then wiped his hand dramatically across his forehead. She laughed. Okay, it was hot out! She grabbed her water bucket, stepped away from the sculpture, and dumped the water over her head, then grinned up at Max as she shook the water out of her hair. She couldn't be sure of his expression from that distance, but she thought he looked wistful at the thought of cooling down. She pointed to the ocean, then back to him, then to the ocean again; but he shook his head. He would stay and watch and root for her until she was done.

* * * * *

"First place! First place! YES!!!" Thea jumped up and down, waving her arms, looking incongruously like a cheerleader, while Max whistled and clapped. He took yet another picture of Thea's completed sculpture: twin dragonets hatching out of the same egg and looking toward each other, the mother's intricately patterned tail a barricade curled around them. Meanwhile, Thea, not content with the actual trophy, quickly sculpted a sand replica next to the trophy itself. Max photographed that as well, then grabbed Thea and hoisted her into the air, squeezing her tight before setting her down again. She grinned ear to ear, then grabbed him as soon as her feet touched the sand and hoisted him in turn. She carried him a few steps up the hill before dropping him and running ahead to her board. All those hours of concentration, with only a quick pause for a sandwich, and she still had energy to spare.

He caught up with her as she lifted it onto her head; she put it down again to grab his hand and pull him close for a kiss, then asked, "Do you want to ride with me for a bit? I'll take it easy."

"Naah, I'll just body-surf with the other land creatures. You go out and rule the waves."

* * * * *

Thea rode the crest of the wave—a beautiful big wave—almost all the way to shore, then jumped off and grabbed the board to head out again, letting the receding water take her along. She lay on the board and paddled out farther, to give herself an even longer ride next time. The sun beat down, but the water was cool, the breeze cooler. All the temperatures and sensations and sounds and smells blended together in a perfect cocktail of sensation. If she could bottle this day, she'd douse herself with it over and over.

Had the digital storage company made any progress lately with its environmental simulations? And should she respond to the RFP for software contractors to join that effort? Working on music so much had been terrific, and it was something she could share with Max, but her computing skills needed some exercise as well.

Time to pay attention! After a few waves not worth bothering about, here came a good one—not monstrous, but worth the trip. She scrambled up on her board—

For a moment, she thought her board had somehow struck her in the head, but she could still feel it beneath her feet. Had another surfer ridden into her? But along with the piercing pain in her head came a horrible nausea, worse than the flu, worse than the time she and Max had eaten that chowder . . . .

Something terrible was happening.

* * * * *

Max scanned the waves, looking for Thea—paddling out, waiting for a wave, riding it in—and couldn't find her. Just how far out had she gone?

Then he saw her board. Just her board, gliding on in as if it had decided it could do without its rider.

He raced down to the water, tripping and stumbling on sand, shouting her name, whipping his head left and right.

And then he saw something tumbling and bobbing and, finally, bumping onto the wet sand.

Thea, crumpled in a ball, gasping and moaning.

Max dropped to his knees and put his arms under her shoulders and knees. He had to get her out of the surf before she breathed in any—any more?—water, but what if moving her did more damage than whatever had already happened?

To his unutterable relief, he saw lifeguards converging on them, two with a stretcher, one with a standard medical kit, and another holding some less familiar device., They slid Thea onto the stretcher with smooth swift motions while one gabbled something into the phone on his wrist. Then the man holding the strange device fastened it somehow to the top of Thea's skull.

An ambulance came rumbling along the beach, people in swimsuits scrambling out of the way. The guards handed Thea over to the EMTs and practically threw Max in after her, and they screamed away down the beach.

" . . . an aneurysm. I don't see any indication of external injury, no impact with a surf board or anything of that kind."

Max had been sitting in the waiting room long enough to imagine an entire lifetime without Thea, day by day, year by year, his birthday, her birthday, making music alone, turning to share with her and finding no one there. . . . When he could bear no more, he relapsed into memories of their life together: high school, the final blissful release from high school, college apart, his quitting college, his joining her, college together, quitting together, finding the first miserable apartment, finding the next apartment, setting up the studio, getting a client, losing the client, getting more clients, panic that Thea might be pregnant, excitement that Thea might be pregnant, blank deflation when Thea wasn't pregnant . . . passing a wedding chapel and abruptly running in to get married, then making it up to their friends—if not so successfully to their families—with a truly epic reception party . . . Thea and her computers, music and more music, the succession of birthday tattoos . . . Would he ever be able to give her the next tattoo?

And finally, the weary middle-aged doctor had come to talk to him, sitting in the faded orange chair beside his own, and he was too stunned and exhausted to ask the right questions.

"How bad is an aneurysm?"

She had that almost-neutral sober expression they must practice in medical school. "Most of them are bad. Some of them are worse. This is one of the very bad ones."

Max stared at her, dimly aware that he had forgotten how to breathe. He managed to gasp in some air. "I don't know what to ask. Tell me what you'd answer if I asked the right questions."

Maybe she did. But he couldn't concentrate. A few words got through: surgery . . . poor prognosis . . . odds against survival . . .

His face felt frozen. And he had stopped breathing again.

Had Thea stopped breathing? Was that why he

couldn't seem to breathe?

"Are you saying she's going to die?"

"I'm afraid that outcome is likely."

Max started to his feet and walked away from the words, toward the window, or the door, or anywhere except next to this doctor who was saying something utterly unacceptable. But as he moved away, he thought he caught another word, a hideously incongruous one: " . . . lucky . . ."

He must have misheard. He would assume he had misheard, and not ask her to repeat it. Because if she had said that he was lucky, or that Thea was lucky, no matter what the reason, then he would probably try to kill her with his bare and trembling hands.

Instead, he turned, slowly, and asked as steadily as he could, "Were you trying to explain something to me just now?"

His expression must have warned her. She paused, looking for the first time like a vulnerable human being; then said, in carefully measured tones, "I was trying to explain how important it was that your wife has already been recorded."

He stared at her some more. "Recorded? What does that mean?"

And then, suddenly, he understood.

Like the flutist.

Because alive was better, no matter what. That's what she'd told him. Had she already gone and done it, that morning? If he'd been more understanding, if he'd put aside his own feelings and listened, would she have told him more?

He stood over the doctor, probably too close, looming over her. "Tell me. Tell me what it means. Tell me what happens now."

The doctor looked to Max's left, then to his right; and Max, following her gaze, realized that the room had other people in it. They had probably been there all along. And now, some of them were obviously craning to hear the conversation. The doctor stood up, moved her hand as if to place it on his shoulder, then visibly thought better of it. She took a step toward the door through which she had come. "Please follow me to my office, and I'll tell you everything you need to know."

The chair in the doctor's office was a lot more comfortable than the ones in the waiting room, and he could smell something like cinnamon instead of the waiting room's antiseptic odor. Was that supposed to compensate somehow for the news to be delivered?

Max had not managed to ask many questions, but the doctor ran through the sequence of events, and that answered a few.

When he and Thea first got the ad agency job, there had been something in the paperwork about a chance to make baseline recordings at a substantial discount. Thea had taken them up on it. His guess was almost right: she'd had the recordings made right after, rather than before, the two of them had talked about stored people and the quality of their existence. And Max's attitude probably explained why Thea hadn't told him what she'd done.

Had she had some sort of premonition? Probably not. He was the superstitious one; she was simply thorough. She made contingency plans, and did it for both of them. When would she have gotten around to suggesting that he get a recording done?

Should he do it now? He shuddered and shook his head to throw off the idea. The doctor paused in mid-sentence, puzzled. He felt himself flush. "Sorry. Please go on. Did she get any more recordings made?"

"Not exactly. Not until today."

Of course. How dumb could he be? That's what that weird device had been, at the beach. Did the lifeguards do that for anyone in bad enough shape, or had she had some sort of info, an embedded chip or something, to let them know?

Not that it mattered. "So what got recorded today?"

The doctor looked uncomfortable for — surprisingly — the first time so far. "I don't know all about the process. My, um, educated guess is that the equipment confirmed that the basics were unchanged, then recorded new memories since the last time. The devices are networked, so her previous files would have been available."

Max might not be the computer expert Thea was, but that didn't sound good. "If they're networked, could someone with that portable gizmo read her files?"

The doctor took a visible deep breath. He should lighten up. None of this was her fault. He made a feeble attempt at a smile and gave up on it. "Never mind. That's not what we're here for you to tell me."

The doctor nodded slightly, almost-smiling back. "As I was saying, her memories up until the accident have been mostly or entirely preserved. The damage from the aneurysm affected many critical areas, I'm afraid, making Thea's prognosis very poor indeed." She paused, probably because Max had finally burst into tears. He shoved back his chair and hid his head in his hands. The doctor placed a box of tissues in front of him — she must have them handy every time she brought someone in here for this sort of talk. He didn't much care whether he wiped tears and snot on his sleeve, but he grabbed a tissue and blew his nose. He looked around, but failed to see any waste basket. The doctor must be human and fallible after all. . . . He stuck the used tissue in a pants pocket, then looked up at the doctor, biting his lip. "You can go on now."

"The damage, severe as it is, hasn't—at least, not so far—affected the areas where we know that memory gets stored. Of course, we're learning more about the brain all the time, but it's likely that any damage would affect redundancies rather than unique memory information."

That must have been the luck the doctor had started to talk about.

But now what?

Max noticed a pain in his hands. He looked down and saw that he was gripping the arms of the chair so hard that his knuckles were white. He forced his fingers to relax and folded them together. "So what happens now? Do you just go ahead and . . . reboot her in some computer somewhere?"

The doctor tapped a button on her wristband. Max heard the smooth whir of a printer, though he couldn't see one. It must be built into the desk somehow. In a moment, the doctor was sliding papers across the desk. "What happens next, Mr. Cooper, is actually up to you."

"*What?*"

"Ms. Lee—Thea—hasn't signed an agreement for actual storage and all that goes with it. She was planning to leave that decision for some while later. But in the event she hadn't decided when something happened to her, an untimely event like this aneurysm, she left the decision up to you."

Max couldn't move. He could barely speak. He couldn't think. And all he could feel was the overpowering feeling that none of this was happening.

He would wake up any minute, and Thea would be there, maybe sleeping and looking the way angels would look if they could sleep, or maybe snoring with her mouth open. . . .

The doctor was talking again. "It's not as strange as it may sound. The—" The doctor strangled some word before finishing it, a word starting with an "n." Max's stomach clenched as he filled in the blank: next of kin. "A patient's loved ones are often called upon to decide whether we should perform high-risk surgery, or how long a patient should be maintained on life support."

"And this is a high-tech form of life support."

The doctor cocked her head and looked faintly reproving. "As I understand it—and I don't claim to be an expert—it's significantly more than that. It's a chance to continue a fully conscious existence, and to interact with those who remain alive in the more conventional sense."

It didn't make sense. "I know that's how she thought of it. She told me. Even though she didn't tell me what she was doing, she told me that much. So why would she leave it up to me?"

The doctor sighed. "You can probably answer that better than I. But could it be that she didn't want to survive if you wouldn't want to be part of her, ah, her new life? That she wanted to live, but not to live without you?"

Max grabbed another tissue, managing to bring it to his face before he started sobbing again. It went on longer this time. When he glanced up, his chest still in spasms, he saw that the doctor had disappeared somewhere. There was a door in the back of her office: she must have gone through it to give him some privacy.

Good. He could cry himself out. Except he couldn't imagine that would ever happen. Not without Thea.

What would she do to comfort him, if she were—here and not here? If she couldn't touch him, couldn't put her arm around him, couldn't haul him to the couch or the bed and hold him close until he recovered?

She would still know him well enough to find the right words. She would have woven a spell with her voice—

Would she still have her own voice?

He would have asked the doctor, but he couldn't face trying to track her down. And even if she wouldn't sound like herself, that wasn't important enough to make the difference. He couldn't let something like that be the deal-breaker.

He'd known almost since he first knew Thea that under the logic and the formidable intellect, she was as romantic—or almost as romantic—as he was. If he'd had any doubts, she'd proved it to him, here, while she was lying in a coma or whatever—

Was she? Or was she awake? Surely if she was awake and could talk to him, they would have taken him to her instead of just putting him in an office and making him decide all by himself?

He had to get answers to some of these questions. In a minute, when he'd pulled himself together, he'd go find the doctor. And he'd try to figure out whether the answers she gave him were what Thea had known, or had expected, when she went as far as she'd already gone down this strange, strange road.

And then he would sign the damn papers. What else could he do? Tell the doctor to let her die—die completely, die forever? With no chance to change his mind later, or for her to change hers?

He would have to sign.

Chapter 3

MAX SAT by Thea's bed. Maybe it wasn't her bed, exactly, if all that was left in it was a disintegrating shell. But you couldn't tell that just by looking at her peaceful face, and her chest still moving up and down under the sheet; though the purplish antibacterial glow gave her face an eerie, unnatural cast. The window added little light—somehow, it had become evening.

She was still breathing. Once all the recordings had been made, the doctor had asked his permission to take her off the machine that had done the breathing for her. He had waited for a few minutes, clutching her hand so hard that it would have hurt her if anything still could. Maybe he had hoped it would hurt, that the pain would reach her, in spite of everything the doctor claimed. But it hadn't.

Once he finally forced out the words, he had made himself open his eyes and look at her as the technician punched the buttons. He had thought she would—die— finish dying—whatever the hell he should call it, right then; but her face did not change, and her chest kept rising and falling. The doctor said it could take a while, maybe hours.

So he was still here with her.

But wasn't something missing?

Oh, my God. He hadn't called her parents.

Did the hospital even know who and where they were? Even if they did, they would have left it up to him. They'd see him as "next of kin." Even if her parents took a very different view.

All the time he'd spent in the waiting room, the time that felt like eternity: how long had it actually been? Plenty of time to have called them. Time they could have spent getting here, to see their daughter before she died.

Shit.

They would probably have had plenty to say about his decision. Even if Thea had made clear it was his decision, not theirs.

He had not brought a phone to the beach. After one too many lost in the sand or submerged in salt water, he had left it to Thea to make or receive any necessary calls.

Not this time.

Where was Thea's phone? He checked her bare wrist, staring at it as if a phone might somehow materialize; then hauled himself out of the chair he found himself sitting in, and searched the room until he found the shelf on which her phone lay abandoned.

Hands shaking, he fumbled with the phone, dropping it, retrieving it, and finally managed to put the call through. Just in time, he set it to show his living image rather than a stored photo of their daughter, to give at least a moment's warning that something was amiss.

They had never invited him to call them Mom and Dad, rather than Bill and Linda. Would this, finally, be the time? Or the worst possible moment?

One tiny thing went right, on this day of everything wrong: Thea's mother answered her phone. She might not be a whole lot more impressed with Max than her husband was, but she liked Max at least a little because he loved Thea so completely.

And unlike Thea's father, she understood how tough Thea was, and that she didn't need someone to protect her from every little thing. She understood because she was a pretty tough lady herself. That's where Thea got it, more than from her muscle-bound father.

"Linda . . . Mom . . ."

Max managed to choke out the essential information: the accident, the aneurysm, the doctor's denial of any real hope. There was a horrible silent moment; and then, in a flat, robotic voice: "Where?"

He gave her the name of the hospital, and the street, which was all he remembered of the address. She had hung up before he could find the words to tell her the rest.

Maybe Thea's father had been right all along. Maybe some other guy would have protected her somehow. And maybe that other guy would be driving home with Thea right now, while she waved her trophy out the car window and hollered with glee.

But Thea had chosen him. If he started believing she'd been wrong, what would she have said about it? She'd have been in his face, telling him off . . . .

How long had it been since he looked at Thea? Was she still breathing?

She was.

She kept breathing until ten minutes after her parents burst into the room.

And in those ten minutes, even though they tried to shut him up, even though they shouted at him (Thea's mother must have moved past the initial shock, no more robot voice now) to be quiet, he managed to tell them just enough that they let him keep going.

When he had finished, Thea's mother turned her back on him and laid her upper body across Thea's chest. Thea's father stood beside her, his arm stretched out, his large gnarled hand on Thea's shoulder. And there they all waited until the soft sound of breathing gave way to silence.

And then, after some period of time that must have been laid out in a written or unwritten hospital rule, the staff, gently and persistently, required them to leave.

They huddled in the waiting room, though there was nothing left to wait for, not there. None of them took the first step to go out into the vast and empty world with no Thea in it.

To leave behind her body, the body to which Max had taken such pride in bringing delight, the arms in which he had sheltered, the delicately beautiful breasts, the radiant skin, the embodied energy coiled up and centered in one warm place . . . .

Her mother must be remembering, instead, a bundle in her arms, lips suckling, the clutch of a tiny hand. And her father—Max had seen the photos, so many pictures of Thea riding upright on his shoulders, fearless, her hands thrust upward as her father clutched her strong slim legs.

"Her body." For a moment Max thought he had spoken his own thought, but it was Thea's father who spoke, in a quiet mumble nothing like his usual loud bass. "What did she want—did she say something, make arrangements?"

This, Thea had told him ahead of time. "She wants—wanted to be wrapped in a cotton shroud and left in a treetop. There's a place that does that. She picked a tree." And had picked one for him, right beside it.

Her father stared at him, then shook his head in a slow rhythm. "It isn't right."

Thea's mother took a deep and shuddering breath. "But it's what she wanted. And—she, or whatever—" She was shivering now, hunched with her arms crossed, her hands squeezing her arms. "The program that's going to think it's Thea, it'll know whether we did what she wanted." She looked up at Max, or looking through him. "But we'll have a stone, a marker, in the cemetery where we'll lie someday. She wouldn't begrudge us that."

And then, slowly, as if in slow motion, she collapsed, Max and Bill converging on her to catch her as she crumpled toward the ground.

Chapter 4

THEA woke up. At least, that was how it felt, except that she was standing on her feet.

She had not known what to expect, even though she had tried to find out. She'd requested a face-to-face with the flutist, the only stored person with whom she already had a connection of sorts; but she had not yet received a response by the time she—what had happened? Had she drowned in some freak surfing accident? Or had it been the aneurysm?

Maybe she should have told Max about the aneurysm. She'd only found out about it during the exam that preceded her initial session with the storage company. They'd said it would be riskier to attempt a repair than to just leave it and hope for the best.

Thea was—had been—fairly skilled at putting unpleasant realities aside, if nothing remained to be done about them. But Max would have fretted, at the very least, and made pointless efforts to protect her; and that would have changed their lives in ways she didn't want.

Well, their lives had certainly changed now.

If she'd had to guess, she would have guessed that she would awake disoriented, out of touch, maybe reliving some forgotten infant state. Apparently it didn't work like that: her thoughts made sense. Her intellect seemed to be in its usual working order—or even a bit better, clearer. Was that the result of the analog-to-digital transition? Had there been some sort of tradeoff? She could think, but could she feel?

She had only to bring Max to mind to have that answer.

Poor, poor Max! What must he be going through? And how long had it been? How long had he been alone?

She had to talk to him. And she missed him, already, with an intensity that reassured her. The recreation of her brain had not omitted whatever signals would from now on substitute for hormones and other chemicals.

In fact, she could still cry. And crying felt wonderful and terrible at the same time.

She let herself cry for a few minutes, examining the process at the same time. There were tears, but her nose didn't run. Had some programmer decided to clean things up?

How many other "improvements" would she discover in what it meant to be human?

But it was impressive that the programmers had analyzed the brain in enough detail to make such tweaks.

Not until she thought of wiping her tears did she discover that she had sleeves. Had clothes. They looked like the clothes she had worn to that initial screening. But while she could see them, she could scarcely feel them: they had minimal weight and texture.

Thea looked around at her environment, such as it was. The first thing she noticed was a chair, a swiveling desk chair; she poked at the back, then carefully sat down. The seat just barely registered as having any sort of mass, and lacked texture, just like the clothes. The walls around her were a light gray that reminded her of the background in dully designed software. And she heard nothing, nothing at all.

If the programmers could play with her nasal secretions, surely they could do more with clothes and interiors. Were they simply not bothering? Or would she have the chance to make tweaks of her own?

She could make her own aural background. At least she knew there would be some way to make music.

But all of that could wait. She had to talk to Max. How?

There! In the corner, on a table—something like a sturdier card table, but hard to see because its color matched the walls—sat a wristband with the usual controls. She rose from the chair; the movement felt different in some way she couldn't immediately define, some subtle way, but it got her upright. And she was able to bend down, and to pick up the chair, and to lift it. It was absurdly light (another "improvement"?). She almost lost her grip and hurled it upward, but managed to move it over to the corner and drop it in front of the table.

Thea sat back down with some reluctance. The thing just didn't *feel* like a chair. No matter. First, she would find out how long it had taken for them to . . . not to revive her. Resurrect her? Reboot her? She felt something like a laugh building, a hysterical laugh she did not want to hear.

She fought it back and flicked the controls on the band to the tablet setting. Help, FAQ, About, Search: options so familiar that the incongruity made her smile. At least, it felt like a smile. She would not worry just now about how it would look.

She touched the controls, which felt more like real controls than the chair felt like a real chair. A screen appeared, and she saw the small matter-of-fact numbers showing the date and time.

Four days. Four days had passed while they checked and double-checked and possibly debugged. Four days of purgatory for Max.

9:30 p.m. Nighttime, even in summer. (Was it summer here? Was there summer here?) She looked for a window and found one, a small window with white blinds pulled shut. She stood up again and braced herself for the sensation of walking.

One step, and then another. It felt the way walking had always felt, or almost. Perhaps she was already becoming accustomed to how movement felt. Or forgetting how it truly felt to move. . . . She closed her eyes, bit her lip, and shuddered. (She could still shudder, and feel something like fear.)

Then she forced herself into motion again, reached the window, and opened the blinds.

She saw darkness, interrupted by street lights along a winding foot path. The lights showed hints of trees, and the shape of a manicured lawn. Odd, for them to bother with lights at night; but of course, there would be no energy expended, no more than for any other feature of any other scene. Perhaps some customer had been wooed with the promise of evening walks. And walks by moonlight? Would there be a moon?

She allowed herself one sigh, then returned to the task at hand.

The FAQ proved satisfactory for her present purpose, and in fact went considerably beyond it. She had never been able to read just part of a FAQ, but this time was different. Max needed to hear from her as soon as possible. So she scanned the document quickly, finding out how to access a Contacts list based on the information she had already provided.

But now she had to face the problem she had pushed aside when she filled out the Contacts form. Max was something of a throwback where phones were concerned: he could not be counted on to wear one, even when she bought him a flattering earring or a detachable tattoo. Would it occur to him, confounded and troubled as he must be, to keep a phone handy?

* * * * *

Max had somehow fallen asleep. He must have, or the buzzing sound could not have awakened him. But it took him too long to locate its source, and the buzzing stopped. He let his head thud back against the pillow. It had probably been his phone, lying somewhere about. And no one who knew him well tried to reach him by phone, at least not right away. They always tried Thea first.

The bolt of memory blazed through him, and he jerked upright, gasping.

And then the buzzing came again.

A friend calling to offer sympathy? The hospital, with some new and horrible detail? Thea's parents, ready to re-fight the battle over their daughter's remains? Or the corporation, the one that held what remained of Thea in its digital depths?

Max staggered out of bed, tripping over garments, searching for the sound. He found the phone in a shirt pocket after five rings and jabbed at the answer button, looking for the caller's image or logo.

Then he dropped the phone.

And scrambled frantically to pick it up again. And couldn't speak.

"Max?" A pause. "Baby?"

Thea's face, frozen in a still image; and her voice. Really her voice. Or as much like her voice as he could expect on the phone.

"Oh, baby, don't cry."

He must be crying again. He was sick of crying. And there was Thea, telling him to stop. What Thea wanted was usually the right thing to do.

"Thea. Oh, God. There you are. *Here* you *are!*"

A small chuckle. "Yup. Here I guess I am. Max, I'm sorry for how awful this must have been for you. I was hoping it wouldn't happen—or not for years and years."

That what wouldn't happen? Her dying? Or—he started to blurt out a question, even an accusation. Maybe she had known about the aneurysm and hadn't told him. Some time or other, he would ask, and ask why, if she'd known, she'd made a secret of it. And he'd ask what other secrets she had. Maybe they'd even have a fight.

He would rather fight with her than make love with any other woman.

But—"I wish you were here. Right here, in our bed with me."

Another chuckle, or a small sob? "Me, too, baby."

Before, when one of them had traveled and the other couldn't go along, they had lain on their separate beds and talked each other into frenzy, then to satisfaction. They could try that now. Except . . . .

"Thea, do you have any, any *privacy* there?"

A moment of silence, then: "Hold on. Let me see if the FAQ covers it."

"The *FAQ??*"

Now he could hear her laughing, though the still image remained static. "I know. It's all so crazy, isn't it?

But give me a minute. Maybe it'll really tell us. Hold on."

And then, silence again. A silence, he could not help noticing, unlike any silence on any phone call, ever. Thea wasn't moving a phone against her hair, or swallowing, or breathing.

No more breathing for Thea, ever.

Unless she could. Maybe she felt like she was breathing. And maybe she could learn how to make it sound as if she were.

And if he kept thinking like this, he might start screaming. Which would scare her, or upset her, even if it couldn't hurt her ear.

Just in time, there came Thea's voice again, as the still image morphed into motion. "I found out how to turn the camera on while I was looking! Anyway, I've found a sort of an answer. There's a confidential setting. But there's some sort of monitoring even then. Here's a link to another document about restricted subjects. . . . Got it. I'm just going to skim it for now. . . . How would I even find out about proprietary info? Never mind . . . . Corporate business, blah blah . . . ." She was drifting off into a muttered monotone, the way she did when she was processing something at top speed. He stopped trying to follow the words and let the familiar tones wash over him.

"Well, we can't be sure, of course." Now she was actually speaking to him again. "Shit. That's going to be our new refrain, isn't it? But if they're being straight with us, the system probably isn't keyed to notice—personal private talk. And if someone *is* listening, well . . . ."

Max chimed in. "To hell with 'em!"

They laughed together, and when they stopped laughing, Thea's voice went soft and sultry, and she asked him, "Now, honey, are you lying back in bed?"

"Uh-huh." He lay back to make it true. And then gritted his teeth, as he wondered what he could ask her, whether this made any sense, whether it could work, whether his idea had been a lousy one.

Once again, they were thinking the same thing at the same time. Her voice was still soft, but she had dropped the seductive tone. "This is going to be different, isn't it? We'll still be pretending. But we'll be pretending in a whole new way, both of us. Do you think we can do it?"

Max took a deep, shuddering breath. "I want to. I want to try. We may never be able to—" He would *not* cry, not again. "—to touch each other again. But we know how it feels. I can help you remember, and you can help me."

"I love you, baby."

"I love you. Forever."

He heard the sound of her kiss as her lips moved; then came her voice again. "Lie back, baby. Imagine me touching you. Imagine my hand, running down your chest, and lower, and lower . . . ."

He had guessed right. They could.

* * * * *

Thea awoke, this time in a bed.

She had made another quick scan of the FAQ the night before, even as she began moving Max toward arousal. It did include information about creating furniture; she settled for a bed she could manifest quickly, and then focused on herself and Max and what they could do for each other. Including what, to her relief if not really her surprise, he could still do for her. It made sense that a digital duplication of her brain would include all the portions necessary for arousal and orgasm, but it would not have astonished her if the lack of an actual body proved problematic.

Afterward, naturally, Max had fallen apart again; but not for long. She had switched gears and talked him to sleep, and disconnected the call as soon as she heard him breathing slow and steady. Then she had wrestled with her own emotions as she imagined the warmth of his sleeping body next to hers.

It might actually be possible for her to create some simulacrum of a sleeping Max. A ghoulish idea, perhaps, and one raising interesting if tricky issues of consent. Would she need to ask him first?

Instead, to distract herself, she had improved the bed. To avoid more frequent attacks of homesickness, she refrained from duplicating their bedding, instead designing an abstract and angular design in purple and black on white and applying it to an indulgently fluffy comforter. And she was able to create exactly the right thickness of pillow, which she had never managed (or bothered) to do before.

Then, she had settled in to find out if she could sleep. She had hoped so, and expected so. Humans needed sleep, and the ability to copy the massive intricacies of the human brain did not imply the ability to go beyond and substantially readjust it.

And here she was, waking up from what certainly felt like sleep. Or to be more precise, it felt like waking up, since sleep itself had that uniquely frustrating quality, an interlude she passed through repeatedly and yet could never consciously experience.

What should she do with what, in an utterly novel sense, constituted the first day of the rest of her life?

She would have to contact her parents. But before she did that, she needed to know what they knew. Max must have told them something. She bit her lip (which felt, well, like biting her lip) at the thought. Of all the things to have to do, and all the people to have to do it. . . .

It might be too early to call Max. And when she did call him . . . she needed to find the right balance, a way to stay in his life without letting him rely on her presence, such as it was, throughout his days.

Yes, it was too early. And in the meantime, she had a great deal to learn.

She had gone to sleep naked, after noting with only a touch of embarrassment that the program had faithfully duplicated her body, literal and figurative warts and all. But now she used the knowledge acquired yesterday to provide herself with some cozy flannel pajamas. Then she sat in the inadequate chair once again, called up the FAQ, and got back to work. She needed to learn how to make a flute.

Before long, however, she found herself distracted by a welcome sensation: hunger. When she had first wrestled with the decision to have herself stored, she had asked whether she would still hunger and thirst, and had hoped the positive response could be trusted. After all, she would apparently lose some functions, such as eliminating bodily waste. What focus group had led to eliminating elimination? . . . In any event, now that she was hungry, she checked the FAQ to find out what she could do about it.

Apparently the digital equivalent of room service required some special procedure. To start with, at least, she would need to venture forth and seek out a dining room—which would presumably mean meeting some of her fellow digital constructs.

The morning, if she could call it morning, looked appropriately sunny; but the sunlight failed to warm her skin as much as it should. And she could feel no breeze.

(Would there be seasons? Which clients' norms, or what marketing decisions, would drive that decision? Would their actual location—somewhere in Idaho—make any difference?. . . As a Californian, she had been used to what others might regard as muted and minimal seasonal changes. If this bland and temperate morning proved the norm, she would have less to miss than those whose lives had featured bright autumns, frozen winters, and humid summer nights.)

The path she had seen the night before came equipped with helpful and somewhat tantalizing directional signs. "Tennis court," "swimming pool," "movie theater"—and "dining hall," her current destination.

In a few minutes, she found herself at the door of a large building, one apparently containing several of the amenities she had seen on the signs. She opened the door and took a hopeful sniff; but if breakfast came with odors, they did not reach so far. The hallway did, however, include its own signage, and she followed that.

The door to the dining hall stood open. She stood in the doorway for a moment, reliving old memories of arriving at a new school and gathering the courage to enter its preexisting social circle. Then she took another sniff—there, a faint whiff of something like toast!—and stepped inside.

The food proved barely palatable, the company more welcoming than she had feared. With new arrivals frequent, there was little opportunity for cliques to form and harden. She did not, however, linger for long, but excused herself with the quite accurate excuse that she had social obligations not yet fulfilled.

By now—if her time had any connection to that of the world she had left behind—Max might have awakened.

* * * * *

Max woke up, his nose buried in a damp patch of pillow, and struggled to remember his dream. He had dreamed of Thea. A good dream, not one of the nightmares. Had they made love in the dream? But no, he could not remember touching her.

Looking around the room as if it held a clue, he saw his phone, lying on the empty side of the bed; and he remembered, all in a moment like a thunderclap.

Not a dream! He rolled over and grabbed the phone, fumbling for the call history. The most recent entry showed an unfamiliar number and nothing else. Did this uncanny arrangement work both ways? Could he call Thea?

He touched the phone, gently, as if touching Thea lying there in bed; touching her to see if she was awake, touching her without waking her if she slept.

And after waiting as long as he could stand, he called; and she answered.

Thea waved her new flute in the air. "It took me a while, but I figured out how to make it! And it sounds pretty good. Want to hear?"

"Of course, babe. Anything you want to play."

Thea grinned and started the triumphal march from *Aida*. He laughed and listened. It did sound pretty good, even if didn't sound just like her real flute, the one still sitting in its case on the bedroom shelf. He tried not to wince at the thought—Thea would see him.

Thea got to the end of a phrase and stopped. "All right, enough of me performing." She smirked at him, if that cute an expression could be called smirking. "Your turn."

Max had a better idea. "No, *our* turn. Let's play together."

Thea's face lit up. "Yes! Pick something."

There was a duet for flute and guitar, an arrangement of a flute concerto by, of all people, Frederick the Great, King of Prussia. It wasn't the most inventive of pieces, but it managed to be both lively and soothing. He grabbed his guitar, resting against the nightstand, and played the first few notes. Thea laughed. "Why not!" She put her flute to her lips and joined in.

When they reached the end of the Allegro, she stopped and laid her flute aside. "Have you written anything new?"

Max split the screen and called up his composition program. "It happens I have. Want to hear it?"

Thea nodded vigorously and bounced in her chair. A faint grimace crossed her face, maybe because of something about the chair, and then disappeared. Max queued up the track and hit play.

He had used guitar, his go-to instrument, along with cello. Flute would have added to it, but he had left the flute part for Thea. And she would recognize the melody. They had never had a single song they called "theirs," but songs often brought back shared memories. This one recalled one of their first road trips after they started getting serious, a trip to the wine country. Both of them had overestimated their capacity to taste and drive—hell, they were young and pretty new to drinking—and they'd ended up with an overnight motel stay that neither had planned. Which had been one of the best nights he'd ever had up to then.

Thea put a hand over her heart as the first notes played, then clasped her hands together and listened. Soon she was humming along, not so much a harmony as a complementary lyric line. It would sound great on a flute.

It was perfect.

* * * * *

The last thing Max said to her, before their closing exchanges of "I love you"s, was a question. "Have you called your folks?"

Her answer was an admission. "I will."

In the old days of land lines, Thea could have called a phone jointly owned by both her parents, and left it to fortune which would answer. She was glad not to have that option. She needed her mother's advice before she tried to talk to her father.

What would her mother see when Thea called? She had not thought to ask Max. She called him back. He looked startled as well as pleased to hear from her so soon.

"When I call you, what shows up before you answer? Is it any different from when I called you—before?"

"It's different, but it's still your picture. I had one of my favorites that popped up. This one looks like something that company—LiveAfter or whatever they're called—might have taken."

Thea thrust aside the temptation to linger, to let their conversation wander where it would. "I'm going to call my mother. That's why I wanted to know."

Max donned an encouraging expression. "It'll be hard for both of you. But you'll pull it off."

He probably meant it. She would have to rely on his faith in her to shore up her own.

Her mother answered on the first ring; then stared, eyes wild and wide, and said nothing.

Up to Thea, then. "Mom? It's me."

Still nothing. She could not remember her mother ever being at a loss for words. But then, she had never faced a conversation remotely like this one.

Remotely. There was the right word.

"Mom, what can I say to help you with this?" *To make you believe I'm here. That it's me.*

The image floating in front of Thea jittered as if her mother had dropped heavily into a chair. "Explain it to me. Please. Tell me how they . . . copied you, or whatever they did. Tell me how it works."

That was Mom, analytical even in crisis. Once she understood the process, she would assess whether she was in fact talking to her daughter, or at least a close enough facsimile.

"They used nanobots. . . ." She ran through the summary she had memorized when she was deciding how to talk to Max about storage, before she concluded that such details would make little impression on him.

Her mother listened quietly, then asked, "Did you ever see it tested, this—this software, this model?"

What a good idea that would have been. If she had

consulted her mother back then . . . . Too late now. "No. I never gave the matter that much thought. I didn't expect it to matter so soon."

Mercifully, her mother made no comment, this time, on the dangers of surfing. "Of course not."

"But you know I'm thorough about things. Like you. I looked into it enough to verify the essential claims."

Silence again.

"Mom, have you . . . have you decided? Do you believe I'm me?"

Now her mother was crying. She so rarely cried. But probably that had changed. . . . Thea fought back a sob of her own, closed her eyes, and waited.

The softly percussive sounds of crying faded away. Thea opened her eyes.

"Yes, Dandy. I believe it."

Dandy, short for dandelion, a reference to Thea's light and fluffy hair. The only nickname her mother had ever bestowed on her, or on anyone. And at this moment, the most precious of gifts.

"Thank you. Thank you so much. And I'm so sorry for how hard this is."

"I hope you never know how hard." Then she gasped. "Oh, my God. You never will. You never can. You'll never . . . . And we'll never . . . ."

They wept together, the young woman and the older, one never to be a mother, the other never a grandmother.

Thea's mother regained her self-control first. "Hush, love, hush . . . ."

Thea focused on her breathing (and she could not let herself think about breathing and not actually breathing, not now) until it was steady. For a few minutes, neither of them spoke. Then, while the subject still hung in the air, her mother asked quietly: "Would you have?"

Thea gulped and nodded. "I think so, in a few years. Max would have loved it, even though the idea still scared him. And he'd have been wonderful with children — though not very much like Dad was with me."

Her mother's gaze flicked away, probably to another room, and back again. "You haven't tried calling your father. He'd have told me. Have you thought about how to approach him?"

Thea rubbed her forehead with one hand. "I didn't even know how to start with you. He'll be a hundred times worse." She hated to ask, but she desperately needed the help. "Will you talk to him first? Tell him to expect my call? Or if he's willing — do you think you can get him to call me?"

Her mother heaved a heavy sigh. "That might be best. He can work himself up to it. And honey, he won't want to hear the details, the way I did. He'll care about memories: the special times, and those little moments you wouldn't have mentioned to anyone else but never forgot."

Thea might well have told Max about such moments; but her father would not know that, nor need to know. "I'll go sit myself down, right now, and start remembering."

When Thea reminisced about her mother, it was her words that came to mind: so many words, about so many things, spoken in so many moods (though rarely, very rarely, in any histrionic mode).

Her father was not exactly taciturn, but words, for him, were secondary. She could talk to him, rattling on about anything or nothing, but only because he enjoyed watching her speak.

It had never before mattered so terribly much what she said.

When he called, his voice hesitant and hoarse, his face pale, she dove into the memories and let her tongue follow.

Fireflies flickering in the trees like escaped and feral Christmas lights.

Stars, dozens of them or even hundreds, up in the hills beyond the city lights.

The ocean, her first true sight of a horizon, blue-gray under clouds, then translucent and startling blue-green in sunshine; and her father's large hand reaching down to point at the sandpipers scuttling up and down the beach, their spidery footprints left behind in the sand.

Those hands, so firm in their grip, holding her in the surf, letting her ride lightly at the surface, bobbing up and down.

Those hands, squeezing her arms in reassurance and letting her go, to be tossed and tumbled toward shore.

A campfire, and a crowd of families around it, and her father playing some wild, stirring tune on his grandfather's balalaika while the wood popped sparks into the air.

Another night, another campfire, and Thea improvising along with her father, playing her first flute.

Her father looming over her and shouting, the night she wandered off into the woods in a thunderstorm and a tree fell across her path home, and she had to climb over it, scraping her hands and tearing her clothes.

Her father looking out the window at Max and their loaded car, standing in front of the door with his back to it, unconsciously blocking her way, as they made ready to move into that first apartment.

"Not exactly. I knew I was doing it."

She had almost forgotten, riding the river of memory, that she was speaking to her father, and why. What had she been saying? Oh! "You did? What was the point?"

Her father gazed at her, and it was the same gaze she remembered from that day. "I needed one more moment with my little girl. I wasn't ready to let her go."

"I'm here, Daddy. I'm still here."

He closed his eyes, heaved a heavy sigh, and opened them again. "I know." But he looked at her, still, as if she were lost instead of found.

Chapter 5

LIVEAFTER's Vice President for Client Relations grabbed a patience inhaler and took two deep puffs before taking the next call, the fourth one of the morning, and with her luck, probably another complaint about the same damned thing. The clients must be coordinating this assault. She glanced at her reflection in her office window and practiced her smile once more, then hit the button. "Good morning, sir! How may I serve you?"

"Morning, is it? One could hardly tell from the landscape here. And service? Ironic wording. I have played tennis three times a week for the last forty years. And what passes for a tennis court, and a racket, in this place is an insult to the sport."

They none of them appreciated the difficulties in synthesizing experience. Of course they took for granted the incredibly complex and groundbreaking nanotechnology that had traced and recorded their neural contents and connections. Most of them never bothered to begin to understand it. So they didn't realize how different a task it was, how much more research still remained, to reproduce the type and quality of experiences they were demanding.

"I distinctly recall the promises your sales representative made. And I have verified that your promotional materials included such promises. My family, whose resources have been significantly diminished by your fees, are more than prepared to pursue appropriate legal remedies."

For far from the first time, the VP cursed the sales department, silently and without moving her lips or changing her expression. The "promise first, deal with it later" mentality got the sales, certainly — and saddled the rest of the company with consequences like these. The legal costs had no doubt been included in the budget. But there was no budget item for the length of vacation she would need to recover from the aggravation.

Meanwhile, the client's rant continued. "If retirement is to be forced on me, I at least expect — I *demand* — the amenities that could make retirement acceptable!"

A brain wave struck her with such force that she forgot, for a moment, the irate customer on the line; then, seeing his eyes bulge out further, said hastily, "Sir, please give me a moment to check on a possibility." Without waiting for a response, she put the call on hold and checked his file. Yes, she had remembered correctly: the man had been heavily involved in politics, though not actually an officeholder. And someone at their ad agency had suggested something close to her idea — which meant she'd get less credit for originality, but also less risk of being thought *too* original.

She put the caller back on and waited for a pause in the spate of angry words. "Sir — sir! I completely understand that retiring before your time is a major hardship. But what if your unfortunate demise did not in fact force retirement upon you?"

A momentary silence, and then, in a quite different tone, perhaps even a bit tremulous: "What was that?"

Now she had to decide whether to over-promise in

her turn. . . . Maybe just a little. And now that she thought about it, she'd heard some rumors; so she might not be exaggerating. Much.

"Sir, I believe the time has come for me to disclose to you an exciting new program we have in the works. If you, and our other clients with similar concerns, could just be patient. . . ."

The Vice President for Client Relations made a pitch to the CEO. The CEO met with the Board of Directors.

The idea had marketing potential. The politically active might find storage more attractive if the stored retained the right to vote. Those who had, in life, been wooed for their money would find some comfort in being wooed for their votes. And as the VP of Client Relations had discovered, the promise of political engagement might provide some compensation for, or at least distraction from, the current shortcomings of the virtual environment.

The Board voted to proceed.

* * * * *

The senior member of the ad team reread the client's new request for the third time. Arrange a favorable political climate for a push to let stored people vote? LiveAfter must think the agency had done a damn good job on the last campaign, to be asking them to pull this off.

She had the authority to limit which members of the team took part in followup projects, but she never liked to exercise it. Excluding anyone led to hurt feelings, and often to rumors at least as lurid as those a well-informed team member might start.

Her young co-leader had better stay in place. It would do her career too much damage to oust her, whatever the explanation provided. The DA could also remain: he would have a head start at predicting the difficulties ahead.

She brought up the video of the team's first in-person meeting and watched it from start to finish. She'd forgotten that wisecrack the copy editor made, toward the end. At least, that's what he'd probably thought he was doing. But now, he had better be kept in the loop.

They were likely to need some actual legal assistance, whether from LiveAfter's legal department (if they could get access to it) or from outside counsel. Would the law buff be good at working with lawyers, or would his or their egos interfere? It might be just as well to leave him out. At least, she would check around for other projects where his skills could plausibly be in demand.

As for the others, she could decide later, when the details of the new campaign started to emerge and the necessary skill sets became clearer.

She looked at the client's paperwork one more time and smiled ruefully. If they could pull this off, it'd be a hell of a coup; but the agency might not want to (so to speak) advertise their role.

The senior team leader opened two windows on her screen, one for the latest sketches and one for the audio, and studied the sketches.

The first showed a healthy, subtly muscular older man, with gray-to-white hair and plenty of it, and even a well-trimmed mustache. He wore casual but well-fitted pants and an argyle sweater, and sat in an expensive-looking armchair, facing the camera. The second sketch showed a brother and sister, the brother about four years old and the sister no more than two, standing in some sort of field and looking off into the distance with wide eyes. Attached to the sketch was a note: "Alternative: suburban setting, in playground or waiting to cross street." The last sketch showed the same older man close up, his gaze more intent, with another note: "Dissolve to slogan, still in progress."

She took another look at the first sketch and jotted down a note: *too much wealth here, especially that chair. We'll be fighting resentment of rich folks. How about old pants and a flannel shirt, sitting at a kitchen table?*

She started the audio, the strong and confident baritone of a well-established voice actor, and wrote another note: *Less recognizable voice might be better.*

"I've always been involved in my community. All my life, I've made sure to keep up on local politics. I served on the school board even after my children graduated from high school. I've volunteered at soup kitchens and bookmobiles, not to mention the polls on Election Day, and shown up at city council meetings.

"I take enormous pride in being an American citizen, and I've always done my best to make the most of that privilege. Because I care about my country and my community. And I care about the town, and the country, and the world that my grandchildren are going to grow up in.

"I don't like to brag—but I think I have something to offer my fellow citizens. I don't want to waste it."

Ensure video not too static.

"If not for LiveAfter's amazing technological achievements, I would have no chance to know about my grandchildren's future, let alone participate in it."

Avoid contradicting still-common religious notions such

as *"grandpa watching over us."*

"But I'm still here. All of me—my love for my family, my concern for my country, and any small portion of wisdom I may have acquired over the years.

"I would hate to have to sit by, helpless, the next time my town, or my state, or my country is faced with an important decision and calls upon its citizens to make that decision. How would you feel?

"I still have a voice. Let me use it. Don't condemn me and those like me to silence. Don't discard our experience.

"Let us vote."

Too long. Could use smoother transition to main point. Needs more visuals. Show participation he's talking about. Q. Any patriotic symbols still effective with majority of viewers?

She ran the audio again and added more notes. *Who else? Young voter, only voted once, pleading not to be deprived of long-anticipated political rights? (Credible?) Mother of teenager? Let's aim at a total of four.*

Then she sat up and called the lawyer they'd found. Once connected, she hurried through the pleasantries and asked as soon as she could, "Are the stored still citizens of wherever they used to live?"

A short pause, then: "Damned if I know. I'd think they're as likely to be 'resident' in whatever computer's running their programs. Why?"

"I just needed to know for the ads. Thanks." She ended the call and dashed off the draft of a memo to the client, urging them as tactfully as possible to work their legislative contacts. The stored would be less invested in politics if the issues had nothing to do with their previous lives. And practically speaking, the agency could hardly generate a nationwide legislative consensus if all the stored were deemed citizens of one state and county, instead of their widely distributed original communities.

She saved her notes and put them aside. Time to spend time on some task with fewer unsettled questions, and a more immediate payoff.

* * * * *

The new ad campaign hit more snags than the earlier ones. The first focus groups made zombie jokes, a few members even dredging up the old stories of "cemetery voting." The more academically inclined members of the team attempted some psychological research, with inconclusive results; then the team as a whole tried to agree on a level of negative response that they, and LiveAfter, could tolerate.

Finally, after an all-night virtual brainstorming session, they came up with a new approach. Instead of more ads, they scheduled virtual town halls, using every stored person both willing to participate and — according to LiveAfter, which insisted on the final say — suitable for the task. After some initial missteps, they avoided providing scripts.

The team tried working with LiveAfter's lobbying people, who knew the concerns that most needed assuaging among the influential and politically connected. That attempt did not last long: pitches that would strike a favorable chord with political elites were less well suited to those leaders' constituents.

The polls moved slowly; but they moved. By the time the senator from Delaware proposed legislation allowing verified stored individuals, registered to vote prior to their demise, to continue voting, popular sentiment was sufficiently balanced that senators and representatives could contemplate supporting the legislation.

The dot-com millionaire turned representative raised concerns about stored personalities voting simultaneously in multiple locations; the lobbyists (after hurried consultation with the technical gurus) assured him that fail-safes made (or from now on would make) such manifestations, for voting or any other purpose, impossible.

The bill passed; and after a suspenseful nine days, the President made known to its sponsors that while she would not actually sign the bill, neither would she veto it. It became the law of the land for federal elections; and states began following the federal lead.

But that was only the beginning. The rules implementing the new statute threatened to become byzantine even by regulatory standards. And the focus on those rules reminded the regulators that LiveAfter's basic role as guardian for its clients needed further micromanagement, which must then be reconciled with the rules specifically addressing voting. . . .

The team leaders, sitting back and watching the show, thanked their currently lucky stars that the agency would play no role in the efforts to get a working structure in place before the next Election Day.

* * * * *

The leader of the technical team in charge of the voting arrangements sat at her ease in the executive vice president's office, despite that august official's startled expression. "Yes, that's correct. We've had three separate attempts, traceable to overseas actors, to put software in place that would override our clients' votes."

The executive vice president cocked his head. "And you don't appear concerned because?"

The young woman made a graceful fanning gesture with her left hand, suggestive of Italian ancestry. "I don't know for certain, of course, but it's highly likely that the same foreign countries are working even harder to hack the votes of the living. It's inevitable with digital voting and tallying of votes. If we need to, we can ask for assistance from whatever agencies are fending off those attacks." She waved her fingers again, less elaborately. "Or we can just take for granted that voting is a more uncertain business than it used to be."

The executive vice president grunted. "More than in my antediluvian era, I assume you mean. No, don't apologize! But despite the temptations—and the financial savings—offered by such cynicism, I prefer to make some efforts to guard against future incursions. See to it, if you please."

* * * * *

The Vice President for Client Relations approached the COO's office just as three technical people left it, all with variations of the same hunted expression. When she had dodged them and made her way in, the COO gave her just enough time to sit down before barking his demand. "Too many customers are still bitching about the environmental features. We need a distraction. What have the customers been requesting?"

She only wished she could feel surprise. "I've been filing reports that include discussion of that question."

"It's quicker to ask you than to wade through reports." She suppressed the urge to roll her eyes, or even glare, as he went on. "And I want the hottest topic, the frill they'd be most excited about."

She, at least, knew the contents of her reports. "Many of the clients had assumed—and I wouldn't be surprised if some sales people helped them assume—that they'd get to choose their appearance, or at least roll back their apparent age. When they woke up with the face and body they'd had toward the end of their lives, they were disappointed, some intensely so. Most of the customers who felt that way still do, and complain regularly. In fact, I've tried to flag this issue as a potential legal exposure." She paused, then could not resist adding, "In my *reports*."

"Why haven't we already obliged these people?"

Couldn't he have asked the technical people before he drove them out of his office? "It turns out body image, including facial features and all the rest, is more than one isolated bit of stored information. It's distributed, and related to a number of other things. Changing it means monkeying with areas we can reproduce but don't fully understand."

Clearly, this was not what the COO wanted to hear. "I'll goose the technical people to study the area. But unless they can tell me about why it's a problem, and tell me soon, we'll be giving these people what they want. Start hinting, without actually making any promises just yet. That's all."

He dismissed her, probably to summon back the technical staff who had so recently escaped his presence. She would take them out for a drink, later, to show her sympathy.

* * * * *

The COO watched the VP hasten down the hall and

cursed quietly to himself. Hadn't the whole point behind the voting initiative been to keep the customers occupied and take the pressure off on the environmental front? But apparently not enough of them really cared about politics.

That suggested another question he could put to the technical staff. Would it be quicker, more practical, simply to increase political interest among the stored? It would be a new technical frontier, certainly — but for all he knew, a less challenging one.

* * * * *

The general counsel had had many occasions to congratulate herself on her arrangements to review internal memos on whose circulation list she did not appear. If she had any way to calculate the millions of dollars she had undoubtedly saved the corporation in outside attorney fees and damage awards, not to mention the impact of adverse publicity, she could make a compelling case for a substantial raise. And while the practice was of necessity known to the various corporate officers whose harebrained ideas she had scotched, there had been no concerted movement to terminate her access.

This time, as on too many previous occasions, the current COO was the culprit. The general counsel did not even pause to imagine, with any specificity, the legal and political consequences of tinkering with their client's established habits and preferences. It should suffice to make clear that she would involve the CEO, and if necessary the Board, in her quest for an unequivocal veto.

CHAPTER 6

THE GROUP had gone by various names in the decades since it initially formed. The details of its political orientation and goals had also shifted this way and that over time. What remained constant, however, was the members' proud consciousness of radicalism and their impressive level of technical expertise. No government department and no corporate entity could count on keeping them at bay.

Some of them had regarded the nascent digital storage technology with deep suspicion, while others reserved judgment. But when the promise of indefinitely extended life was expanded to include the continued exercise of political power, the group approached a consensus of dismay.

What to do, however, remained a contentious topic. Those who still bothered to engage in conventional political activity, and who had to some extent been caught napping as the voting legislation was rammed through, did their best to organize a belated resistance. But even some of these, and many others, considered it both necessary and irresistible to take more immediate and dramatic action.

To be sure, LiveAfter's officers and directors were most directly responsible for this dangerous societal development. But attacking them would be unlikely to gain a great deal of attention. Who cared about the personal peccadilloes of this or that boring businessperson? Besides, the true danger would come from the growth of the stored population, their increasing usurpation of the political process. Better to discourage the living elite from joining the ranks of the stored in the first place.

Better to make digital existence less desirable.

"What the hey?" Thea paused in mid-chew, a half-eaten bagel in her hand.

She had been playing poker with a few new acquaintances, and had brought a few snacks from the dining room for them to share. And one of them, a well-known race car driver, had just scrambled out of his chair, running out of the room so fast that he bashed against the door frame. The programmers must not have bothered with great auditory detail for this room: the impact made only a dull thud.

Thea and the woman to her left exchanged baffled looks. The woman waved a hand toward her own plate. "Okay, it's bad, but it's not *that* bad."

Thea swiveled to look where the man had gone. Should she go check on him? She gulped down her mouthful, took a swig of apple juice, and put the rest of the bagel back on her plate. Yes, she had better go. She could always back off if he didn't want her company or her concern.

She found him in the far corner of the adjoining room. He sat, if that was the word, curled up in fetal position on the floor, panting and trembling, looking from side to side in apparent panic.

Thea took a small step toward him. His head whipped

around, and he stared at her with eyes wide, the whites showing. But he said nothing to warn her away. She took another step. He looked at her face, and then lower. Without intending to, she had reached toward him, palms out in the (universal?) gesture of intending no harm, and he was looking at her hands. Then his body began to relax out of its curl, and he muttered something. Had he said, "No food"?

Another small step.

He spoke again, louder this time. "Please! — Close the door."

She backed up to obey, then moved forward again to the point she had reached before. The man seemed to be recovering a little: some color had returned to his face, and his breathing sounded less frantic. She took the chance of kneeling down a few feet away from the corner.

The man shrank back, then relaxed again with what looked like deliberate effort. He spoke once more. "They're still eating, aren't they?"

Thea nodded, utterly at sea.

The man shut his eyes, and a tear trickled down one lean cheek. "It's the noise. It started yesterday when I went for a walk in the park. I passed a woman eating pizza. It wasn't even crispy pizza — I don't think there is any, here. . . . But the sound of her biting and chewing made me want to — to *attack*! I wanted to grab the pizza and trample it! And then, today, instead of that rage, I felt as if I had to get away from all that chewing and lip-smacking, or something terrible would happen. . . ."

Thea reached out and gently grasped his hand. She had to pry it loose from his knee; and when she had managed, he squeezed her hand so hard it hurt. "Could you apologize for me, in there? And then . . . could you come tell me when all the food is gone?"

Back in her room, Thea tried to find out if the driver's problem had any sort of precedent. She soon discovered that it did. It even had a name, misophonia, from "hatred of sound." Eating noises were a common trigger, but far from the only one. It wasn't only sound, even, that could trigger the fight-or-flight response. But misophonia usually developed gradually, and in early adolescence.

Two days later, the former marketing director of a Fortune 500 company confided in Thea, his voice shaking and his eyes averted, that he would no longer be able to attend any poetry readings because people kept *blinking*. . . .

* * * * *

Thea so rarely seemed frightened — and this time he could not reach out and hold her.

He waited for her to finish her story, so he could provide whatever comfort his words and tone could give. But in mid-sentence, moments after she said something about misophonia and before she could tell him what it meant, the call broke off. The screen switched from Thea, biting her lip, to some sort of logo, and then a swirling pattern of color behind the offensively cheery words, "Whoops! Something went wrong! Working on it. . . ."

What the hell? They'd never had a glitch before.

He had never been one to default to paranoia. But before he could be sure the timing was coincidental, he had better find out what misophonia was.

He looked it up. And it looked bad.

He took the easy way out and called Thea's mother; but she didn't answer. So much for that: he would have to call her father instead.

When Bill answered, Max couldn't resist asking whether Thea's mother was busy. Bill, who probably shared Max's preference that Max talk to his wife, showed no surprise. "Linda's out back, elbow deep in mulch. Do you want her to call you back?"

No, that would be wimping out. "I just wanted you both to know about something."

Max didn't get far before his father-in-law started cursing. Max persevered, speaking louder than came naturally to be sure he wasn't wasting his breath. When he had finally got through a short definition of misophonia, he waited until the older man ground to a halt and an even more awkward silence followed.

Bill broke the silence first. "It's a devil's bargain you made."

Well, he hadn't exactly made it. But he had, in the end. He'd made the decision. And what did that matter, at least right now?

Bill wasn't through. "Of course the company's pulling this shit. Did you, either of you, really think they'd care about what she was entitled to know?" He turned his head and appeared to actually spit.

The last thing Max had had the time or perspective, or much of a reason, to consider that day was what Thea's parents would think. Now, he wondered. "If she'd left it to you, made you decide, what would you have done?"

The power of rage drained away from the older man and left him diminished, shoulders slumped, his face a decade older in an instant. "I'd have cursed the fate that put me in that place. And I'd have danced with the devil, all the way to hell, to keep anything I could keep of my little girl."

He pulled together the strength for one more momentary glare. "But that doesn't make it right."

* * * * *

The engineers had faced their share of setbacks, even crises, in the company's short history; but nothing had approached the intensity, the urgency, and the resultant camaraderie of this mobilization. Identifying the hacked code, fixing it, finding the hole through which the hackers had entered, plugging it, fortifying the system against future attack: the endeavor pushed aside all other concerns, for the company and for its staff. By the time every affected client had been restored to proper functioning, and the strengthened defenses had withstood multiple simulated attacks, two engineers had suffered the loss of longterm relationships, and several more were going to special trouble and expense to repair lesser damage. But every engineer received, at his or her option, either a generous bonus or a vacation in which to recuperate; and if not for the prudent scrubbing of the corporate records, the saga, all felt certain, would have gone down in corporate history.

In the ancient world, scientific and mathematical epiphanies often faded from public awareness. The Chinese (for example, and one of many) accurately described the structure of snowflakes around 135 B.C.E., a feat not replicated in the West until the twelfth century

C.E. By that time, the Chinese were extracting hormones from urine for medical purposes, an achievement at which Western medicine did not arrive until some hundreds of years later. In ancient Greece, Aristarchus of Samos posited the heliocentric solar system (placing the sun, not the Earth, at the center) in the third century B.C.E., a discovery forgotten and then rediscovered — amid life-threatening controversy — many centuries later.

But in our modern world, knowledge rarely lies fallow for so long. Inventions, once they exist, refuse to disappear. They are discovered, despite any efforts to the contrary, or rediscovered; and they are used.

The panic brought on by the malicious hacks had barely subsided when new anomalies presented themselves.

The grunts tasked with routine monitoring of digital feeds noticed the phenomenon first. A small number, perhaps no more than five percent, of the stored were sometimes showing an unusually wide range of higher brain system readings, an increase in random associations and interaction between different brain areas, and/or distorted perceptions of time and space.

When interviewed, some of these clients denied any subjective experiences corresponding to the readings, while others claimed to have been meditating. A few, apparently ignorant of the differences between readings for sleep and wakeful states, claimed to have been dreaming.

Before long, LiveAfter's engineers grew curious enough to research what situations might correspond to such readings. Soon, most of the technical people knew that someone was supplying the stored with the virtual equivalent of "shrooms." And given the new precautions against outside hacking, the supplier almost certainly worked for the company.

It took another week before an engineer said the wrong thing in the wrong place, and the word percolated up to management levels.

The Board of Directors met to consider the corporation's response. The chair got straight to the point. "Once we track down and crucify the son of a bitch who's peddling this stuff, should we offer the same experience ourselves?"

The stuffier members appeared taken aback at the suggestion, while the rest chuckled appreciatively. One of the former, embarrassed to find himself out of step, cleared his throat and said, "Paying engineers to come up with an authorized version costs us money that we would need to recoup somehow."

The chair dropped his smile and nodded. "We'll keep a lid on this while we find the culprit. That'll give us time to do some preliminary studies, possibly with the — cooperation of whoever created this, ah, product."

* * * * *

LiveAfter's CEO had known the caller since college. They had protested together; they had spent late nights earnestly examining society's failings and sharing their hopes for turning things around; the caller had once given the CEO a ride to the emergency room after an ambitious prank gone wrong. The CEO took the call with a warm feeling of anticipation.

The feeling faded quickly.

The caller's uncle, it appeared, had been one of

LiveAfter's earliest clients. The uncle had not been directly affected by the misophonia and other maliciously induced symptoms; but he had apparently mentioned the matter to his nephew before appropriate information screening had been put into place. At least the uncle had not mentioned the more recent breaches in their security, 'shrooms apparently not being among his indulgences . . . . The CEO yanked his attention back to what the caller was saying.

"Of course I don't want to make trouble for you. I know how damaging this news could be if those of us in the know proved indiscreet."

Which was as much as to say that his old friend had some alternative to suggest, something the CEO might have otherwise been less willing to entertain.

"But this news did get me thinking. Would I be correct that you're still somewhat short of the profit projections your investors want to see?"

Whatever the CEO had been expecting the caller to say, that wasn't it. Nor did he want to confirm the caller's information. "Let's say, for the sake of argument, that the figures added up that way. What then?"

"Well, I have an idea that could beef up your revenues, at least in the short term and possibly longer. Which would let you improve on your cybersecurity, wouldn't it?"

The CEO nodded warily.

"And at the same time, you could serve some other goals. Remember all the things we used to talk about and hope for? You haven't left all that idealism behind, I'm sure. You're in a unique position to make a difference, in a way that only your scientific breakthroughs have made possible."

The caller kept talking; and the CEO kept listening.

The CEO managed to extract himself from the call without making promises, except the promise to call back in the morning. Then he instructed his secretary to cancel his meetings and appointments for the rest of the afternoon, and double-checked that one of his former favorite hangouts remained in business.

When he reached the bar in which he and his comrades had spent so many hours, he wondered why the owners had bothered to keep the name while changing so much else. Instead of comfortably shabby decor and low lighting, pale yellow walls and larger windows; instead of the long list of foreign and domestic beers, a few local brews and a host of drinks with cutely unenlightening names. He almost turned on his heel and left, but where would he go instead? He ordered a brown ale, hoping it would bear some resemblance to his old British standby, and found an uninhabited corner in which to brood.

Of course the place had changed. How much, after all, had he himself changed? He had immersed himself in the fascination of technical challenges, and then in the demands of the business to which those challenges had led. When was the last time he had made time for politics, let alone for its revolutionary extremes? Had he even voted in the last election?

It struck him as ironic, now, that their clients could vote, even if he did not. He had accomplished that. But how many would bother, whatever persuasion Marketing came up with? And when they did, had he, by making those votes possible, injured the progressive causes once dear to him, causes in which he still believed? Many of their clients, to be sure, held views similar to his own; but enclaves of the privileged still clung to the old American myths of self-reliance and market forces, private charity and limited government. And LiveAfter could hardly afford to neglect that customer base, nor to be caught excluding it.

Was his friend's proposal so extreme, or was it, rather, the logical next step? Having given the stored political clout, was it in fact his responsibility to ensure that such power was exercised for the public good?

The proposal had its risks; but the promised payments would greatly increase the company's chance to survive and prosper. And the project would also serve to expiate, even to justify, the financial priorities that so preoccupied him, and which he would once so gleefully have scorned.

That night, the CEO arranged to meet the COO for breakfast at a restaurant whose private dining rooms were well suited to confidential discussion.

He had not expected outright opposition. But neither had he expected such a prompt and enthusiastic endorsement of his plans. Apparently, he had provided the COO with a welcome opportunity to take the general counsel down a peg.

He could live with that. The COO's eager cooperation would more than make up for any dissatisfaction the lawyer might nurse. She was too professional, and too practical, to get in his way, now that the die was cast.

* * * * *

First, the COO met with the general counsel in her soundproofed and electronically protected office. The lawyer sat in grim silence as her earlier advice was recalled, recited, and dismissed, and the CEO's complicity in the new scheme established. Then the COO summoned the senior project engineer, treating the office as if it was his own, and gave the engineer a brief synopsis: how the CEO and the founder of a prominent nonprofit had come to be having a highly confidential and potentially explosive conversation, and where that conversation had led.

No one else spoke, at first, when the COO had finished, nor made any sound, even to cough or clear a throat. The COO shook his head in irritation and pointed to the project engineer. "So tell me: is this kind of attitude alteration possible?"

The project engineer held up his hand, palm outward. "Just give me a minute to think." He sat back without awaiting a response and gazed out the window. The COO suppressed his irritation at the disrespect: he needed the fellow's expertise, just now. After three or four minutes, however, he was nearing the end of his patience. Fortunately, the engineer emerged from his near-trance and looked back toward the COO, assuming a somewhat pedantic tone and posture. "I think it is. What you want ties in with evolutionary psychology. We evolved to be hunter-gatherers living in small tribes, sharing very limited resources. If someone somehow ended up with more, that meant everyone else ended up with less. We lived like that for millions of years, probably. And even though humans eventually settled down and started creating new resources, with farming and then craftsmanship and then industry, most humans haven't really evolved beyond the hunter-gatherer mindset. They still tend to equate 'equal' and 'fair.' So all we have to do is strengthen that tendency, for those clients where it needs strengthening, and connect it to more detailed outlooks." He paused. "As for boosting their desire to vote in the first place, that may actually be a bit trickier. But if you set the ball rolling, get some of the already political people to start organizing, then we can amplify the tendency to follow the crowd."

The COO took a deep breath for what felt like the first time in hours. "Is there anything about the proposed interventions that would undermine the stability of the digital persona? Obviously there would be changes made in a number of files, but what's the likelihood of unwanted additional changes occurring as well?"

The engineer sat back again with interlaced fingers, tapping his thumbs together. "It's too soon to answer that question. Our tests will have to be very carefully monitored." He had begun to look excited. "But even if the project proves impractical, we're likely to learn a good deal in the attempt."

The COO turned toward the general counsel. "Are all the necessary patents in-house?"

The general counsel tapped her wristband to display a screen, oriented in the COO's direction. "We own the patents jointly with the employees who actually wrote the code. But the employees' employment contracts preclude them from exercising any sort of veto on how we use the patents."

The COO nodded, then frowned, a familiar expression using lines already etched deep. "I'll be talking to Personnel Management about those employees; and I'd like you—" He jerked his chin toward the general counsel. "—to be part of that meeting. For now, please give me your thoughts on the extent of our legal exposure."

The general counsel sniffed and tapped her wristband again to make the screen disappear. "You already know that I consider this an unnecessary risk.

But there may be a window of opportunity here. We're quite early in the roll-out of storage technology and the regulatory response. It'll probably be years before any restrictive statutes or regulations make their way through the bureaucratic process and go into effect. As for lawsuits based on the stored folks' constitutional rights: where the statutes involved impose criminal penalties, those statutes have been interpreted to require that the defendant knew their actions were illegal or violated established constitutional rights. At this point, it isn't even clear the stored *have* constitutional rights—although that's where the law is heading."

The COO's eyes had started to glaze over by the time she finished; he turned his attention back to the project engineer. "Get started mapping things out. Give me an update by this time next week." He stood up to signal the end of the meeting. The engineer hurried to stand as well; the general counsel moved more slowly, and dropped back into her chair as soon as the COO had left the room.

Three days later, the COO's office received the security upgrade he had long considered his due. As soon as the technicians had checked and signed off on the system, the COO summoned the Human Resources manager.

"You received the memo?"

The manager glanced up at the new equipment, tucked into a corner of the ceiling. "Yes. And I'm glad you flagged it as highly confidential. I've treated it as such."

The COO narrowed his eyes at the suggestion that the man might have done otherwise. "What difficulties do you expect when the technical people are apprised of this project?"

The manager stuck out his lower lip a trifle. "At least a few of them will be somewhat conflicted. They love pushing the envelope and solving new problems, but they also tend to be on the libertarian and contrary side. So they may object to what they would view as a reduction in the independence of the stored individuals. We're going to have to treat them very well during this phase, and defer to them on everything feasible short of actual project goals."

"Emphasizing the carrot, I see. What's the stick?"

The manager brought his holo to life and peered at the floating text. "They've all got airtight noncompete and confidentiality clauses in their contracts. And the orientation sessions when they were hired made clear that we enforce those clauses consistently and vigorously. If they want to use their skills and expertise, they have nowhere else to do it. And anyone who starts blowing whistles is going to spend the rest of their potentially productive years in litigation hell."

CHAPTER 7

ESTHER Boccara came from a long line of problem-solving women. She had turned that gift to software and nanocoding, but earlier generations had found their own ways to make use of it. And while Esther's cultural traditions might not exactly include the idea, she always thought of her maternal grandmother as the "wise woman" of her clan.

That wisdom encompassed, but ran deeper than, the family's practical genius. If the family had an old story worth remembering, Grandma would remember it. If some bewildering mystery arose, she would have a useful insight to help solve it. And the one time Esther had desperately wanted a love potion, Grandma had invited the boy over and fed him her special Purim cookies. The boy had followed her around like a puppy for the next six months, until Esther thoroughly regretted having wanted his attention.

But Grandma had probably known that would happen.

So now, with the disturbing rumors about the new project team, a team to which—if it existed—she might be assigned, Esther came for a visit. She brought one of Grandma's latest favorite treats, stuffed prunes wrapped in fake bacon, from a deli closer to Esther's apartment than Grandma's; and once they were ensconced in the sunny breakfast nook, she asked her wise woman, "What would it take for people to change their minds about something important overnight?"

Grandma popped another prune in her mouth, chewed, swallowed, and smiled like a saint on a shiny day in heaven. "*Thank* you, child. Now, let's see. Funny, but I can actually tell you about the time I changed my mind just about that quick. Do you remember the day we old folks call 9-11?"

Esther did. Her parents and grandparents might not agree on everything, but they all insisted she learn as much about the society around her as she possibly could. She could play around with software and write games as much as she chose, but not until she finished her history and sociology homework.

"I was a grown woman by then, and living with your grandpa. I grew up when all the young folks thought it was clever to think the worst of our country. I didn't go as far down that road as some, but you would never have seen me salute the flag or say the Pledge of Allegiance or anything of that kind.

"And then came 9-11.

"We lived in New York, where the terrorists were most successful. The world seemed to come to a stop: subways shut down, businesses shut down, schools shut down. The New York Stock Exchange, where people traded shares in all the big corporations—it shut down too.

"Not until six days later, on September 17th, did the Exchange reopen. And I can tell you, I would never in a million years have expected to get choked up about a bunch of rich people, as I saw it then, getting to throw around their money. But I did. I actually cried.

"And even before that happened, from the very day

the towers fell, I felt a whole lot different about the flag, and the national anthem, and the idea of being patriotic.

"If you'd yanked me out of my life on September 10th and plunked me down a week later where I could see myself, I would have thought I'd been brainwashed." Grandma cackled and reached for another stuffed date. "Or maybe replaced by one of the pod people."

Esther recalled another bit of family lore, the subject of much head-shaking among some members of the family. "Didn't you change your mind about some other things? Politics?"

"Sure did. About nuclear power, and guns, for example. My folks blamed it all on your grandpa—but I didn't just agree with everything he said, whatever they thought."

Esther opened the bag of chocolate rice cakes she had brought for her own snack and poured both of them some more iced tea. "But for all those changes, you knew they'd happened, and you more or less knew why."

"That's right. But you know, there's probably always been ways of changing folks' minds for them. I just mentioned the idea of 'brainwashing.' That's an old word, and it doesn't mean any fancy tech for messing with actual brains."

"Then how does it work? Is it something like hypnosis?" Esther, whom neither magicians nor dentists had ever been able to hypnotize, had always wondered if the hypnotic state even existed.

"Sorry, love. I never dug into it enough to know how it was done. But I think it worked on weak and wounded people—whether the brainwashers found them that way, or made them that way."

Esther shuddered.

"Fetch me my tablet, and I'll show you what I'm

talking about."

Esther hid a smile. Grandma liked to affect the frailty and limited mobility of a far older woman, or perhaps of her own grandmothers. Maybe it was her way of going along with the "wise woman" persona. Esther brought the tablet from the kitchen counter a few steps away and plunked it on the table. Grandma picked it up.

"Now you've got me curious about the how. . . . Says here that they used a combination of isolation, total control, exhaustion, uncertainty, and physical and emotional torture. Hmmm. I don't think you need all those methods every time, not from what I remember." She tapped away for a moment, then turned the tablet to show what looked like prisoners at some sort of trial. "Communists used to brainwash other communists into confessing all manner of things whenever they had a falling out. I'd bet they went the torture route. But look here." A group of young people in long loose dresses and pigtails sat in a circle around a stout well-dressed man with oily hair. "Fellows like this one managed to recruit young people, idealistic types searching for meaning in their lives, by posing as holy men. They'd turn the kids into beggars, pestering strangers for money or handing them flowers and then asking for donations, so they could support the leader in luxury. The kids would give up their families and everything else in their lives to do it."

Esther peered at the photo. "They certainly don't look tortured. They look happy, or maybe stoned."

"Yes'm. Throw in religion, and you don't need the harsher methods. And cutting the youngsters off from their families, that's where isolation and control came in."

Esther focused on one girl with a particularly

beatific smile, holding hands with a fairly good-looking (if scruffy) young man next to her. "But where do you draw the line? If we could talk to that girl right now, she'd say she was happy, doing what she wanted and being where she belonged."

"It did get complicated, as I recall. Sometimes the families got so worried they'd hire folks who called themselves 'deprogrammers.'" Grandma called up another photo. "I think this is from a movie, but it'd be something like." She slid the tablet over to Esther. The scene showed a burly man hauling a girl, a girl much like the one in the other photo, into a van. "They'd essentially kidnap the kid and take them somewhere, like a cabin in the mountains, away from other people, except sometimes a mother or sister or such. Then they'd try to break the leader's hold on 'em." Grandma looked thoughtful. "In fact, what the deprogrammers did looks a lot like brainwashing in reverse. Isolation, control . . . And if the kids were too upset to eat or sleep, you'd get the exhaustion, too."

Esther shook her head, her stomach too uneasy for even another rice cake. "What a mess."

Grandma, unruffled, took the last stuffed date. "People are, dear. It's best not to draw lines around them, unless you can erase the lines once you know them better." She wiped her fingers and tapped the tablet. "But I don't mean to say you shouldn't ask questions if people seem to change all of a sudden. Especially if some of the signs are there, the isolation and whatnot."

Later, in her bedroom, Esther pulled the quilt closer around her shoulders and sipped the hot tea. When her stomach felt better, she would try some hot tomato soup, or maybe a casserole. Comfort food.

She couldn't stop thinking about the stored. They were, in a way, more isolated than human beings had ever been. But was it isolation, if they didn't feel alone?

And would a brainwasher need isolation or exhaustion or torture, given sufficient control?

* * * * *

Max answered the call with an anticipatory smile, then did a double-take. "Your hair's black!"

Thea looked smug. "Yup. We just got appearance tweaks. They're still pretty buggy, but I managed to get a decent black on the second try. I remembered that you liked the look, that time I experimented."

So he had, though it had not, in the end, been worth the hassle. Thea had to shave her head to get rid of the dye, and while she'd looked pretty cool that way, sort of a foxy alien vibe, he'd missed being able to bury his hands in her hair. Now, of course . . .

That train of thought led to a familiar and desolate place; he forced it away. "Would you widen the view? I want to see more of you."

Thea smiled and obliged; and obliged further, whether or not she realized it, by changing the subject. "I've been doing more 3D drawing lately — since I don't have a beach worth calling a beach, let alone sand I could sculpt with. Want to see what I made?"

"Absolutely!" Maybe he could work something she'd done into his next tattoo design — for her, if that could be managed now, or for both of them, even.

Thea switched Max's view to show only her own screen. Max yipped in protest. "Hey, I still want to see you! Can't you do a split view?"

Thea reappeared, grinning. "Sure, lover." Then her

upper body occupied only the left half of his screen, with a 3D image on the right. He had thought she might choose the sort of subject she would have used for sand art; and it could be, he supposed, but she had never before chosen the sea itself. The arch of the wave rose tall, its depths glowing green, foam curling at the top. Looking at it, he could almost hear seagulls call, and breakers dragging pebbles along wet sand, and the distant yells of children playing. Thea rarely went so literal. She must be missing the ocean even more than he had known.

Max swallowed the lump in his throat. "It's gorgeous, babe."

She read his mind, as usual. "They're not all like that. Some of them are more my usual style. Let me pull those up."

He watched her on the left of his screen, wishing the lighting in her usual "room" were warmer, that it would light up her hair the way sunlight would. But at least he could see her. He must never come to take that for granted.

But something was off, different—more than usually different. Was it the lighting, still? Or something else?

Thea had put up the next image while Max's mind wandered: a thick, somehow muscular serpentine shape atop a rugged mount, intricate patterns suggesting snake skin. Max bent forward to admire it. "Cool!"

"Thank you, kind sir." She bowed and smirked. "Here comes another."

Her clothes? No, she wore a familiar outfit.

Then he realized. Since she had switched over to the wider view, showing more of herself, he hadn't seen her twitch.

The tic did come and go. Sometimes she went a lot

longer without it showing up . . . But not usually, unless she was sculpting or surfing or playing an instrument. Had he seen her tic at all, in her new life?

He kept watching, furtively, as Thea showed him two more images. But of course she noticed his distraction. "Don't you like them? It's okay to tell me. More than okay." She had her almost-stern face on, though he thought he saw some hurt behind it. "You'd better!"

Now he'd done it. "No, baby! They're terrific! I was just wondering about something."

"So! Spit it out."

"Have you noticed, since you . . . got there, whether you've been ticcing? Because I haven't seen it, at least not lately."

"Huh." Thea sat back in the chair, not bothering to complain about it as she sometimes did. "Now that you mention it, I don't think I have." She paused, waiting. "And usually, once I start thinking about my tic, I start ticcing. Not happening." She beamed; then stopped when she saw his very different expression. "What is it?"

Max took a deep breath and blew it out. "It's nothing. I'm being silly. It's just—I love you, every which way, just the way you are."

"You mean just the way I *was*." She glared at him with her head lowered in a familiar, though rare, about-to-charge posture. "Does it matter that I never liked that tic? Don't I get to change, even if I think it's for the better?"

"Uh . . . They didn't ask you, did they? They didn't know you'd be glad to get rid of it. They just assumed."

To his relief, the gleam of battle faded from her face, replaced by a look of concentration. "All right, that's a point worth thinking about. . . . Though it's not as if they had much of a chance to ask me about it, not unless they noticed the tic when I came in for my baseline reading. And even then, the tech who handled the reading probably had nothing to do with the programming end of things." She gazed at Max, intent, serious. "If you notice anything else that's different, tell me. Because yeah, I'd like to be consulted. But if they change something, don't assume I'll want to change it back."

Another day, another call.

"I wrote something for you."

Max beamed in delight. "What sort of something?"

"It's on the flute. I'd love it if you'd sing a harmony. All right?"

"Of course I will!" And if he missed the days when he would do his harmonizing lying in her lap, gazing up at her as she played, he would just have to push that aside. Again. "Ready when you are."

But when she started to play, the haunting minor tune put such a lump in his throat that his first notes were hardly even notes. She stopped. "Are you all right?"

"Just give me a minute." He fumbled for the glass of water he'd left nearby and drank half of it. "Okay. Sorry. Would you mind starting over?"

She answered by playing the first notes again; and this time, he was able to fill his mind with the music, and make it theirs.

When the last notes echoed and faded away, he cleared his throat. "Thank you! My turn next. Tomorrow, okay?"

She took a moment to respond. "Absolutely. But now . . . Would you just talk about something? Anything?"

The sadness in the music had been no accident. Max cast about for a cheery subject, or at least a neutral one. A flier for the upcoming election caught his eye. "So you can vote. And here I thought I was going to have to do the voting for both of us."

"That'd be two more of us than usual." Thea's mouth twisted in a wry smile. Neither of them had ever paid much mind to politics, except for a few issues that touched their lives in obvious ways.

Max searched his mail. "I got some sort of message about the ballot issues coming up. Let me see whether I deleted it already. No, here it is. Did you get one?"

"If I did, I probably deleted it—but I think I remember something about enlarging the public easement to and from the beach, though."

"You would remember that one! I can guess what you—Wait a minute, I'm getting another call."

* * * * *

Thea scrolled through her notes while waiting for Max. He was back in moments, his voice louder and higher with excitement. "We got that soundtrack!—the one where the director found us from the sand art promo. He loved the scene we scored on spec. We're in!" He stopped short, and when he spoke again, his voice shook just a little. "We've still got it, babe."

Once again, as so often, Thea ached to put her arms around him. "Of course we do! I can call in when you and he watch the film and get into the details. Why don't you let me know ahead of time if you have thoughts about where you want to steer him on style and instruments. And I'll speed up my work on generating different instruments. It'll be fine."

Max hesitated. "He wants me to meet some of the other people working on the movie, informally, over dinner. I'm supposed to head out soon."

Thea shoved down the surprisingly sharp pang of envy and managed a smile. "Off you go, then! Charm their socks off. And tell me what they feed you — I bet it's something fancy. Maybe squid eggs. Do squid lay eggs?"

Max laughed the big laugh she loved. "Squid eggs or nothing! I'll make 'em write it into the contract. I'll call you as soon as I'm through, okay? Love you, Thea! Later!"

Thea hung up, smiling more easily. Max sounded almost like himself again . . . and it felt good to be talking about work. To hell with politics.

* * * * *

The leader of the newly constituted technical team appeared rather suddenly behind the junior tech's shoulder, as was her wont. "I understand you have a test subject in mind."

The junior tech no longer jumped or flinched at these sudden appearances. "That's right. I suggest one of our newer arrivals, so the patterns will be up to date. Thea Lee. She's very bright, which may be a factor — and we should also test some of our, um, less conspicuously intelligent clients, but we may as well start with Ms. Lee. We cleaned up her motor tics, so we already know we can tinker with her code and get the expected result, at least in some respects. And there's a ballot initiative coming up in her former area of residence. She was a sand artist and avid surfer, so we can be reasonably confident of how she would have voted without application of our technique. . . ."

* * * * *

"We had some excitement yesterday." Max hadn't been sure whether to tell Thea about it, but Thea always knew when he didn't tell her something. Their now-limited means of communication hadn't changed that, and he was glad.

Thea looked up from her knitting. Yarn was apparently one of the items that existed in satisfactory form in Thea's new world, so naturally she had taught herself to knit. (Thea's hypothesis: one of the programmers liked to knit.) When he didn't immediately say more, she thrust her chin at him and commanded, "Spill!"

"We had a little fire in the building."

Thea set her knitting down in her lap and leaned forward. "How little? Where? Is everyone all right?"

"The laundry room is pretty much a loss, and you can smell smoke everywhere. But everyone's okay."

Thea frowned. "Doesn't that old lady with the rare neurological problem live next to the laundry room? And she's almost always home."

"Yeah. About that. When I smelled the smoke, I went out to look and saw a whole lot of it coming out of the laundry room. So I knocked on her door, and she buzzed me in after a while. And then I carried her out to the yard while the firefighters took care of things."

Thea looked like she was holding her breath. Then she relaxed and shook her head. "I don't know whether to be proud first or scared first. I'll go with proud, since you're okay. My husband the hero!"

Max laughed. "Not hardly. But I'm glad I was home. And that I've been working out. She was kind of heavy."

Thea had her far-off gaze. He waited for her to come back and tell him whatever she'd been pondering. Pretty soon she looked at him again, as serious as he had ever seen her. "If something had gone wrong—or if something else happens, some accident or other—what would you want to do? Want done? I don't know if you've realized it, but you have the same discount I used, if you want it. And that life insurance your dad bought you years ago? You could apply it to the fees, I hear."

Shit.

Deflect. "What would you want me to do?"

Thea rolled her eyes. "Now that is a really dumb question. Of course, for my sake, I'd want you here. You're not dumb; you're stalling. What would *you* want?"

The word "here" stuck with him. "Thea . . . do you know, when two people are both, um, there, stored . . . can they be together? Share space? Touch each other?"

Thea's eyes went wide, and her jaw dropped just a little. "I don't know. I hadn't thought about it. And I guess I haven't found out by trying to shake hands or pat anyone on the back. That would make one hell of a difference, wouldn't it? I'm going to find out. If anyone knows, I'll *make* them tell me. Or I'll just find a good excuse to touch someone." She paused, obviously pondering. "We have the sense of touch, so I don't know why it wouldn't work when people touch each other. But it would matter, a lot, just how *well* it worked. Would it be as good as breathing and the sensation of movement? Or as mediocre as the food?"

"Great questions—of course. . . . We can talk about it once you find out more. Okay?" Time to change the subject, to something a lot less important. "Say, you never did tell me how you voted. You did vote, didn't you?"

Thea chuckled. "Yeah. They lobbied us hard to vote. I guess they wanted to use the numbers in their sales pitches. I almost dug my heels in—metaphorically speaking—but I decided to go along. . . . I voted against the sales tax hike. If someone wants a bigger convention center, they can find a way to make it pay for itself."

"Same here." Max made a check mark in the air as if keeping score. "What about that beach access business?"

"Well, like you said, you know how I feel about that. I'd like—I'd have liked to live on the beach myself someday, when we could afford it. If people care enough about living on the beach to pay those real estate prices, they shouldn't have to have people traipsing through their front yards at all hours. It's not as if there aren't other paths."

Max made another, bigger check mark. "Yup, that's what I thought."

* * * * *

The junior tech stood before his boss's desk and shifted his weight from foot to foot. "You might not want to send my report to anyone just yet."

"So you said in your message. Just in time, I might add, or you'd be in somewhat more trouble. What's the problem?"

"Well, we've been doing some monitoring of our test subject. And it appears we may have jumped to conclusions about her preexisting views."

The team leader listened to the junior tech's rather stilted recital of the mix-up, suppressing her irritation. She should have kept the fellow on a shorter leash, given his inexperience: the snafu was as much her fault as his.

When he had finished, she allowed herself to lift an eyebrow at him and shooed him out the door. "Send me a write-up."

The team leader studied the junior tech's report, thoughtfully tapping her stylus against her lower lip. He had done more than summarize: he had also stated, with reasonable clarity, the decision to be made next.

The threshold question at this stage is whether to run a second test employing the same test subject, either alone or as part of a larger group, despite the miscalculation that prevented clear assessment of earlier results.

Advantages include the ready availability of the parameters already measured, as well as most advantages previously noted.

Disadvantages include the variables introduced by modifying the relevant programs twice in succession, and doing so within this short a time frame.

Including this subject in a larger group would reduce the danger of drawing erroneous conclusions, but would also render such inclusion less significant overall.

The tech had, with understandable prudence, declined to make any recommendation. Nor would any suggestion he made have mattered a great deal. She was team leader. It was her call.

CHAPTER 8

(one month later)

THEA looked adorable in the sweater she had knitted herself. Apparently the LiveAfter environment did include something like seasons, with crisp air and a decorative approximation of snow; a few oversized, implausibly detailed snowflakes lingered on Thea's shoulders.

"Ready to show me your tracks for the next cue?" Max rubbed his hands together in pantomimed expectation.

"Sure thing! I'll play all the tracks together, and then, if you want, I'll play mine by themselves. Ready?"

Max nodded vigorously, then closed his eyes to listen. Thea hit play. Max snuck a quick peek: she was watching him. He closed his eyes again.

The music welled forth. Thea had done a terrific job at picking up and playing with the themes he had used. No surprise there!

But something was surprising him, and he wasn't sure what. He tried to listen more intently without wrinkling his forehead or otherwise showing any unusual reaction.

He still couldn't put his finger on it. But something was different. Good—great!—but different.

The tracks finished. Max opened his eyes and

smiled as broadly as he could. "I love it, babe!"

Thea beamed back. "The team's still got it!"

"Three cheers for the team! . . . Have you been listening to anything new lately? Anything I should hear?"

Thea cocked her head, quizzical. "Not really. I don't, when I'm composing. You know that. Why?"

Max shrugged, trying to keep his shoulders relaxed. "Nothing. I just wondered."

Thea gave him her what's-going-on look; but when he refrained from blurting out any further response, she moved on. "Let's hear your rewrite on that earlier cue."

Max hit play, glad to be let off the hook. He would think about it more later, when he listened to Thea's piece a few more times.

After repeated listening, Max still didn't have a name or category for what was different about Thea's style, but he thought he'd be able to identify it if he heard it again, either in Thea's music or elsewhere. Though he hadn't tested that notion with any "elsewhere." The whole business made him too damn nervous.

He had sent Thea his tracks for the final cue in the movie, and now he would hear what she had added. He closed his eyes and thought about keeping his face relaxed, then realized that would distract him from the music. Thea's music deserved better than that, whatever was happening.

At first, he was relieved: the difference he had been waiting to hear, he wasn't hearing. It got easier to relax not only his face but his body; he sat back in his chair, smiling a little.

Then the smile started to freeze up on him. Something

was still different. It was just a different difference than the first time.

The music shut off in mid-phrase. "Max, open your eyes and tell me what the fuck is going on."

Max jumped in his chair and opened his eyes. Thea was glowering at him. She looked royally pissed. What was that old phrase her mother sometimes used? The jig was up.

While he was trying to decide how to start, Thea spoke again. "If you don't like what I've written, do you really think it helps either of us if you try to hide it? Not that you could!"

"That's not it! I love it! It's just . . . your style's been changing, and I wasn't expecting it, and it surprised me. That's all it was."

Thank all gods, the anger faded and she got her boy-that's-interesting expression. "Changing how?"

Max waved his hands in confusion. "I don't know. I've been trying to figure it out. I thought I had, kind of; but then it changed again. Today seemed a little more . . . hip, maybe? And last time . . . it was maybe more classical, or referential, or something. But still original and exciting, don't get me wrong!"

If either of them could figure out why, it would be Thea. "What do you think is going on? Or am I just imagining things?"

"You could be. I'll do my own listening, with the question in mind, and see what I think. But if my style is changing somehow, is that so surprising? My life is so different now. I'm more on my own than I've ever been. I have fewer distractions, but also fewer inputs and influences. Why wouldn't that have an effect? Or different effects at different times, not always in the same direction?"

"You're right. As usual. I feel a *lot* better." Max smiled at her; but she didn't smile back right away.

"I don't know if I'm right. I'll have to think about it. But for now, let's get back to work."

* * * * *

The Cerebral Management Project team met in a room superficially like any other. The coffee, good if not excellent, was as usual. And the team members were all accustomed, by now, to the security scans as each of them entered the room, and the barely audible hum of the electronic interference mechanism installed within it.

The team leader position had rotated since the team was first established—although a couple of members, like the slim Sephardic woman who so conspicuously kept her thoughts to herself, had declined their turn. This month's leader might not have been ideal for the moment that had finally arrived. He seemed uncertain, perhaps overwhelmed, as he stood before them; he fidgeted with the beaded necklace encircling his thin throat, and played with the ends of his untidy hair, and waited a moment too long after conversation had ceased before beginning to speak.

"You've probably all heard this news in some form. As rumors or whatever. But I wanted to announce it in case anyone had doubts."

The room, already quiet, seemed to get quieter, the mechanical hum now clearly the loudest noise to be heard. The gulp as the leader swallowed, then swallowed again, seemed impossibly loud by comparison.

"The testing is complete. The kinks have been worked out. The process works.

"So." More fidgeting, more hesitation, and finally the announcement that no longer needed to be made. "We can get started."

CHAPTER 9

THE POLITICAL analyst ran the numbers one more time. No, it wasn't a glitch. But she was damned if she knew what to make of it.

The numbers from several districts in the Northwest and the flyover states, districts that should lean conservative or libertarian, had varied from predictions. Of course, those predictions were based on polling that hadn't kept up with recent developments: the newly enfranchised voters, the stored, were underrepresented, especially given their unexpectedly high voter turnout. But if anything, that made the results even stranger. The stored were disproportionately wealthy, and had been (should still, or again, be) powerful. Why would they be supporting more liberal, even what she liked to call communitarian, candidates and initiatives?

What the hell was going on?

* * * * *

It was never too late, Thea had realized, to get politically active. And according to the calendar and the sudden appearance of flowers, it was spring, an appropriate time for new beginnings.

It seemed that quite a few of the stored had felt the

same urge. Not just one but two new discussion groups had started up to keep track of local, state, and national politics. Thea wasn't sure which one she wanted to join, though. Her moods seemed to shift around a lot, at least where politics was concerned.

Max wasn't likely to be too interested. But one advantage of sorts to their new separation was her freedom to do things that disturbed him without having to explain, at least not as often. There were enough aspects of storage that undeniably sucked: she might as well enjoy those few that could be viewed as silver linings.

It was a bit early to worry about the next election, but she did some searching to see who might be running for what, and what the hot issues might turn out to be. Then she could attend both groups and decide which, if either, might be ideologically congenial.

It would mean something close to having real company. And the people she met might share some of her other interests as well. At the meeting she'd attended so far, she'd been tickled and pleased to find that one of the other newcomers was the flutist who'd played her piece for the ad agency proposal. He'd recognized her name and complimented her work, even suggesting that they get together some time to play duets.

She'd also verified her guess that the stored could touch each other, and that it felt a lot like touching should feel. It made sense: if yarn felt like yarn, why shouldn't a handshake feel like one hand gripping another?

Which raised more questions, some she was glad Max wasn't around to notice (though he had never been as good at guessing her thoughts as she was at guessing his). They had never talked that much about fidelity, as as it seemed to come naturally to them both. But now, if her only chance for tangible physical connections—for physical affection—came from other stored people, was she really going to rule it out indefinitely? And did she want to talk to Max about it, or make her own decision and then let him know?

* * * * *

Max didn't realize he had been staring blankly at his recording equipment until a clattering outside, on the stairs, jolted him out of his daze. He hurried to the door and opened it to find the new neighbor, a woman who had moved in a couple of weeks before, staring at a busted cardboard box and at all the items that had fallen out of it down the stairs. Just as he took in the scene, she started cussing with a fluidity and inventiveness that made him want to start clapping. Instead, he skirted the mess to get to the bottom of it and started picking things up.

She stopped swearing and flashed a broad smile down at him. "Thanks so much! I should have checked that box, especially once I hefted it and felt how heavy it was. Let me run and get a couple of others." She pattered off down the hall. Max paused once his armful of items threatened to spill back onto the stairs; his neighbor reappeared moments later and slid a box down toward him. He stopped it with his foot, dumped the stuff in, and resumed working his way up the stairs, filling the box to the brim. Then he hoisted it and waited for her to finish with the second box before following her up the stairs and down the hall to her apartment.

From that position, he couldn't help but notice what a great shape she had on her. And her hair was a really cool darkish red—chestnut, he thought it might be called—that caught the sunlight when they passed the hall window.

The woman paused, balancing her box on her hip, to unlock her door. But before she actually put the key in the lock, she turned toward him and aimed that smile at him again. "I really appreciate this. And I'd like to start getting to know the neighbors. Do you have time to go get some coffee or something? You could show me where the good coffee is around here."

It would have been easier to think without the edge of the box digging into his side. And without the scent of sunlight and clean hair drifting toward him.

Max was used to telling women "no" in a nice way before they actually asked a question that would get them embarrassed. Thea wasn't the only woman who'd found him attractive. It sometimes surprised him how many women seemed to. So he shouldn't feel as if some new problem had arisen.

But that's how he felt.

He fell back on a noncommittal excuse. "I'm kind of expecting a call." Which was almost true. Thea's and his afternoon call usually came a little later, but she wasn't anal about hitting the same time every day.

The woman didn't stop smiling. That must mean that the way he'd responded, his body language and such, had left a door open.

And speaking of doors . . . He shifted the box to his other arm. The woman noticed and shook her head, hair swinging. "Sorry! Here I am keeping you standing around, weighed down with all my crap." She opened the door quickly, then stood back just enough to let him in.

Not enough that he could avoid brushing against

her a bit as he staggered past to put the box down on the nearest piece of furniture.

He backed out, searching for an exit line, and found a pretty feeble one. "Well, I guess I'll be seeing you around." Then he fled back down the hall to his apartment.

He checked for missed calls. None. Good. He hoped, for once, that Thea didn't call just yet. He wanted to think.

He'd been attracted to that woman. No hiding from that. And what's more, he hadn't shoved that attraction to one side the way he was used to doing.

It was time he sat down and talked to himself for a while.

Thea wasn't gone. But her body was. She would never have one again. All the wonderful things their bodies could do together, they would never do those things again.

And Max was a young healthy guy with a body that needed to love a woman. Well, not only a woman, necessarily, but that was how it had always worked out so far.

If the aneurysm had taken Thea away from him, and she hadn't secretly had herself recorded, he would simply be a too-young widower. And apparently, he would be starting to notice other women again. Because he just had.

Thea would never have expected him to live without women forever. Without sex. If she ever thought about it before she died, she might hope he'd wait a few months; but she wouldn't have wanted him to swear off sex forever. Or love.

Of course, he could talk to her about it. She might call any time now.

But the thought of that talk made his stomach squirm.

Sometimes phone sex worked. Sometimes phone sex was great. Not tonight, not so far.

Max had set up pictures of Thea to look at. He had just one nude photo of her, and it was a terrific shot; but it was artsy, black and white, with Thea stretched out on one of her sand sculptures and almost disappearing into it in places.

They'd made love the afternoon he took the photo, right out on the beach, on a blanket big enough to keep the sand out of everywhere, the air soft and humid and no one anywhere around. . . . Sometimes remembering that day could get him off all by itself, even without Thea murmuring in his ear. But other times, memories and photos weren't enough.

And today, his memories of Thea kept getting interrupted. Memories of how his neighbor's behind had looked in those tight jeans, ahead of him on the stairs, would break in. And that would heat him up, all right, but it felt too much like cheating.

And all this trying and thinking distracted him so he couldn't do much good for Thea either.

Max fell back against the pillows and shook his head at his screen. "I'm sorry, babe."

Thea's breathing slowed (maybe she'd been closer than he thought; maybe he shouldn't have quit), but she didn't look frustrated, or sympathetic, or whatever he had been expecting. Instead she had her Plan B look. "Just a minute, sweetie. I want to try something."

Then the image of Thea's face disappeared, and Max was looking at Thea sprawled on a bed. A water bed, moving her just a little up and down as she moved.

And she was indeed moving, a slow sort of squirm, sprawled across the bed, her legs open, her breasts round and spilling a little to each side.

And her right hand, her first and middle fingers, poised, and then, touching . . . touching . . . .

"Ohhhh." He hadn't seen her move in so long. He had *never* seen her touching herself like that, bringing herself . . . bringing him . . . .

He had grabbed his cock without even knowing it, and now he was stroking it, stroking, faster, groaning . . . (Call her name!) "Thea! Omigod, omigod, baby, baby. . . ."

He came like a rocket taking off, shouting.

He'd been looking at her, and then he'd been so lost in the blast that he hadn't even noticed whether she came too. He looked now. She was lying on the bed, no longer wriggling, her hands loose at her sides. He couldn't see her face.

Should he ask?

Slowly, Thea pushed herself up onto her elbows, the motion making the bed toss her up and down. She looked sleepy, the way she sometimes did after they made love. But whether she'd climaxed or whether she was just glad that he had, he couldn't tell.

And neither of them seemed to know what to say.

* * * * *

Thea gave up on trying to sleep and hauled herself out of bed. The bed reminded her too much of the strange, sad session she and Max had shared earlier. Yes, they had both come, but the afterglow had faded more quickly than any she could remember.

If he had been asleep beside her, she could have

soothed herself by watching him sleep. He was so cute, sleeping—boyish, almost childlike, despite whatever beard or stubble he might sport. And he snored so softly there should be a gentler name for the sound.

She'd snapped a photo of him sleeping once. If only she had that photo now, at least.

She could ask Max to send it—if he could find it. Had she shared it with him, or backed it up somewhere? Had her wristband been recovered, or had some lifeguard or bystander trodden it into the sand, to be forgotten and ruined?

There were other photos she could ask for, ones Max should still possess. He had been taking pictures on that last day, pictures of her final sculpture, her final victory, and probably of her as well. A bittersweet reminder those pictures would be. . . and what she wanted were pictures of Max, not of herself, or not only of herself. There was that lovely one her cousin took of the two of them at a campfire, Max on his guitar, Thea on flute, both golden in the firelight. And the posed portrait by one of their oldest mutual friends, a girl whose pictures rose to the level of art, with Max positioned like an ancient Greek statute and trying not to smile. And the shot Thea took of him in high school, bent over with his hands on his knees, laughing at his own exhaustion after a run.

Max would have that, and every other photo she had ever sent him.

And hadn't one of the witnesses taken a picture of their wedding? She'd been glad to have that picture, it turned out, as little as she'd thought she would care about the ceremony. She would be glad to have it now.

* * * * *

Max sat in their—his—saggiest armchair, legs folded up and arms around his knees, sleepy and afraid to sleep. He did not trust his dreams, not tonight.

If only he knew that he would dream of Thea the way she used to be, or of the two of them together! But as he'd been drifting off, tonight, what had suddenly come to mind was Thea washing up broken on the beach.

Max groaned and pried himself out of the chair to fetch his tablet. If he could not trust his mind to show him the pictures he needed, he would look at them another way. He took the tablet to the couch and stretched out with his head on one end, resting the tablet upright on his chest.

He had so many photos, from all their years—

But Thea had none. How could she? Unless her preparations had included providing copies. But she had probably not bothered, not yet.

Would she want them? Would she, like Max, cherish visible reminders of their lost past?

He would send her some pictures; and if she already had them, no harm done. And if not, she could make her own decision about whether to look at them, or store them, or ignore them, or delete them.

He should not send too many. He would scroll through them all and pick just a few of her favorites.

Start with high school. Thea had always enjoyed that photo of him trying to catch his breath after a run. Let her laugh at him one more time! It was laughter with love, and he had always loved to hear it. . . . That photo at the bonfire was just plain pretty, and if it called forth vivid memories of singing together, at least that was something they could still do. . . . The Greek-sculpture pose did, he had to admit, make his bod look good, and

Thea might find a use for that. . . . Not much point to a photo of him sleeping . . . .

What about their wedding? They only had the one photo, and Thea had been looking over her shoulder at something, so her face didn't show. He wouldn't bother with that one.

Those should be enough to start with. He'd send more if she wanted them.

He scrolled to the end, to the very last photo of Thea on the beach, Thea triumphant with her trophy, and then grabbed a blanket off the back of the couch. He would lie there and cry a little, and then he could probably go to sleep.

CHAPTER 10

IF MAX had spent a solid week guessing what might happen if Thea ended up stored—not that he would have wanted to dwell on such a possibility for a minute, let alone a week—he would never have guessed she'd get so interested in politics. If he didn't want them to grow further apart, he would have to work up some interest of his own. But that would take some time; for now, he just made encouraging noises as Thea rattled on about the meeting she'd rushed off to attend after their morning call.

"All these bigwigs are going to join forces, and resources, lobbying for a series of publicly funded Utopian communities. They'll start with one, see how it goes, learn from its growing pains, and start some more. It's pretty exciting."

"That's cool, I guess. Depending on who decides what's Utopian."

Thea looked slightly miffed. "Well, the principles made sense to everyone involved. I'd actually expected more disagreement, but as people chimed in with their ideas, they all seemed to be heading in the same direction. I guess ideas really can have their moments in history."

Max couldn't, offhand, remember having lived through any such moments, but he vaguely recalled books he'd read in school that talked about them. "So what are these ideas everyone felt good about?"

Thea bit her lip, the way she did when she tried to remember something. "Rotating leadership; communal ownership and pooling of assets; hi-tech farming; making and selling handcrafted goods; invitations to artists and artisans to come live and work; solar-powered everything .... That's all I remember right now. But we're meeting again in a couple of days. I'll take notes this time, so I can tell you all about it. Maybe you'll end up one of those artists in residence!"

Max had a hazy feeling that some of those pieces might not fit together perfectly; and he wasn't sure such communities could support themselves, unless the government was supposed to support them indefinitely. But if it made sense to Thea, it probably made sense, period.

* * * * *

The most junior worker in the Oversight and Retention Department (what everyone except the stuffier management types called Peep and Keep) looked over his notes for the second time, finding three more typos. He should probably break down and use Spell Check like everyone else; but he could still hear his mother's rants on the subject, all about homonyms and real-but-wrong words chosen by accidental free association. And rereading also let him see where he'd drifted off into bureaucratese. Not that his supervisor would mind. In fact, she'd probably prefer it: bureaucratic jargon seemed to relax her.

He was supposed to pay as little attention to the substance of the conversations as possible. Right. "Don't think of brown monkeys!" But most of the time, it was boring enough that nothing lodged in his memory. Lately, though, he'd noticed a change, a fad of sorts, with politics replacing much of the complaints and nostalgia and bragging one-upmanship that used to fill his reports. The johnnies in charge had tried to whip up this sort of political interest when the voting rights legislation passed; maybe it had finally happened.

Well, it wasn't his job to spin hypotheses, and even if it had been, how was he supposed to know just why these rich leftovers of people were becoming more interested in changing the world they'd left behind?

* * * * *

"I thought you were going to have that segment arranged by now. Even with your meetings and all, you said you could manage." Even to himself, Max sounded like he was whining. But he'd never had to worry about Thea sticking to a schedule before. He wouldn't have taken on this new project if he'd expected such problems; and he'd made promises assuming she'd have her piece ready.

Thea looked stricken, which made Max feel even more like an asshole. "I'm so sorry, baby! When the group asked me to work on the charter for the first planned community, I was so excited that I must have lost track. Can you get just a couple of days' extension?"

He should be glad that she'd found a consuming interest, one she could still pursue. That she wasn't pining for all she'd lost. That it didn't tear her up inside, the way it did him, to think of her never riding her surfboard again, or cooling off by rolling in wet sand and then diving into the waves to wash off.

He should be happy for her.

But damn it all, he'd never thought Thea would leave him hanging! And how could she care more about writing rules for people she'd never met than about the music one of their best friends would conduct at his first really big concert?

"Max? Can you get more time?"

For the life of him, he couldn't pretend that everything was okay. "I guess I'll have to try. If you still want to be part of the project."

Thea actually gasped. "Of course I do!"

Had he hurt her feelings? He never wanted to do that. But he had feelings too; and he hurt.

*　*　*　*　*

One of the regulars at the meeting, a man who had recently started up a theater troupe as well, started things off with an announcement. "I'm changing my name. So from now on, please call me Jim."

The woman to Thea's right cocked her head to one side and said, "O-kaaay . . . . Would you mind saying why?"

The man flushed. "Because my family and friends keep complaining about how much I've changed! Why am I doing this, why am I saying that, why do I care about anything I haven't cared about for the last twenty years!"

Thea's ears pricked up. "So you're sort of calling their bluff. Saying that if they can't accept you as the person they know and love, even if you've changed, then you'll take them at their word."

"Exactly!" The man's shoulders relaxed, which showed Thea how tense he had been when making his announcement. He hesitated, then added, "Though I have to admit I hope the gesture gets through to them. I'm not sure I'm ready to be Jim for the rest of my . . . Well, you know what I mean."

Thea looked around the room. Quite a few people were nodding in agreement or identification.

Their leader for the month cleared her throat. "Well, is everyone ready to get started?"

Thea and "Jim" had living quarters near each other. That made it easy for her to walk with him after the meeting. Thea started out by asking him about the theater troupe, which actually sounded like fun, if not an activity she had ever dabbled in before. Once she had him chatting, it took very little to bring him back to the subject he had raised already. He had plenty more to say on the subject, and she contributed just enough to keep him talking. Outspoken as Thea could be, she had still learned the art of active listening.

"Anyone who keeps up with new science and technology, and thinks about how those developments affect our daily lives and our public institutions, is going to change their mind now and then. I've changed my mind over the years, and I've admitted it. They didn't accuse me of becoming a stranger before. Is change so different when it happens to someone stored?"

And: "People afraid to change will end up hiding from facts! Do I have to turn into a coward to keep my family?"

When she got back to her own quarters, Thea undertook some historical research, checking her memory of a few anecdotes that seemed pertinent.

There was that miner, Phineas Gage, who'd had a

metal rod blown through his head in some explosion. It had changed his personality quite radically, making him short-tempered and unreliable (not to mention profane in his word choices). His friends, it chilled her to learn, had come to feel that he was "no longer Gage." She had also not known that many of the man's personality changes were temporary. At what point had those friends decided that "their" Gage had returned to them?

The great neurologist Oliver Sacks had written about an old woman, around ninety years old, who found herself becoming noticeably less inhibited, more (in her words) "frisky." That turned out to be the result of tertiary syphilis. And after she was diagnosed, she deliberately chose a course of treatment that would arrest the progress of the disease without repairing the "damage" that had changed her behavior. She liked the person she had become. But Thea could find no information on how her family and friends had received those changes.

And the prophets, the "saints" like Joan of Arc, whose visions might well have been symptoms of temporal lobe epilepsy—if they had somehow been cured of that condition, they would have been less historically significant, and possibly would have lived longer, but would they have become different people?

How much could someone change before it was appropriate, before it was fair, to question that transformation? How much, before loved ones had some excuse for changes in their own feelings?

She had thought to raise the subject in her next talk with Max; but in the end, she fell back on the less volatile communication of a written message. She told him about "Jim," and about the history she had checked. And then she reviewed the ways that Max himself had evolved since they met.

You've always loved music, but you used to be all about playing, being on stage with girls going crazy. Now you're a superbly talented composer, and while you still like girls to notice you, you don't always notice them.

(At least, he hadn't when she was there at his side. . . .)

You used to waste money on smuggled tobacco cigarettes. Now you just take a friendly toke with your friends, or a few more with me.

(More on those nights when they knew they would make love for hours before bothering to sleep. . . .)

You used to be close to your dad, but not your mom. Then you started making an effort to learn about her past, where she came from, how she got to be so sharp-tongued and difficult. And now you respect the hell out of her.

You used to think tattoos were pretentious. And now, my love, you design the most beautiful tattoos for me.

She had thought of challenging him outright to tell her whether he believed his love had a limit, how much it depended on the bundle of traits and beliefs she had accumulated during her corporeal lifetime, or those that had characterized her when she died; but her courage did not, in the end, carry her so far. So she simply asked him to write back sharing any thoughts her message had stirred.

In another few minutes, it would be time to call Max. Thea checked her mail and was relieved to see that he had already written. Holding her breath for a moment (and she would stop apologizing, even to herself, for thinking in those terms!), she was further relieved to see the length of the message. He had not evaded the question or retreated into his less articulate mode.

You sure gave me plenty to think about.

I looked up that miner and the old lady. And I thought about the saints.

We all change. And when we promise to love someone and stay with them no matter what, we know they'll change, and that we will too.

If someone gets sick, so sick they turn into someone they wouldn't want to be, then the people that love them should show that love by fighting the sickness and helping the person get back to who they want to be. But I don't think you're sick, and even though you've changed, there's nothing about you now that either of us should have any problem about loving. So I'm sorry I've been a dick.

Thea laughed and dabbed away tears, then went on reading.

And if, somehow, you change so much, or in such a way, that I think you wouldn't have wanted it to happen, then I'll fight for you. Because I love who you are, and I won't let either of us lose the fantastic person you are, if anything I can do would save you.

That was all, except the drawing at the end, a sketch of two people, of the two of them, sitting on the sand, cuddled close together, watching the waves come to shore.

* * * * *

Max read over his message, even though he'd already sent it, and waited for Thea's call. He could have called her first, but he could use more time to get ready for talking to her again.

If he hadn't written that one thought, if he'd had a reason for not writing it, then he probably shouldn't say it.

Yes, he had to give her room to grow. Yes, her new life and new friends were bound to change her. Yes, being involved in politics was usually a good thing, and even more so for people who had little else to tie them to the world of the living, or whatever.

But Max had a bad feeling about all this, and he couldn't say why. With all the explanations and reasons and logic Thea had given him or he had recited to himself, something was still bugging him, making him more than a little nervous.

He'd said that if the time should come, he'd fight for the Thea he knew and loved. He hadn't said how unsure he was that he would know when that time came.

CHAPTER 11

THEA returned from the meeting pondering once again how good it felt to talk to people in person. The simulation might be imperfect, in some way she couldn't quite identify, but it came close enough. Of course, it helped that she was finding the subject matter so absorbing.

Before, when she'd more or less disdained politics, she would have expected meetings like this to be full of status-seeking and posturing and pontificating. Were the members of this group more focused, less egotistical, than the average citizen? Was that why they so often reached a consensus? And did the self-selection process at work, the decision to be stored, somehow result in people who worked together well? That seemed counterintuitive. She would have thought people so determined to survive that they would choose to live after (ha, the company name cropping up again) their body had died would be more self-focused and individualistic than average, rather than less.

Her mother had been just as surprised, when Thea filled her in. And she'd been so pleased to find herself and Thea more in agreement than in the past. Thea had long since learned to ignore her and her mother's political differences; she hadn't realized the effort it took, the energy diverted to maintaining a wall against her mother's quiet disapproval.

Should she try again to discuss the group's work with Max? They'd reached an understanding, more or less, about her political activities, but she had the sense that he was still more bothered about it than he would admit.

But she had better stop woolgathering (an apt term, for a knitter . . .) and call. She was running a little late.

Max's line rang a few times, more often than usual. He must be busy with his own activities. That was good. Sauce for the goose and all that. Though she could hardly help wondering what he was doing, and if he was doing it with people she knew or with new people.

"Thea!" He still answered by almost shouting her name, that special joyous lilt in his voice.

These calls had a routine, by now. They took turns telling the other about what they'd done that day. Did he ever tailor, or even censor, his accounts? Had she been doing the same, without altogether realizing it?

Thea listened to Max's account of yet another pitch session, one that didn't sound likely to lead to a job, and of the neighborhood cookout at which he'd proudly taken charge of the grill. The most surprising news: he'd started taking surfing lessons. He'd always declined her offers to teach him, saying he'd rather watch and sketch her instead. Damn—she'd have liked to be his teacher. "So who's teaching you?"

He looked faintly uncomfortable as he responded, "Just one of the neighbors. No one you've met. They moved in later."

She noted the pronoun with amusement. Max tended to use gender-specific pronouns, probably because he was old-fashioned straight in his preferences and couldn't help noticing gender before many other characteristics. So the neighbor was probably female and cute. The time might be coming to discuss how they should deal with their sexual needs in the future.

But this woman had better be careful about Max's safety! "Gotten hit in the head with the board yet? Or thought you were drowning?"

Max chuckled. "Yes to the first, no to the second. It's all good, except the water's still a little cold. I tried on your wetsuit, but it's too loose. No matter. Now your turn. What have you been up to?"

"Well, I just came back from another meeting. We're taking a break from the new-community development and preparing for the next elections. We each took an elected position or a likely ballot issue and talked about the options we expect to have. It's something of a waste of time, I suppose, since we don't actually know what the options will be. But I presented the issue of raising local taxes to fund public support for artists."

Max um-hummed along as she spoke. When she paused, he threw in, "That's a subject you already know inside out. If you want to follow up, I can send you the letter you wrote last year, explaining why artists shouldn't depend on public funding. You could bring it to the next meeting, or distribute it beforehand."

Thea sat back, stunned. Max had been looking to one side, no doubt searching for this supposed letter on a split screen, but her continued silence made him glance back at her. "What's wrong?"

"Hon . . . are you sure that's what I said? Could you be misremembering it?"

"I don't think so. I remember because you got interested in something political for a change. And because you made your point so well. There were a bunch of comments about that. You changed some minds. . . . Here it is! I'm sending it now."

Thea waited, holding her breath, until her mail program pinged a moment later. She skimmed the message, then read it again, her heart pounding. "You're right. That's what I said. And I sounded very sure of my ground. So why don't I remember?"

And why had she been so casually and confidently presenting the opposite position?

* * * * *

The technical meeting did not take long to devolve into a shouting match. The current leader had expected as much, and had brought along a police whistle. She blew it now. "That's enough! This isn't about who made what decision and who did or didn't express any doubts how clearly."

The various combatants settled back in their chairs, some grumbling, others obviously relieved. When she had as close to silence as she was likely to get, she went on. "The memory deletion approach had fairly obvious advantages and disadvantages. The advantages of neatness, lack of internal conflict, and so on hardly needed demonstrating. The disadvantages were predicted by some, and have now been demonstrated. So the next phase, as I see it, is to proceed without erasing previous contrary views. We will leave it up to the subjects to reconcile any contradictions. I'll be sending round the research about how naturally people adjust their own memories to reduce cognitive dissonance. And then, we'll watch to see whether the results confirm what that research suggests. Comments?"

One of the more senior programmers raised his

hand. She nodded at him, but he had started speaking without that permission. "What about their memories of this latest fiasco? Do we leave those alone as well?"

The leader pointed to the team member in charge of monitoring and collating information. "How many of this round's subjects discovered the discrepancy on their own, without assistance from others and without informing anyone or making any written record?"

The team member tapped away at her holographic keyboard, then looked back up. "About one-third."

"Good enough. Delete the relevant memories for those, so we'll have a clean slate. As for the others, we risk too many complications, and too much reinforcement of what may already be troubling them, if we intervene. Let them come up with their own comforting versions of events."

* * * * *

Dane Andresen took a bite of his sandwich and tried to ignore his feet. He didn't walk enough, and his floppy old shoes had no arch support to speak of. But he and his coworker Esther hadn't even had to discuss the matter: they couldn't touch this topic at the office, or in any restaurant or plaza where their coworkers or bosses might be found at lunchtime. That is, if he wasn't imagining that she found their current project as disturbing—no, make that outrageous—as he did. He was taking a hell of a risk based on expressions and body language, along with political comments from before the project landed on them.

Esther slurped her smoothie, then glanced up and down the sidewalk on which they walked. "I think we're far enough away."

Well, that was reassuring. "Okay. I guess—well, let me put it this way. Are we out here because you have a mad crush on me, and you can't wait any longer to tell me?"

Esther's eyes went wide, and then she grinned. It made him realize that he had never seen her smile. "Sorry to break your heart, big guy, but no."

Dane relaxed and grinned back, a grin he could only sustain for a moment before remembering just what they were here for. "Then I guess we feel the same way about what we're doing. At work, I mean."

Esther, somber again, gave one short nod.

"Do you know of anyone else on the team who agrees with us?"

He had inadvertently pulled ahead of Esther; she double-stepped to catch up, her short brown legs moving fast enough to remind him of a sandpiper. "If I were guessing, and I could easily guess wrong, I'd think at least a few others were upset about it; but there's no one else I'm sure about. Better to start out with just the two of us, and keep our eyes and ears open. . . We may as well jump to the really tough question. What the hell can we do?"

Dane took another bite of his neglected sandwich and took his time chewing and swallowing. He didn't want to insult her by suggesting a difference in how far they were willing to go. But he was pretty sure that difference existed. "Did you know my mother's one of them—stored?"

"Ohhh. I didn't, but it makes sense. I know she was sick for a long time. You let her use your discount?"

Dane ground his teeth. "I did. She wasn't too sure she wanted to, but I talked her into it. So if we help someone muck around with what she thinks and feels, it's on me. Even more than it would be anyway."

Esther didn't argue. She just brought them back to the point. "So what can we do to change things? I can't think of anything except going public. And aside from how dangerous that could be, I'm not sure what would happen to the stored if people started thinking of them as—I don't know, as robotic voting weapons or something like that."

"Damn. You're right. What about some sort of sabotage? Keep the code from working?"

Esther obviously didn't buy that suggestion. "Isn't it a little late for that? I mean, it's already working, isn't it? And besides, we'd need to have everyone on board, or the ones who weren't would find the problem. And it wouldn't be hard for them to figure out where the problem came from."

They had been walking more and more slowly, to stretch out the time they had for this discussion without running out of lunch break. But when the idea came to him, he stopped short as if it had shoved him backward. "What if we recruit some of the stored?"

Esther had stopped walking when he did, and now turned toward him, excitement dawning in her face. "Like going public, except we'd be telling the people with the most to lose, the people who'd care the most. I like!"

Then she shrank back a bit. "You are talking about *telling* them, right? Not about using the code to *draft* them or anything?"

He stiffened, and made himself count to ten before speaking. Then he responded as calmly as he could. "I am not talking about forcing anyone to do anything. Ever."

"I'm—"

He held up a hand. "Don't apologize." He had never thought apologies made much difference. He would just have to remember that she didn't trust him yet.

He, on the other hand, had to trust her. It was too late to work alone. So he raised the obvious objection to his own scheme. "The company's monitoring communications, aren't they? The stored don't have much privacy, whether they know it or not."

Esther looked thoughtful, then smug. "Then that's where we start. I'm sure we can find ways to hint to people that their calls are monitored. And once we manage that, I have some thoughts about stage two...."

* * * * *

(six days later)

The park, several miles from the office, was not exactly empty on this warm summer day, but there was room enough to be sure no one would overhear. Dane had picked the place and time; Esther waited for him to speak, throwing one penny after another into the fountain, stray flower petals bobbing up and down on the resulting ripples.

"The time has come, the walrus said, to start leaking information." Dane smirked. Esther turned to throw a penny at him. It bounced off his chest and fell onto the stone bench ringing the fountain; he picked it up and put it in his pocket, earning an exaggerated glare from Esther.

Esther dropped the remaining pennies in her own pocket and sat down on the bench, sitting sideways, facing the path they had taken to the fountain and glancing around the plaza. "I did some checking to see if any of the stored were LiveAfter stockholders and still had control of their stock."

Dane, still standing, gave her a thumbs-up with his gloved hand. Esther smiled a little and shook her head. "Thanks, but I don't think it'll work. From what I could find out, they all gave up their stock as part of the deal."

Dane lowered his head and growled. "Careful bastards, aren't they."

"No big surprise, that. So should we go back to Plan A?"

Dane sat beside her, his back to the fountain, his legs stretched out, kicking his sandals together. "Yeah, I still like Thea Lee. She knows something weird has happened. They won't be erasing that knowledge because her husband knows too. We have plenty of measurements and other data because she was one of the first test subjects. And she's good with math and computers, so we can hide the message in a way she'll notice without it being obvious to the Peep and Keep folks."

"I was thinking: why not double-team them? I could go see Max this weekend, wearing a scrambler. It's not that long a trip on the maglev."

"Great idea! Picked out a pseudonym yet?"

Esther raised an eyebrow. "It's not about picking one. I had one randomly generated. It wouldn't do to leave any unconscious hints."

Dane waved one hand outward in cavalier dismissal of such practical concerns. "Me, I'm going to be Leif. It's a good Viking name."

Esther stood up and planted her fists on her hips, glaring at him. "That's just stupid! A name based on Danish history? Do you *want* to get caught?"

"If you insist, I'll find something else. Worrywart."

"I do insist! It's not just your ass, you know — it's mine. And you might put Max and Thea at risk as well."

* * * * *

At first glance, the message on Thea's screen looked like yet another promise of how much better the environment would be getting, with this or that new feature supposedly available at some unspecified future time. But this one, unlike the others, included several cartoonish sketches. The first showed a skier zooming down a slope, a slope that looked rather like a Chi-Square distribution. Then came mountain climbing. The mountain was weirdly skinny, its sides somewhat concave — wait a minute.

If she ignored the surface detail, the mountain looked a whole lot like a double exponential distribution.

Not that those were especially unusual shapes. What came next? A woodsy setting, with a tent and a campfire, and in the foreground, a hammock. A hammock that didn't sag much at all in the middle. A hammock shaped like a beta distribution.

It could all be coincidence; but it might not, and she had nothing better to do than investigate. If these shapes were supposed to get her attention, they'd done it. Why? If anyone wanted to send her a message, why not just send it, without playing games?

Unless . . . .

What if her messages were monitored? If someone was trying to alert her, they couldn't do so in any straightforward way.

In which case, the very fact of something surreptitious constituted a warning.

She could be imagining all this. She could only hope that if she weren't, whoever was trying to warn her would find some way to confirm as much.

*****

Max had decided to stay at the beach for a while after his surfing lesson. Partly it was a way to avoid going out to coffee with his teacher. Once every couple of lessons seemed about right. More would feel like, well, more.

So he lay on his towel, a towel worn thin enough that he could feel the warmth and shape of the sand through it, and let his mind empty out, then fill again with the sound of the surf.

After a few minutes, he realized that the surf had picked up a musical accompaniment. He looked around for a musician or for any source of recorded sound, then realized the music was in his head. Good thing he'd brought his tablet with him, just in case! He scrambled up and fished it out of his beach bag. Opening his composition program, he dashed off the main melody and some of the harmonies, though more of them kept popping up as he worked. Finally he figured he'd done enough that he could pick up with his better facilities back at the apartment. That's when he realized that a pair of feet, slender coffee-brown feet, were standing about three feet away from him.

He looked up from the feet to see the rest of a petite girl with close-cut, curly black hair, her hands folded in front of her, apparently waiting for him to notice she was there. He hauled his jaw back into place and started to get to his feet. She waved him back. "You don't need to get up! Do you mind if I sit and talk to you for a moment?"

If he said no, he'd feel rude. And if he didn't end up enjoying this conversation, if she was peddling something, he'd be closer to stuck than if they'd been standing. This girl was sharp. (Also cute.)

He waved a little toward the towel. She looked at it with a measuring expression, then plopped down on the sand instead. Nice of her (and, again, smart) not to crowd him.

"My name's Esther."

"I'm Max."

She waited a beat, then said, "I hope this won't freak you out, but I already know. I came here hoping to talk to you. And I have a question I kind of hate to ask; but do you go around linked all the time? That is, right now, are you transmitting anything to anywhere, beyond what that tablet has to do just to keep working properly?"

Max stared at her and shook his head. She relaxed a bit, which was his first clue that she hadn't been relaxed before. "That's good. You'll understand why in a minute. And please just listen for a while before you jump to any conclusions."

Max closed his eyes, then opened them again. No, he hadn't fallen asleep and dreamed all this. The girl, Esther, sat in the sand beside his towel, cross-legged and patient, waiting for him to absorb the news.

News that sucked. Thea didn't have any privacy, not even what they'd thought she had?

He wasn't sure he had the whole story, even now. Esther had explained about how a few of the programmers didn't think it was right to spy on the customers. But would she have gone to all this trouble, and taken what she seemed to feel was a risk, just to get the word out about it?

Well, whether she had some other agenda or not, he would have to do something. Max pounded his fists on his thighs, then winced, then smiled a little. "Thea's going to be soooo pissed off. Except—wait a minute. How can we tell her? Without anyone knowing we've done it?"

Esther paused, started to speak, paused again. Finally she said: "I've got a somewhat odd question to ask you. I hope you won't find it offensive. I'm asking because one of the better ways to tip her off is to bury the subject inside another one, but handle the apparent subject in a way that she'll recognize as artificial. And I had an idea for a subject that might provide a hint. . . ."

* * * * *

Max seemed a little jumpy this evening. Thea put down her orange juice (not too bad a facsimile, considering) and studied his face. "Hon, is there anything wrong?"

She saw him shake it off, whatever it was; and then, as if donning a mask, he looked at her in an almost condescending way that absolutely did not belong on his face. "I did want to bring up something we've talked about before. You always get upset about it, but I've been hoping that with all the changes you've been through, you might have, you know, loosened up."

Thea took a deep breath and blew it out slowly. "Max. What. The. Hell."

"Just hear me out, okay? I was thinking that the next time we have one of our, ah, our sexy talks, you could forget about that confidentiality setting. Just relax, and we can show them what sexy is. You're so hot, baby. Why did it always matter so much that no one else know it?"

This conversation made absolutely no sense. Max had never cared that much about sexual privacy, but he'd never asked her to turn exhibitionist. It just hadn't been an issue, let alone some sort of years-old bone of contention.

Before she could find the words to start interrogating him, he was saying, "Just think about it, okay? I'll leave you alone now so you can do that. Later!" And he actually hung up. Max hung up on her.

Thea jumped out of her chair, sending it crashing back against the foot of the bed, and paced back and forth, fuming. What had happened to Max? Was he turning into some sort of obnoxious stranger, just because she wasn't around?

Of course not. She stopped in mid-step.

How could she be thinking such a thing? It was an insult not only to Max but to her. She would never have lived with him so long without knowing him better than that.

She sank down onto the edge of the bed and did her best to recall the bizarre phone call, as close to verbatim as possible.

As she finished, the ad she'd seen the other day popped into her mind. The ad she'd thought just might be a warning, a warning about monitored communications. Which still seemed a bit far-fetched as an explanation— until she added this new datum. Max had been talking about confidentiality. All the rest, the inappropriate tone, the bogus personal history, that had to be just a vehicle for conveying a message. A message about what was confidential and what wasn't.

And if he'd focused on the times she'd thought she had privacy, he must have been trying to tell her that she'd been wrong. Misinformed.

Misled.

Lied to.

And even now, she was no doubt being monitored: her actions, her emotions. And her words.

She jumped to her feet again, punching her fist in the air. "The bastard!" Hopefully that would help the watchers, whoever they were, mistake her anger at this intrusion as anger at her husband.

But as much right as she had to be angry, she wanted a cool head to think through the ramifications. So she went through what the watchers would recognize as a calming ritual, heating up water for tea, sitting in bed, leaning back on her pillows, sipping the tea and bathing her face in its steam.

There. She actually did feel calmer, and the change shouldn't appear anomalous. Now she could think.

Unless they could actually follow her thoughts in real time. She stopped (felt as if she had stopped) breathing for a moment, then shrugged. If they could do that, she and Max were thoroughly out of luck. There was no point in worrying about it. She would assume otherwise, because she was damned if she were going to try to censor her thoughts for fear of anyone or anything.

All right. First of all, where had this information come from? Max had neither the access nor the skills to discover it on his own. And for that matter, the message-within-a-message gambit was a bit too devious to be his style. So he'd had help. Someone had gotten in touch with him, and helped him get in touch with her.

The someone might have sent her the ad with the significant shapes, or the two might be working together.

There was nothing she could do to find out. Much as she would rather be investigating and making plans, she was too damn helpless to do it.

Helpless and vulnerable. At the mercy of someone else's agenda.

And now she was furious again. She had better provide some cover. Hating to say it, she muttered under her breath, almost hissing: "That bastard. How could he do this to me."

Hours later, sleep impossible, Thea put the finishing touches on the angriest percussion impromptu she had ever written, sent it to Max, and pondered her alternatives.

She could reread the storage contract, scrutinizing every last bit of fine print, to see whether the company had violated any of its terms. But that unusual activity, in itself, would probably set off alarms somewhere. And Max, after consultation with the mystery insider, had taken pains to keep his warning from attracting such attention.

There were sure to be lawyers here. If she did more socializing, she could find natural ways to ask them what they had thought of the contract. Maybe she could even arrange to be walked through the contract as part of an ongoing project of expanding her intellectual pursuits.

Which would be a good idea in any event. She should be making the most of her survival. And she could combine it with getting to know more of her neighbors, so to speak. The more people she got to know and the better she got to know them, the more opportunities she would have to assess them as potential allies.

There was an active bridge circle that met once a

week or so. She could join it. She had taught herself to play bridge some years back. She'd never actually played that often, but that might be all to the good: she was less likely to alienate the existing players by swooping in and conquering too swiftly. She added the event to her calendar and was relieved to find herself yawning. Having a plan of action beat frustration and insomnia any day.

CHAPTER 12

THEA'S friend Jim, as she was now used to calling him, turned out to be a lawyer—a former litigation partner of a small but prestigious firm—and when she discovered as much and approached him, he seemed almost pathetically glad to talk about his field again. Apparently the theater troupe, while giving him an occasion to perform for an audience, wasn't a fully adequate substitute for practicing his profession. In fact, he explained, he was working on proposed legislation to let stored attorneys continue to practice. "Or it might be a court case instead of a bill. One of my partners likes that idea. She's a real hot-shot, loves the cutting-edge cases. If I know her, she'll find a constitutional angle."

"What about jury trials?" Thea asked, recalling that the lawyer had been famous for his ability to charm and persuade a jury.

He gritted his teeth for a moment, then resumed his genial and paternal expression. "If things look promising, I'll start exploring the extent to which holographic appearances would be feasible and effective."

Now for the pivot. "Do litigators like you"—she made sure to use the present tense—"ever write contracts, or review them for clients? Or is that too dull for you adrenaline junkies?"

Jim chuckled. "We actually like to prevent problems sometimes! At least, I was always happy to vet a contract *before* our client ended up signing some godawful, one-sided mess. But all too often, we only hear from clients once a deal turns around and bites 'em."

Another careful step: "And I guess the clients aren't too good at reading contracts for themselves. That's one thing lawyers probably do better, when it comes to their own affairs."

An outright laugh, this time. "Not all of them! We can be as careless as anyone else, and with less excuse. But I'd be ashamed to get caught napping that way. For example, you can bet I read LiveAfter's contract from first to last!"

Score! With some difficulty, Thea suppressed any signs of glee and instead tried for a rueful expression. "I wish I could say the same. What did you find that I should have known ahead of time?"

Jim's rather mordant sense of humor conveniently led him to concentrate on any provisions he guessed she would find dismaying. And even expecting trouble, she found her expectations falling short of the reality.

"See this language here?" Jim must have learned his trade before voice-activated programs and holos became ubiquitous: he had obtained or created an old-fashioned screen, complete with mouse. He scrolled down and let the cursor blink in the indicated spot. "This disclaimer of implied warranties? That means that even if you'd normally have a right to expect something, you're out of luck if it hasn't been explicitly promised. And here, this cross-reference? That brings in the terms of a separate document that they probably didn't spend much time showing you. It's full of technical software terminology, and if there are more than three of us here who read *and* understood it, I'll at least try to eat my hat."

Thea ground her teeth. "I'd have understood it if I'd read it. But I didn't bother."

Jim tsked at her, grinning, and scrolled further down. "Here's a 'hold harmless' clause. You see these in all sorts of contracts. This one says that if someone connected to you, like your husband, sues the company, say about invasion of privacy" — Thea hoped she managed not to twitch — "or insufficient access to you, you end up paying for the company to fend him off. And here's another clause, saying that if you manage to sue the company yourself — they've thought that far ahead — you have to pay their lawyers. Unless, of course, you win."

"But —" Thea sputtered for a moment, then found words. "I had a will! My assets were supposed to become Max's assets if I died! How could they get hold of them?"

Jim leaned back in his chair (which looked considerably more comfortable than the one Thea was still putting up with). "I remember this part without checking. The obligation goes with the money. By signing the contract, you bound anyone who ended up with your money to honor it."

Thea stared at Jim in bewilderment. "You knew all this before you signed."

Jim nodded, with a soft sniff a bit like a chuckle. "All things considered, I'd rather be in Philadelphia. But storage was the best I could do."

* * * * *

Max ran up from the waves, dripping, to find Esther, the cute skinny programmer, sitting on a towel next to his. She'd warned him, last time, not to expect many visits—after all, she worked in Boise or some such place. If she'd shown up again, there was probably some news about Thea; and he didn't have much of a clue what it would be.

Nor was she in a hurry to let him know. Instead, she looked him up and down, grinning. "No teacher today! You're a solo surfer now?"

"Barely. Did you see me out there?" He imitated his typical posture on the board, knees pointed every which way and arms waving around to keep his balance.

"Hey, it's better than I could do. Mazel tov! But I didn't come this far just to admire your progress."

Max grabbed his extra towel, wrapped it around his shoulders, and sat down, shivering a little. If Thea had been here, she would have been draped behind him, warming him and rubbing his shoulders. . . . He shrugged off the image; Esther noticed, but was nice enough not to comment. He prompted her. "Has something new happened?"

She answered his question with one of her own. "Do you think Thea figured out what you were trying to tell her about the monitoring?"

"I'm sure of it." She'd been clever about letting him know. The next time they talked, she'd put on a little show, saying how sorry she was for overreacting, and that she knew he just wanted what was best for her. He'd had to fight to keep from laughing.

"What do you think she's doing about it?"

"Um . . . ." Of course she'd be doing something. Thea never let people mess with her without taking action. But she hadn't been able to tell him—or had she? "She said she'd met a lawyer who was starting some sort of drama club, and that she was thinking of joining."

"She didn't just meet him. She met *with* him, and they spent an hour talking about the contract they both signed. The storage contract. Which, by the way, has some wrinkles you should know about—I learned a lot reviewing that conversation. But that's not the problem."

Shit. "So what is?"

Esther sighed. "From everything you've told me about her, she probably tried to be subtle about it; but she underestimated how paranoid the company is. That conversation got her placed on an alert list. It doesn't take much: any change in behavior patterns gets the person tagged for review. Well, not any change. We aren't sure what the exceptions are. But most changes will do it. And so will any attention to any sort of legal document. So she got tagged twice."

Max made himself keep breathing. "What happens now?"

Esther smiled, a surprisingly wicked little smile. "Well, we—a friend and I—we were able to do a little editing. We got rid of the tags and took her off the list."

Max found that he had switched at some point from sitting to kneeling. He relaxed and sat back again. "That's good. I don't know quite what it means, the tags and the list and all, but I like it better this way. Thanks. Thanks a lot!"

But Thea would probably keep pushing. "What if it happens again?"

Esther paused, as if unsure whether to confide in him. Then she looked him in the eye, face grave, and said, "We've been thinking, my friend and I, about leaving a program in place, something that would prevent her from going on the list. But we're not sure how long it could run undetected."

"And it might get you, you and your friend, in

trouble. Thea wouldn't want that."

Esther raised both eyebrows. "Would I be wrong in thinking that Thea is a little more practical than you are? She knows now that she needs help. She might be willing for someone to take a risk to help her."

Max shook his head violently. "It's not about practical. Thea cares about what's right. Don't do it, please. We'll take our own risks."

"But that's not what we want. Let us keep working on it. We'll try to come up with something—say, I just had an idea. It'd be great if you and Thea could talk openly, plan together, and if you could pass on warnings to her. What if I could make that happen?"

Max furrowed his forehead. "How?"

"I don't want to promise anything. I'll have to talk to my friend. But we might be able to plant some phony conversations. We'd synthesize your and Thea's voices, and sometimes throw in other people as well. We wouldn't want to make the fake conversations very long —but we could give you two at least some privacy, the privacy Thea thought she was getting."

"That would be *great*. Please let me know as soon as you can."

And if they got those private talks, they should probably spend them plotting and planning. But maybe, just maybe, they could steal a little time for other, private matters.

* * * * *

"Why shouldn't we tell them what we really think is going on?" Dane tended to walk faster when he was frustrated, and Esther had to scurry more than usual to keep up, fallen leaves scattering in her path.

"Dane, be realistic. Max is intelligent in his way, but he isn't ideal conspirator material. He's impulsive and—and open. In retrospect, we should probably have started with someone else. Someone older and cagier."

"Well, that ship's sailed, hasn't it? And the sort of person you're talking about might have been suspicious of *us*. Which could have gone all kinds of wrong."

"I suppose. As you say, there's no going back, anyway."

The two walked on in silence, Dane fortunately slowing down somewhat.

Then he spoke again, more quietly, almost muttering. "It may not matter. I think they may be figuring things out for themselves."

"*What?*" Esther stopped and pivoted to face him; but he kept walking, and she had to follow.

"Last week, when you were out sick? Max told me about some political subject that came up, something where Thea'd changed her mind and hadn't realized it. It had them both pretty freaked out." He glanced at Esther, then whistled softly. "I guess that's not what you wanted to hear."

Esther took a deep breath and blew it out in slow puffs, as if trying to blow smoke rings. "And I guess that sooner or later, we'll have to bring them all the way into the loop. But please, Dane, wait for one of them to say or ask something first."

He didn't answer; but he didn't argue, and that was close enough to winning the point, for now.

* * * * *

Esther and Dane had managed to install their phony-conversation program. The relief, however temporary it might be, left Thea and Max both somewhat giddy. Soon enough, they would have to use their freedom to talk about the difficult and important; but not just yet.

When their game of swapping bawdy limericks finally wound down, Thea leaned forward and stage-whispered, "Baby, I need you to talk me out of something."

In this mood, he would have trouble discouraging even the most foolhardy plan. "Fire away!"

Thea smirked, then composed her face in who-me-propose-mischief serenity. "We haven't decided for sure about my next tattoo. Though I did love that meta-design idea, a tattoo of you giving me a tattoo. This could be an extra instead of a substitute."

"What could?"

"Well . . . I was thinking of an ear."

"An *ear*?"

Thea was losing her battle with a grin. "Yup, an ear. A big one. With an earring — something like a megaphone. Or maybe an insect, an earring like an insect crawling into the ear."

What the — OH. He got it now. An ear, listening. Listening to Thea, to both of them. And the insect, the "bug," just to underline the point.

"Just where were you thinking this tattoo should go?"

The grin broke free. "On my ass."

Max broke down and laughed. "Are you sure you don't want to add some lips next to it? Just as directions?"

They both ended up giggling. It was hard to stop even when the timer went off. But the conversation the program had been feeding into the system might not have anything in it to explain their laughter.

* * * * *

The abrupt end of their shared hilarity jolted Thea into a glummer frame of mind. It was no joke. Talk about bugs — she and the others were like bugs in a terrarium, insects in glass cases.

And then there was that other, more frightening possibility: that somehow, her thoughts, her feelings, her beliefs were not entirely her own any more.

Maybe the tattoo should be a robot.

A robot in a voting booth, pulling the lever.

Thea would have liked to speak directly to Max's contacts; but they had all agreed that the less she knew and the more attenuated the contact, the safer all of them would be. Any message would have to go through Max.

"Hon, I need you to ask what's-their-name for something."

Max bit his lip. "Is it important?"

"Your guess is as good as mine, so let me tell you what I want. I'd like to start looking at my own software."

Max looked confused. She'd been playing with the idea for a while, but of course he didn't know what she meant. She could be referring to any of the code she'd written over the years, to improve their recording studio or to speed up their networks or to add options to their environmental controls.

"Honey, I mean the software that's *me*. The code that replaced my neural connections."

Max shuddered. Her poor lover. Of course he wouldn't want to be reminded. But it was time they both got used to their — to her — new reality.

"We're both wondering whether I've changed in certain ways because of how my life is changed, or for some other reason. We can just sit and wait for our new friends to figure everything out, if they ever do, while maybe things get crazier; or I can try to find out something on my own in the meantime. And you know I'm good with code."

"That's an understatement." Of course Max would say that; but it happened to be true.

"Do you have a way to reach them?"

Max got his put-on-the-spot face and hummed for a moment. "For emergencies, yeah. Otherwise . . . ."

Thea barely managed to catch an exasperated sigh before it escaped. "Okay, when do you next expect to hear from *them*?"

Max's face brightened. "Not too long. Today's what, Thursday? Next Tuesday, I think."

Their private time was almost up. "All right. I'll do some thinking tonight about how to put the request. I'll tell you tomorrow. And then, I guess we'll have to wait."

* * * * *

"It's a great idea!" Dane realized, belatedly, that his excited gestures might be attracting the attention of passersby, and reined himself in. "She can help herself and the others. She may not be a professional, but she's got some relevant expertise, right? And we could use the help from someone who won't inform on us."

"She may not do so intentionally." Esther looked at the sidewalk ahead, rather than at him. "But she's in an especially vulnerable position as far as security goes."

"We've already intervened to give her some protection. And as far as either of us can tell—and we should be able to tell—no one has looked at that code, let alone meddled with it."

"But do we really need to increase the risk, to her and to us? We may not have confirmed Thea's suspicions in so many words, but we know that at least some of the stored have been hacked, whether or not Thea's already included. Shouldn't we focus on ways to put an end to the hacking, rather than on whether one individual has already been affected?"

Dane fought back a wave of anger. "What if your significant other was in Thea's place? Or Max's? Wouldn't you want to know what was actually happening?"

Esther rolled her eyes. "Of course I'd want to know. But that doesn't mean I'd put my desire for knowledge above operational security."

Dane gritted his teeth. He needed to find some sort of baby step that wouldn't scare Esther so much. "How about this? Max can send her the code, but call it something else. He can say it's software he's thinking of buying, or something that popped up on his system. We'll check first, but I bet LiveAfter's system doesn't screen for incoming mail that happens to duplicate code already in the system."

Esther finally looked intrigued rather than disapproving. She did like novel, sideways-type approaches to problems. "All right. Congrats. That just might work."

Chapter 13

THEA swore under her breath as she looked around the increasingly quarrelsome theater troupe. They'd warmed up with a set of three one-act plays, and now the group was ready for a meatier challenge. But the newest members were more interested in writing plays than acting in them, so the possibilities were expanding to the point of chaos.

Some of the original members clearly disliked the idea of a brand new production. "It'll take, what, weeks to write even a draft, won't it?" grumbled the woman Thea had privately labeled The Diva. "That's time tacked on to what we'll need for rehearsals. If we go too long without another performance, people will forget we exist!"

One of the would-be dramatists actually bared his teeth. "Are you kidding? You're worrying about *time*? What do we all have more of?"

Someone needed to come up with a compromise. Someone like Thea. But what? Ah—"How about this? Let's take an existing story, maybe even a film, and adapt it. That will give one or more of our writers the task of adapting the work, without taking as long as starting a play from scratch."

Of course, not everyone liked the idea, and those who did now had something else to argue about. Which movie? Whose favorite?

One of their newer members, a soft-spoken gentleman with long white hair, put up a tentative hand. (Thea noted with approval that he hadn't thought it necessary to turn his hair a more youthful color.) "Why don't we see what our founding member recommends? After all, this troupe might not even exist if he hadn't taken the trouble to start it."

Jim lost no time in speaking up. "Thank you for that very kind suggestion. As it happens, I've just been watching an old favorite of mine, and I think it could make a truly riveting stage production. Have any of you seen *The Manchurian Candidate*? I'm talking about the original, from the 1960s, not that crappy remake a few decades later."

A couple of people nodded, some vigorously, while the rest looked expectantly at the lawyer or blankly at each other.

Thea had heard the name, but had never seen the film. As the lawyer described the story, with its coalition of Communists brainwashing captured soldiers, she grew increasingly alarmed. Did the lawyer know, or suspect, the same thing she and Max suspected? Or did his choice of story show just the opposite? Surely, if he shared their suspicions, he would have been more circumspect.

But coincidence or lack of discretion, this could be trouble.

Thea quickly ran through the story as Jim had summarized it. She needed to find some disadvantages. Maybe—"There don't seem to be many female roles."

The lawyer waved his hand dismissively. "Back then, soldiers were mainly male, but we don't have to stick to the Korean War context. It could be a modern war, with soldiers of all genders." He looked toward The Diva. "And the mother, the worst of the conspirators—now there's a real plum of a role. You could do something great with that."

The Diva, to Thea's dismay, glowed with satisfaction. This play might be happening. She could only hope it was her own sensitivity to the topic that made it seem so dangerous.

The movie made a hell of a play. Well, that wasn't quite right. The troupe's dramatists had made the movie into a hell of a play. And while the acting quality varied, The Diva chewed the scenery most effectively as the female villain. Jim was almost as good as her brainwashed homicidal son. After all the years of performing for judge and (especially) jury, and then the months of forced retirement, getting to indulge his theatrical streak so fully must be gratifying.

Their makeup and costume coordinator did have some unusual challenges with which to cope, due to the limitations of certain software.

The Diva sashayed into the rehearsal with longer, fuller hair, in a fiery red shade that Thea thought unfortunate with her complexion, and with her already substantial chest now narrowing to a dramatically slim waist. The director stared, then shrugged. "I guess it'll do. But your costume will be loose in the middle."

The Diva waved imperiously toward the assembled cast. "I'm sure someone can fetch me a belt to cinch it up. Something spangly."

While The Diva changed into her costume, Thea rummaged through the accessories the troupe had assembled and saw nothing sequined or bejeweled, but did unearth a black patent leather belt. The Diva sniffed qualified acceptance and donned it, the director tapping his foot while she adjusted the fit for maximum snugness. Finally she vouchsafed him a regal nod, and he smiled tightly and flourished the script. "Act Two, Scene 1! Places, everyone!"

They had made it halfway through the scene when The Diva suddenly gasped, her hands fumbling frantically with the belt. The Diva's waist had abruptly regained its original girth, while her hair, now falling out of its hairdo as she struggled, had resumed its previous bottle-blonde color.

Appearances continued to revert at unpredictable intervals, removing makeup and causing costumes to fit poorly or even disappear. The members of the troupe coped as best they could, standing ready to serve as emergency makeup and costume assistants; the dramatists wrote several short bridge scenes to throw in as necessary while any repairs took place backstage.

And now opening night was almost upon them, with just one more tech rehearsal this morning and the dress rehearsal tomorrow. They'd be recording the dress rehearsal and all the performances, so they could choose the one to distribute to friends and family "outside" (the most popular euphemism for the corporeally living). Or rather, they'd be intentionally recording, along with whatever monitoring was always going on, going on right now. . . .

By the time Thea showed up, almost everyone else had arrived. (The Diva, of course, had not. She would be at least a little late.) Jim stood by the costume racks, handling—almost caressing—the uniform he would wear. He noticed Thea noticing him, and chuckled.

"Yeah, I can't wait. Don't you think we need an extra dress rehearsal, like today?" Thea couldn't help but laugh along, even as she shook her head.

Ah, here came The Diva. She made an entrance, of course: no simple opening a door and walking through for her! Thea refrained from raising an eyebrow, then turned back to Jim.

Jim disappeared.

The Diva screamed. Thea flinched at the sound and stared at the spot near the costume rack. She looked rapidly around the room, in case she had had a momentary fugue and he had moved in the meantime (but then why would The Diva have screamed?). She saw a room full of startled and, even as she watched, frightened people. But no Jim anywhere.

About half the people turned toward someone else and began jabbering questions and exclamations. The others simply stared at each other, or straight ahead, in shock.

And then the door opened once more, and a stranger came in, a nondescript man of indeterminate age, medium height, unremarkable coloring.

"Excuse me. May I have your attention, all of you?"

The room slowly grew quiet. The man waited, shifting around a bit as if suppressing discomfort, until all the talk and exclamations ceased, then went on.

"I'm sure you're wondering what just happened here. I'm very sorry to tell you that we've experienced a serious technical event. Your friend's digital profile has somehow been deleted."

More exclamations, some frightened, some furious. About a quarter of the actors started to cry.

Thea waited for him to say something about backups. They must all have backups. It would be inconceivable negligence not to back up everyone's files. But the man made no mention of restoring Jim from existing files, or even of some additional calamity having affected those files.

The man was still talking, but Thea could not bring herself to listen. Instead she replayed in her mind the moment when Jim had disappeared. She had read, in fiction and in various articles, about what happened when people died. The fiction rarely dwelt on some of the details, like the opening of the sphincter at the moment of death. (Brain death, or something else? She had never inquired . . . . This must be a form of shock, this sudden obsession with minor details.) And most ways of dying took a good deal longer than the one-shot-and-gone portrayal in many a movie.

But there had been no prolonged agony, no pungent odors. And no warning. Just a vibrant, almost larger than life personality, an apparent body full of apparent life; and then, an empty space.

Thea sat down heavily on the nearest chair, shivering, hugging herself, feeling herself shiver. Could she get up? Could she control her limbs? Because all she wanted, as much as she had ever wanted anything, was to get out of this room. Yes, and to run to Max. She needed his arms around her, not her own.

She could never have that. (Not unless . . . but that must not happen, not for many years. She must not even think of yearning for it.) But she could run to her room and call him. And she would tell him what happened, unless something prevented her.

As Jim had been prevented from taking the stage. . . .

She must get control of herself. The man had not left yet. She must ask him whether she could tell anyone about Jim's death. And if not, she would have to wait until the next private call, impossible as waiting seemed now. Her life might depend upon discretion.

* * * * *

Max had just gotten the strangest call from Thea.

It wasn't so much the timing. While they had their rituals about phone calls, either of them would sometimes call the other to share an anecdote, ask a question, or just say hello or I Love You.

But when Thea called him only an hour after their morning chat, all she had to say was that she'd call him again later. Which he already knew. That later call would be one of their precious private sessions, and he always waited impatiently for those.

And she'd sounded shaky. Scared, even. It took a hell of a lot to scare Thea. What could have happened?

* * * * *

The COO had been able to vent some of his anger on the Human Resources manager. Even if the man hadn't directly hired the moron who'd endangered the company, he was in charge of employee supervision. But the COO still had anger to spare.

There came the knock. He barked an order to enter, and the door opened to admit a scrawny woman in (per her file) her mid-thirties. She must know why she was here, but she showed no signs of nervousness, let alone remorse.

"Sit."

She sat down and crossed her legs, apparently quite at her ease. Damn the woman.

"I've already heard about this incident from others, but I wanted to hear your explanation directly." He bit back the rest of what he wanted to say. He must not lose his temper. Despite the COO's prompt attention to damage control, the woman could open up a can of worms—no, of venomous snakes—if she began thinking of the company as her enemy.

The woman tapped her wristband and scanned a screen full of notes. The COO used his own wristband to send a quick email ordering that the woman's band be impounded—no, "replaced with the latest version." He had hit "send" before she actually started talking.

"It's my job to review reports summarizing the activities of the digits—"

The COO clenched his teeth, then caught himself and desisted. The slang told him all he needed to know. Personnel who referred to the clients as "digits" tended to view them as nothing more than copies, copies produced as part of a scam to profit from a credulous population of pampered rich folks. "Digits," to such employees, weren't people, though they could interact with actual people and even cause trouble by doing so.

Of course, according to that viewpoint, the troublesome could and should be eliminated.

He'd missed some of her explanation. He'd be damned if he'd apologize. "Say that again, if you please."

The woman scowled. "As I *said*, my responsibilities include checking whether any of the digits are endangering trade secrets. There have been some rumors going around that come a little too close to actual projects. I checked into this one digit who seemed likely to be part of the problem. He was an attorney, so he liked to hear himself talk. He actually practiced in intellectual property some of the time, so he'd have a nose for sniffing out confidential information. And his drama troupe was about to perform a play that could give people ideas."

The COO drummed his fingers on his desk, noticed it, and kept doing it. "So you thought it'd be a good idea to delete the fellow."

The woman shrugged. "It seemed efficient, at least as a first step."

The COO leaned forward, forcing his expression to remain composed. "Did you get around to any second or third steps?"

"Not yet. I was just writing my report when you told me to show up."

He needed to get her out of here before he said anything his PR people would chastise him for. "I'd like you to go directly from here to Personnel. We've determined that this position is not as good a fit for you as we had initially believed. But we have every intention of taking care of you." (If only that could have its occasional more sinister meaning. . . .) "We've selected several openings for you to examine, all at or above your current pay grade. Or if you prefer, you could leave with an appropriate severance package." Finally, he could unleash just a little of what he was feeling. He looked directly in the woman's eyes. "Although I would advise you to review the noncompete clause in your contract. You might find it quite restricting. Your future will be much more promising if you remain with us."

The woman shrank back just a bit, then got up and scurried out the door. Not so nonchalant now, was she? Good.

At last he could take a moment to think about the woman's reasons for taking action. The idiocy of that action did not mean her concerns lacked validity. The new software they were testing might take care of the problem, but the programmers kept warning him against relying on software still at the testing stage. Best to use the existing cruder methods as well. The supposed technical glitch could be blamed.

He buzzed his secretary. "Send in my next appointment."

The young man who slipped through the still-open door could have posed for an illustrated dictionary definition of the word "geek." In an era when so many programmers looked like supermodels or grannies, it was reassuring that a few still conformed to the stereotypes of the COO's youth.

The man sat down without any introductory chatter, holoscreen already active and stylus in hand.

"We have to activate the backup of this client as soon as possible. But there are some precautions you'll be taking first." The COO ticked them off on his fingers. "We don't know whether this client actually was involved in anything problematic. We've found and preserved the deleted files, and will be inspecting them at our leisure—but that's not your current assignment. What I need you to do immediately is edit out the client's memories of, hmmm, let's say the last eight weeks. While you're at it, do a quick check of his earlier files and weed out any conspicuous changes we didn't initiate. And apply that new protocol, the one that's still in testing, to reduce rebellious tendencies. This can serve as a trial run of that software."

The young man went still for a moment. "Should I make a copy of the backup file and store it, before I do these edits on the file that's going active?"

"Do that." After all, the new software might blow up somehow, and they'd need to try again.

The young man resumed scribbling. When his stylus slowed to a stop, the COO waited another moment, then said, "That's all. Keep me updated on your progress. We want this client back in place by the end of the day. Can you do that?"

The young man nodded as he extracted himself from his chair and hurried out the door.

Yes, the client would be back in place soon. Though the memory alterations would include the lines the fellow had memorized. Someone else would have to step in if the play were to continue. But from what the COO understood, the troupe had not bothered with understudies. The play would probably have to be canceled.

So much the better.

* * * * *

"Jim! Oh, thank *heaven*!"

The Diva rushed across the dining hall and enveloped the attorney in an embrace, then reluctantly released him as a host of others, members of the theater troupe and other friends, followed and surrounded him.

The attorney looked around, appearing somewhat befuddled. "Thank you. Thanks very much. I'm not sure what to say. I've been told something happened to me, some sort of glitch; and while I can't remember it, I'm certainly glad to be here and feeling fine! I appreciate your warm welcome, even though I haven't had the pleasure of actually meeting all of you." He looked around the crowd as a whole; The Diva, though he did not appear to be addressing her, stepped back, bumping three other people, and clasped her hands over her heart as he went on. "But . . . why are you calling me Jim?"

* * * * *

Max's private conversation with Thea would have to end soon, and still she kept repeating the same details. It took extreme stress to bring out that quirk. The last time he could remember it happening had been when her father suddenly took ill on a trip abroad, and she couldn't find a flight to take her to him.

"He doesn't remember his lines from the play. He doesn't remember *suggesting* the play. He doesn't remember the people who joined the troupe recently. And he seems to have no clue that he changed his name, or why he would ever have wanted to."

Max did sometimes have intuitive leaps, and now the word that popped into his head was "scapegoat." Had this attorney somehow come under suspicion because of things that Dane or Esther had done? Or that Thea had done, or Max himself?

And would Thea be next?

He had to talk to Esther right away.

CHAPTER 14

DONGMEI Hu Yang, generally known as Hu, could have been sick of explaining her name, but fortunately, she liked explaining things.

No, Chinese people—at least in China—didn't usually have middle names in the American sense. But then, she was a third-generation American.

She could certainly have used her first name. She liked the sound, and the meaning—"winter plum"—had pleasant associations. She had used that name as a child, ignoring the occasional jokes, of which "ding, dong" was the least offensive. But once she decided on a career in law, and then in litigation, the meaning of "Hu"—tiger—came to seem more and more appropriate.

Of course, now and then some new acquaintance, usually elderly, felt called upon to launch into a rendition of "Who's On First?"

In fact, the first time she got to be first chair in a major lawsuit, her fellow associates had surprised her with an elaborate performance of that number. And a cake. The memory helped her smile, rather than groan, when someone new dredged up the reference once again.

All of which made it more than a little disturbing that when her former law partner, who'd recently changed his name to Jim, answered her last note with such unusual promptness, he not only asked if it had been meant for someone else, someone named Jim, but addressed her as Dongmei. He hadn't called her that in years. When, early in their acquaintance, she had asked him to call her Hu, he had responded with annoying comments about owl sounds, but he had eventually dropped the jest and followed the lead of the other lawyers and staff.

She'd been worried right along that the digitization process, presumably imperfect, might alter her colleague in ways that would be hard to undo. Some of the other partners had thought that was happening when "Jim's" politics started changing, but Hu had reserved judgment, knowing that new activities and associations, not to mention a radically new perspective, might offer sufficient explanation.

That comforting rationalization hardly applied to this latest message, even if it did represent a return to the status quo ante.

She would have to stay in closer touch with her colleague (and remember to use his original name when she did so). There might be something she could do.

* * * * *

Esther came in that morning to find an urgent message from Max. More than urgent: its tone was almost frantic, although he had maintained enough self-control to avoid any real details. She had better make time to see him soon, before that control frayed any further. She could find an excuse to take a day off — if she took pains to be careful.

* * * * *

Esther's message instructed Max to meet her for lunch at a grimy little bar, too rundown to attract any LiveAfter executives who might be in town for some reason, or any of their clients. He'd played at bars like this, when he got broke enough, and eaten whatever free food they threw his way. But he would have no appetite today, even for something more edible.

Esther listened to him with her lips pressed tight together and her greasy bread sticks hardly touched. When he had finished, he slumped back in the wobbly chair and waited for her to say something, anything, that would make him less afraid.

But he knew better, really; and he was not surprised when she finally said, in almost a monotone, "We knew that something had blown up, but not the details. I don't think I can find out any more. And I don't know what I can do, at least short term."

They sat in glum silence for a moment before he remembered to ask, "What about the code Thea asked for? Can you do that, at least?"

Esther reached for a bread stick, stared at it, and took a determined bite. "I'll find a way."

Now Max just had to come up with something to call the code, something innocuous, like a new music processing program.

Not that either of them had been getting much writing done lately.

Damn it, he was *not* going to let the sons of bitches drive him crazy and keep him from writing! Max grabbed his guitar and kicked his front door open. He would head down to the ocean and come up with something.

No, he had better check first to see if Esther had sent the code. He put down the guitar and checked his mail. Yes! There it was.

He looked with longing at the open door, then set down the guitar, closed the door, locked it, and got to work on his message to Thea.

* * * * *

"But you *started* the troupe! Why would you want to drop out?"

The lawyer no longer known as Jim (Thea knew it was pointless, but she refused to think of him by his original name) shrugged and smiled. He did a lot of smiling these days. "I guess I don't crave the spotlight any more."

The Diva drew herself up and puffed out her chest. "Are you saying there's something *wrong* with wanting to shine? To excel? To lead?"

Not-Jim put up his hands, still smiling, in cheerful surrender. "Of course not! We all do what we're suited for. You're suited to take center stage. I'm not. But I'm not really leaving! I'll still help out with building sets and hauling props. I'll be a prompter when we need one. And I'll always be there to cheer you on."

Thea forced a smile of her own, then moved slowly toward the door in the back of the room. She had the distinct feeling that if she could, if she had a body capable of it, she would be feeling sick. But apparently vomiting had been eliminated as one of many undesirable functions.

And in all the turmoil, she'd somehow missed a call from Max. But he'd left her a message. And finally, he'd sent her the code.

In spite of the circumstances and the stakes, this investigation, this sleuthing, might turn out to be fun. She was bound to learn a good deal.

Thea had never worked with the code generated by nanoparticles, though she had seen examples of machine-generated code. Only an expert would be able to analyze it. But she might be able to sniff out unexpected variants.

Did nano-generated code insert punctuation to turn active code inactive, "commenting out" what would otherwise be part of the program? Because she was occasionally seeing such punctuation, spaced the way it would be for that purpose.

And surely that stretch of code, and that one, had a different feel, a more obviously logical flow? It did not look like any coding style she knew, but more like some sort of careful imitation of the machine-generated code, a programming style designed to pass itself off as machine-generated code to the casual eye.

It was almost like reading a musical score—a score into which another composer's work, from a different period, had been intermittently inserted.

What was *that*?

Thea gasped and shoved her chair backward, away from the screen. In the middle of one of the suspect sections, a subroutine name jumped out at her: incPol. A subroutine name including "inc" usually meant something would be increased, just as "dec" usually meant "decrease." Pol. Political?

And there, farther down: decIndep.

And decIndiv.

CHAPTER 15

THEA'S political discussion group would be meeting soon. They had reached an important stage in developing the first Utopian community. Her input now would make more of a difference than ever. And she had made friends there.

But how could she know what her original self, her real self, would want her to do? If she'd seen what she thought she'd seen in the code, she could rely on nothing she thought, nothing she felt.

Should she sit in her room, frightened and useless, counting the minutes and even the seconds until the next private call, hoping that Max's mysterious contacts would somehow come to her rescue? Or join her friends and work on a project she might not have supported without interference?

She would compromise. She would attend, and take copious notes, and see people who cared about her (but would they, on their own?..). And when she had either confirmed or regained her control of her beliefs and priorities, then she would decide whether to rejoin the effort or to oppose it.

* * * * *

Dane had finally managed to nag Esther into

bringing him along on one of her meets with Max. He had a hunch that he had more in common with Max than did Dane's deliberate and cautious co-conspirator.

Though he probably should have guessed that Max would keep staring at Esther when she wasn't looking. Well, Esther was a looker, no denying it, even all bundled up against the chilly ocean breeze. And no matter what sort of epic love story Max and Thea might be starring in, she'd gone on a journey where Max wouldn't — they all hoped — be following her for decades, if ever.

Back to business.

Max could hardly sit still, bouncing his knees up and down as he sat cross-legged on the blanket. At this rate, he would dig a hole in the sand under the blanket, but he probably wouldn't notice until he actually fell in. "It probably *did* happen to Thea, because she saw it happen to her friend! And he's some tough-guy lawyer! At least, he used to be. Now he's mellow and, um, passive, Thea says, and sort of zoned out all the time." Max pounded both fists on the blanket. "If they do that to Thea, I'll kill them, I swear I will!"

Esther reached out and pressed her palm on Max's arm. His eyes went wide for a moment, and he stopped pounding the sand. "We're all here to help Thea and her friends. You know very well she wouldn't want you ruining your own life and putting yourself in danger. And how would you choose your target? No single person in the company is likely to be irreplaceable, not at this stage when the main creative work — if we call it that, which I hate to do — has already been done."

Esther glanced at Dane. "Dane here has an idea. It has some risks, but frankly, so does everything we might try. If you don't mind sharing your private phone time with us today, we'd like to see what Thea thinks."

Thea sat through the introductions with obvious impatience, barely managing to smile at Esther and Dane before blurting out, "I can't be sure, but I think I found something. In—" She looked around furtively, though she must have known how pointless it was. "You know where."

Max closed his eyes and bit his lip. He would cry any minute, and that would probably upset Thea even more. Dane had better say something. "I'll bet you're dying—whoops, sorry about that—"

Thea started and then, to Dane's relief, relaxed and actually giggled. Max's eyes popped open, and he relaxed also. Esther might be glaring at Dane, but he didn't look at her as he rushed on. "Eager, that is, to take some action. And we had an idea about that."

Dane had already drafted the item they would be posting on numerous sites: three concise paragraphs, but loaded with language to make people take notice. And he'd posted anonymously before, though nothing this important. Esther double-checked his precautions, and found one to add (phew). He clicked the final click and sat back while the alarm went off to ring its cyber bell.

* * * * *

Hu habitually kept track of a few underground threads. Some of her partners would never have deigned to get near such sources; but then, some of her partners had no idea why she was so well-informed on the latest tech fads and youth trends and hot-button political issues.

Before she dove in this time, she checked her messages and found the hoped-for reply from her tech guru, a preteen whose mother she'd represented three years back. The links he'd sent gave her a head start on current discussions of storage issues.

She checked the first three, skimming quickly for anything of interest. The thread had gotten more active since her last look a few days before. All the usual participants, and some whose tags she didn't recognize, seemed to be agitated about a post from the night before. She went back and found it.

She hadn't seen the tag before. #PaulRevere. That suggested urgency, and maybe some self-importance.

Moments later, she understood why.

A stored person, a lawyer like herself, had first gone through some political changes, even radicalization, and insisted on changing his name, and had then not just reverted but become a compliant nonentity . . . .

She skimmed the subsequent discussions, looking for any clues to confirm her guess as to the lawyer's identity, but found none. She went on to the next thread, and the next, finding much the same picture: the initial post, the outraged reactions, the same level of detail.

She went back through all the threads more slowly. Naturally some of those posting had suggestions, ranging from an assault on the storage facility to broader publicity to (her stomach turned) trying to find a way to use this technology in pursuit of one or another political aim. But one suggestion made perfect sense. "Someone should sue!"

Someone indeed.

* * * * *

Once again, Max's and Thea's private time would be no such thing. But privacy, and the sweetness it could allow, would have to take a back seat for the foreseeable future.

Another newcomer had joined them: a lawyer, with the shortest possible name (some sort of nickname, or even code?), and glossy black hair cut in a complex geometrical pattern that Thea's curls could never copy. (Though she might be able to look like that, if she chose. Hell, no. Whatever aspects of her identity she could retain, she would.) (Unless—)

She held up a hand in apologetic interruption. "Before we go on—Max, have I always looked like this?"

Max stuck out his lower lip. "Well, I don't know about always, but for the last ten years or so, pretty much. Except you were blonde most of that time."

Of course. It would be too easy for friends and family to notice changes in appearance and ask about them. She needed to keep her wits about her rather than succumbing to hysteria. "I'm sorry. Please go on. Hu, thank you for joining us." It would sound rude, especially after that latest bit of juvenile behavior, to ask straight out what Hu was doing in their conspiracy. No doubt someone would explain.

That someone proved to be the irrepressible Dane. "Hu's a partner of your lawyer friend. She found our post and figured we meant him. She wants to help."

It was good to know that Jim—but would he have taken that name, if not for some manipulation? The ground would just not stop shifting beneath her. Whatever his name should be, it was good to know he had friends who cared what had happened to him, just as she did. "What do you have in mind?"

Hu flashed a smile, showing small white teeth with

a slight inward curve to them. "You may have heard the saying that to a hammer, all the world looks like a nail. We lawyers are like that. I would like to file a lawsuit, exposing and challenging the manipulation of essential aspects of stored individuals without their knowledge or consent." The smile disappeared. "But there are technical hurdles to be addressed."

Thea studied each of them in turn. Esther appeared both tense and excited; Dane, excited and eager. And Max, as so often lately, looked lost.

Apparently she had been assigned the role of prompter. "What sort of obstacles?"

Hu sat up a little straighter, suddenly reminding Thea of a calculus professor from her college days. "In order to bring suit, one must have at least one plaintiff, a person or entity who initiates the suit. And the plaintiff or plaintiffs must have a particular stake in the matter, an injury to redress or to prevent. If the goal is prevention, the threat of that injury must be more than speculative. There must be reason for the court to believe that its intervention is necessary. This requirement is known as 'standing.' So I could not simply file suit on behalf of the entire stored community or some randomly selected individual."

Max piped up. "But what about your lawyer friend? It's obvious he's been, uh, altered."

Dane snorted. "More like mentally raped!"

Esther winced; Hu simply nodded. "Indeed. However, from what I understand of his current mental state, he is highly unlikely to understand what has occurred or to agree to litigation on his behalf. And as he is currently deemed a citizen, able to vote and carry on commercial affairs, I could not claim to be his 'next friend' and sue on his behalf."

"So let me see if I follow you." Thea mentally ticked off items. "You need a plaintiff who's been altered or has reason to fear alteration. And your plaintiff has to be willing to come forward."

Hu tilted her head and wrinkled her porcelain forehead. "Yes, as to the first. As to the second, we could initially file suit using a pseudonym, such as the classic Jane Doe. The defendants will certainly seek disclosure of the plaintiff's actual identity, arguing that only such disclosure will allow proper scrutiny of the plaintiff's standing to sue. I expect they would sooner or later prevail on that point."

Max was now staring at Thea with an uneasy blend of affection and alarm. "I know what you're thinking. And I wish I wasn't thinking it too."

Thea took a long and very deep breath, then faced each of the others in turn. "It's obvious, isn't it? I believe I've already been—affected. We have evidence of one political about-face, and since I had no idea I'd made it, we should be able to argue that my views didn't just evolve. And for what it's worth, there's my impression of irregularities in my current code. Even without either of those facts, there's my close association with J—with your friend. That makes me a natural target, doesn't it? Or would we have to prove what they've done to him to make that argument?"

"Not right away. And if the lawsuit survives the initial hearings, we will be able to demand information from the defendants' files to support our claims. Of course, we can expect various attempts to evade those demands." Hu smiled again, but looking at that smile, Thea could hardly believe that the smooth white teeth were not pointed. "I am, however, accustomed to overcoming such tactics."

Thea tried to remember everything Jim had told her. "If we lose, they'll be able to bankrupt Max, won't they?"

Max's hands had clenched into fists. "I don't give a damn about that—but none of you are talking about the bigger risk. These 'defendants' have Thea completely in their power."

Hu turned toward Max and nodded. "That is why it would be wise to make our move as publicly as possible. So that any reprisals become tactically unwise."

"Do it!" Thea almost shouted the words. Then she looked at Max and had to hold back tears at his woebegone expression. "We have to, baby. It's that or just sit and wait for the next time they decide to change me. If you love me, help me do what I can to stay myself."

Max gazed at her, his face imbued with such love that even his loud sniff failed to make the moment less solemn and precious. Then he turned toward Hu. "You heard the lady. Go for it. Please. And thank you."

*****

Esther and Dane and Hu had all hung up, leaving Max finally alone with Thea for the few moments until the substitute conversation would end. Their connection must be broken before that happened.

Which made what he had to tell her that much harder. Oh, he could just not say anything. As soon as she thought about it, she would realize how things stood.

But he wanted to be with her, in the only way he could, when she found out.

"Lover, once Hu files the lawsuit with your name on it. . . . Things will change."

Did she already know? She looked at him so solemnly. But maybe that was because he sounded so sad.

"We think the private call dodge has been working. But once they know you're fighting them, they'll be on you like lice on a hat."

She didn't laugh. She just waited.

"Once we go public, we won't have any more privacy until it's over." As if some happy ending could be counted on. "Hu isn't ready to file yet. We could talk to Esther and Dane about squeezing in one more session."

"No, lover." Thea held her palm close to her screen. Max put his cheek near his own, imagining her touch. "We don't have to worry about who's listening. I'll say I love you, and you'll say you love me, and to hell with eavesdroppers. You all can do your conspiring without me."

"We won't have to do that. I forgot to say — you and Hu can have confidential calls. Because she's your lawyer."

Now Thea did chuckle. "All right. But she's not as cute as you." A pause. "And don't tell me she is too that cute. . . . Does Hu really think they wouldn't listen in?"

"She thinks with a court order, she can make sure of it somehow."

"That's good. Hey, I had another idea. We can still work on our music. Let's hope whoever's listening absolutely *hates* our stuff."

Chapter 16

KEEPING the secret from Thea's stored fellows was one thing. Keeping it from her parents, she insisted, was quite another, and intolerable. But Hu sternly instructed Thea not to speak to them directly. "It's too unpredictable. They might say something, or you might say something, that LiveAfter can use against us. You can bet the company will be listening."

That left it up to Max.

Thea's father jumped to his feet, shoving his chair back hard enough to knock it over. Thea's mother, who might normally have restrained him, sat with her hands clasped tightly together, her eyes closed and her face turned upward as if in prayer. Max tried to sit very still until both of Thea's parents had their emotions under a little more control.

Her father, however, did not intend to wait that long. He loomed over Max and shouted, "Did you know about this bullshit ahead of time? When you signed those papers?"

"Of course not!" Which he had to admit was evading the real question. Would he have signed anyway?

He had no idea.

Linda opened her eyes, stood up, and moved to stand by her husband with both hands on his left arm—

a gesture reminding Max that Thea's father was left-handed. "Dear, please. It's not his fault. Thea was the one who made the arrangement. And she had far more opportunity to look into the details than Max did, taken by surprise at such a terrible time." She turned to Max. "Does she know it's happening?"

"She does now. And she's—we're—doing something about it."

Linda led Bill back to their abandoned chairs, picking up the fallen chair and setting it upright. Max waited for them to sit, then explained the lawsuit as well as he could. He had memorized some legal lingo, but most of it now escaped him.

When he came to a halt, Linda leaned over to Bill, whispered to him for a moment, received his muttered reply, and faced Max again. "We can help pay for this. We don't know how much that will help."

Max almost replied that Hu had made such assistance unnecessary, but paused at the last instant: they must feel the need to do something, anything, to defend their daughter. Instead, he told them, "I'll talk to the lawyer about that. Thank you. She might want you to help some other way. In fact, I'm just about sure of it. You could testify about what Thea was like before."

A quieter growl this time: "Damn right we can."

Thea's mother smiled a little, which did not make her expression any less sad. "And I can tell the judge, or jury, or whomever about how Thea's been hijacked into agreeing with her mother at long last." Tears had finally gathered in her eyes. "And I was glad. I *thanked* her for thinking things through, and really listening to what I had to say. If I'd known . . . ." She lifted her chin and sat very straight, defiance personified. "I will fight for Thea until she can disagree with me again."

* * * * *

Hu had considered explaining her theory only to Esther for now. Of the current inner circle, Esther seemed the most likely to understand legal points. But Dane, at least, would be sure to demand information either from her or from Esther, and even Esther might garble it. Besides, Hu needed all the practice she could get at getting her points across to lay people.

That would be even more difficult in a phone conference. She would not learn enough about how well she was reaching her audience. So she made the necessary arrangements to assemble Esther and Dane and even Max for a lunchtime meeting, paying for Max's maglev ticket despite his polite protests. As for refreshments, she calibrated the selection to satisfy hunger without distracting: nothing too exotic, delicious, or noisy, but nothing likely to elicit even politely suppressed complaint. She would eat before they arrived—and if she indulged in her favorite takeout of Thai/Mexican fusion, well, that was nobody's business but her own.

As her guests munched sandwiches, peeled bananas, and sipped soft drinks and fruit juice, Hu got started.

"First, let me explain the goal. I'm greedy! I don't just want to protect Thea and the other stored people in the short term. I want to establish a principle that'll protect everyone stored in the future, no matter what clever tweaks are possible in their contracts, no matter what a state legislature or even Congress might do with sufficient corporate persuasion. So we include one or more constitutional claims."

Dane swallowed a large mouthful of sandwich and

grinned, a shred of lettuce still in his teeth. "That means the Supreme Court gets involved, doesn't it?"

Hu suppressed a sigh. She must expect oversimplified assumptions. "Not necessarily, and certainly not right away. We'll be starting out in a trial court—a federal trial court if we can manage it. We still have to decide whether we want a jury trial, at least on those claims that a jury can hear.

"But wherever we end up, we'll have the same initial obstacle to overcome. In general, it takes a government, or somebody directly or indirectly working for a government, to violate constitutional rights."

Max looked up, brow furrowed, and put down his banana. "I'm pretty sure I've heard people complaining about censorship when a bookstore won't carry some book, or a social media site blocks somebody. Isn't censorship about the First Amendment?"

Hu wiggled her hand in a "yes-and-no" shimmy. "The word 'censorship' isn't a legal term. If the government is doing the censoring or is somehow mixed up in it, then you can have a violation of the First Amendment. But whether we're talking about freedom of speech or some other constitutional right, you still need that link to government—what lawyers call a 'state actor'—before you can even start arguing about what the Constitution means and whether it protects your plaintiff against whatever the defendant did."

Hu sighed. "The law about 'state actors' is particularly confusing and confused. I won't drag you through all the details. But there are two concepts I'm hoping will get us somewhere."

"Hold on. Let me grab another sandwich." Dane scooted his chair toward the table with the food on it. Esther rolled her eyes; Max looked from the food to

Esther and clasped his hands together on his lap. Hu waited for all three to look toward her once more before resuming.

"First: 'entwinement.' When the activities of some person or company are so entwined with, so hard to separate out from, government activities, that moves you toward a court finding that the person or company is a state actor for constitutional purposes. What I want to do is emphasize how things have changed in the last several decades. Have you all heard the phrase 'crony capitalism'?"

Esther and Dane nodded in near unison; Max looked uncertain, then said quietly, "I'm not sure. Would you mind . . ."

Hu smiled in what she hoped was a reassuring manner. "It means that some companies, usually large ones, get favors from the government, favors that make it harder for anyone else to compete with them. Sometimes the companies pay for those favors with outright bribery, but usually the quid pro quo is more long-term and subtle. The companies support regulations that give government more power, and the regulators write those regulations in a way that helps the companies keep their market share and stifle competition.

"We've had crony capitalism for a long, long time, but it's expanded along with the expansion of the state and federal regulatory framework. It's now normal for major companies—companies like, and including, LiveAfter—to be protected by government, enriched by government, and, in the end, dependent on government for their prosperity or even their existence. Are you with me so far?"

Max stared over Hu's shoulder, his eyes just a little

crossed, then looked back at Hu. "I think I get it, more or less. LiveAfter needs the government, and the government needs LiveAfter."

"That's close enough. Another way to put it is that there's no clear dividing line between the company and the government. And *that* means — or I'm going to argue it means — that the company is really operating as an arm of the government, and therefore can be held to at least some of the same constitutional standards as a government agency would."

Dane grinned. "Atta girl! . . . Wait, didn't you say 'first'? There's more?"

Hu, unsure whether to bother bristling at the form of Dane's praise, seized on his question as a way to move on. "Yes, I do have another argument to throw in the mix. Legally, LiveAfter is the guardian of all those who've entrusted themselves to be digitized and stored. Like other guardians, LiveAfter is court-appointed, though in a more wholesale way than traditional guardians, and it's accountable to the state for how it cares for its wards — the stored people."

Max stirred in his chair. Hu glanced at her notes and put her finger on the point she would make next. "It's okay to ask a question. Do you have one?"

Max grimaced. "I don't know if it's a question, exactly. I just don't like the idea of LiveAfter thinking it's Thea's *guardian*. Aren't guardians for people who can't do things for themselves, like people whose minds have gone?"

If only she had steered Max toward the seat next to hers, she could have made some physical gesture of support, like putting her hand over his. Too late now. "Of course Thea's as alert as ever, and in some sense as able as ever she was to handle her own affairs. But the brutal fact is: she can't do that, or anything else, without the computer storage space and software that LiveAfter's providing." She waited while Max nodded, bit his lip, struggled for control, and finally sat quiet again. "And that's actually a point in our favor, as I'm about to explain.

"There used to be a fair amount of legal debate about whether state authority over guardians meant that guardians were state actors. Almost all courts decided that no, they weren't—but there was a minority view going the other way. I plan to argue that LiveAfter's guardianships should be treated as state action even if other guardianships aren't.

"You see, normally the state—in most cases, meaning either state government or local government—exercises what's called the 'police power' over all its residents. Making and enforcing criminal laws, settling disputes about contracts and such, deciding who's qualified to practice a profession—these are all part of the police power. And to exercise that power over you or me, they don't need anyone's help—no intermediary. But because of LiveAfter's total control over their wards' interactions with the outside world, governments need LiveAfter's help in order to carry out any of their police power functions where the stored are concerned. And that brings us back to the idea of 'entwinement.' When a guardian is inevitably part of every government action that affects an individual, I'll argue that it only makes sense to call the guardian a state actor as well."

Esther shook her head and smiled a little. "That's quite ingenious. But we're not talking about things the government asked LiveAfter to do. Doesn't that make a difference?"

"Not as much difference as you'd think. As long as

LiveAfter was in a general sense doing what its arrangement with the government required it to do, then we should be all right. It'll be like holding a prison responsible when a guard beats up a prisoner."

Max visibly shuddered. "A prisoner. That's a little too close to home." He squeezed his eyes tight. "It was up to me, in the end. I could have told them not to do it."

This time Hu stood up and went over to Max, putting her hand on his shoulder. "You did the best you could for her." She should make no promises, but the hell with that. "We're going to fix this. We're going to make sure she can live this new life the way she would want to live it."

Dane got up as well, dragging his chair over toward Max and giving him a one-armed hug before sitting down again. Hu went back to her own chair. Esther waited until Hu had resumed her seat, then asked: "Is that the whole legal picture, then?"

Hu laughed. "Not even close. There are all sorts of complexities about what we can get damages for and what we can't, what we'll have to do to try to get into federal court and stay there . . . but those are my headaches. You'll have enough to do just keeping an eye on what happens in the meantime."

* * * * *

Esther found the usual energetic Dane hard enough to handle. Nervous, jumpy Dane was giving her a headache, especially with the early spring pollen already irritating her sinuses. When he paused for a moment in his pacing, she reached up to grab his shoulder. "Stop. Sit. Breathe. And tell me what's going on with you."

He gave a halfhearted grin and sat on the bench.

Esther brushed aside a few twigs and perched beside him. When he said nothing, she took her best guess. "Is your mother all right?"

He jerked his shaggy head toward her. "For now? Maybe. As far as I can tell, they haven't gotten to her yet. But they might, any time. It sounds as if some of her friends are getting more political. . . . Why the hell is Hu taking so long?"

Esther stopped herself from rolling her eyes. "A case like this takes a great deal of preparation. You must know that. And it used to take much longer before the courts streamlined the procedure."

Dane looked away again, staring across the park.

"What do you think would happen if she let us hurry her?"

Dane still refused to meet her eyes.

"If Hu doesn't prepare very, very thoroughly, what would that do to her chances? And Thea's? And your mother's?"

Slowly he turned his head toward her again. "She could lose. They could lose."

Esther laid her hand gently on his knee. "We're not doing all this, taking the risks we're taking, only to make things worse. We have to win. And winning will take patience, and discipline."

Not to mention luck, if not divine intervention.

* * * * *

Hu stretched, turned away from her large office window, and settled back down to work. It was all very well to dream about making new constitutional law, but she had more reliable claims to draft, and procedural mazes to navigate.

Thea might be the plaintiff now, but she couldn't remain the only plaintiff—not if they were going to get some broad relief that protected all the stored. From Hu's limited exposure to Thea, she wouldn't be content with a victory that only covered her. And no way would Dane and Esther be risking their jobs, if nothing more, because of Thea alone. Hu would have to make this a class action, with all the stored who'd been altered, or even all those in danger of it, as her clients.

And she'd need to shore up her access to the federal courts. It might not be a major setback if she ended up in state court, but federal court had advantages she was loath to relinquish. If she defined her class of plaintiffs broadly enough, she could get past the minimum size requirement. And as for the minimum "amount in controversy": she'd be asking for injunctive relief, with the court ordering the defendants to do this and stop doing that. If the cost of implementing those remedies wouldn't get her to the minimum, she could add some large—if ultimately unlikely—figure for "punitive" damages. LiveAfter certainly deserved some punishment.

Her only claims based on federal law were her somewhat ambitious constitutional ones, but she had another way through the federal court doors: diversity jurisdiction, a difference in state citizenship between plaintiffs and defendants. Like so many corporations, LiveAfter was incorporated in Delaware; and with the rapid growth of Idaho as a corporate haven, LiveAfter's principal place of business, like so many of Hu's business clients, was right here in Boise. At least some of her potential class members lived outside Delaware and Idaho. Thea had lived in California. With a class action, "some" was good enough.

Except that notion might be stillborn, if stored

people's citizenship changed with their death. If all the stored were citizens where LiveAfter was incorporated, or—even more plausibly—where the computers that housed their code were located, that'd put paid to the idea of diversity jurisdiction.

Wait, hadn't Max said something about Thea voting? Hu put in a call to Max, and he answered on the second ring.

"Max, when Thea voted, was it the same ballot you used? I mean, the same candidates and issues?"

"It sure was. We discussed some of the details."

"*Yes!*" Hu laughed like a pirate. Max made some attempt to chuckle along. "It's all right, Max. That's just what I wanted to hear. I'll explain next time we meet." She hung up and sat back in her chair, allowing herself a moment to gloat. For whatever reasons, very likely in service of some goal of one or more of the defendants, Thea's continuity of citizenship had already been established. Surely the same was true of her fellows. They had their ticket to federal court.

Aside from the constitutional claims, everything else Hu asserted would be based on state law. The federal court could hear the state law claims, and probably would choose to do so unless it threw the case out of federal court altogether. But as for which state's law would be applied, she'd better be prepared for all the possible alternatives.

Of course, LiveAfter's contract was intended to preempt all manner of claims. So she'd need to dig into the language and find ways around some parts, and ways to turn other parts against the company.

She would start with only LiveAfter as a defendant. Then, once the discovery process yielded more information, she'd add whatever self-appointed social engineers had hired (or otherwise induced) LiveAfter to mess with people's brains.

She would hide Dane's and Esther's involvement for as long as she could; but she would almost certainly end up representing them in whistle-blower lawsuits. At least the statutes covering such suits would pay her fees if she won.

Which was more than she could be sure of in this case, depending on the extent of any victory. But the publicity would be more than worth the investment of time. At least, that was the story she would give her partners. As far as she was concerned, she was doing it for her former colleague, now probably sitting in the virtual sun and contemplating his belly button. And for her new friends. And for herself, against the day when she might hope for digital immortality without the devil's bargain of losing herself.

Hu usually prided herself on an elegant restraint in choosing the causes of action in her complaints. But in this case, she had better make use of any analogies she could and stretch every definition to its limit.

LiveAfter's response took a number of tacks.

Of course, they denied any knowledge of or involvement in the manipulation of their clients. But they acknowledged the possibility that some intruder could have hacked the files of the named plaintiff—in which case she must be considered incompetent and unable to file suit. And they asserted paragraph this, clause that, whereby Thea Lee, like all their clients, had waived the application of any implied warranties.

Time to amend the complaint! Hu promptly roped Max in as next friend, suing on behalf of his wife in the event she were held incompetent.

Max, consulted by phone, showed some initial resistance. "We don't want to admit she's incompetent, do we?"

"That's not what we're doing," Hu explained. "We're pleading in the alternative, just as they are."

"Which means . . .?"

Hu smiled. "Here's one common example. There's a broken vase lying on the rug in the living room. Whoever's accused of breaking it has this to say: 'I didn't touch it. And if I did, I picked it up but didn't break it. Or else it was broken when I walked in.'"

Max laughed outright. "Lawyers do that? It's not just five-year-olds?"

"I'm sure future lawyers are particularly eloquent when they make that argument at the age of five."

For good measure, Hu filed a separate suit with Max as a plaintiff in his own right, seeking damages for loss of consortium, and then moved that the two cases be tried together.

"What's consortium?" Dane inquired, looming over her shoulder.

"Loss of the companionship involved in a familial relationship. For husband and wife, it usually includes sex. But it includes the intangibles as well. Companionship, advice, support."

"Hey, didn't they used to do phone sex? Can you make the defendants pay for interrupting that?"

"Hmmm. That's about the monitoring more than the monkeying. But the contract gave them privacy rights, didn't it? I'll add it in."

Dale pounded his chest. "Me paralegal Tarzan, you lawyer Jane!"

"Do hush up. And back up. I'm afraid you'll trip

and fall and squash me." But she grinned as she worked.

Dane finally took his leave, bowing like a courtier and then drumming a reveille on her door on his way out. Just as well: he was a distraction, if an entertaining one.

Time to review the storage contract again, to be sure she wasn't forgetting anything. . . . Damn it, she had. That hold harmless clause would have Max paying some of LiveAfter's attorney fees unless she could get around it somehow. The judge would probably put that clause on hold until Max won or lost on his consortium claim. If he won, Hu very much doubted the clause would hold up. But she'd better make sure he could afford to lose. . . .

Back to the class action. She would add negligence in allowing the supposed hackers to breach LiveAfter's defenses. And as for the waivers of implied warranties, she couldn't wait to go after those. "How dost thou violate public policy? Let me count the ways."

* * * * *

One of the associates assisting Hu on the Lee case checked his phone in the break room and whistled. "Whoa, our judge bailed! Recused himself."

Hu checked her messages and found the confirmation. "Let me guess: he's got a LiveAfter contract. . . . Yup, that's what it is. Too bad. He's a decent sort."

"On the other hand, if all the judges with LiveAfter contracts are out of the picture. . . ."

Hu gave the half-voltage version of her evil laugh. "Indeed. The message doesn't say who we'll get instead. Check on it, will you?"

The associate popped his head back into Hu's office in less than five minutes. "This really *is* your lucky day!"

* * * * *

"I don't understand." Max was getting tired of saying that, and the case had barely even started.

"Judges have to avoid 'the appearance of impropriety,' no matter how fair they think they can be. If someone would look at the stock they own or the club they belong to or whatever, and wonder if they could still treat all parties equally, then they're supposed to step aside. That's what our original judge did. And in this case, we traded up, and got one of my favorites as a replacement. This lady is sharp as a tack, and keeps lawyers on a pretty tight leash. That means I'll have to play it straight, no pushing the envelope—at least not unless it's crucial. But it also means she'll understand our arguments and the technical facts underlying them."

"I guess that's good. But does the judge matter all that much? What about the jury?"

Hu looked briefly taken aback. "Didn't I tell you? I'd already been leaning against a jury trial, and even more so with this change of judges. I'm sorry—I explained it to Dane, and forgot you weren't with us that day."

Hu had tackled Dane first, on a hunch that he would be the hardest to convince.

"But don't we *need* a jury? Judges are powerful people. We need folks who understand being pushed around. We'd just need to pick some jurors who like to push back!"

Hu had absolutely no doubt that Dane was

imagining himself in the role of heroically combative juror. "It's not that easy. Jury selection is like multiple simultaneous tugs-of-war. Your opponent knows what kind of jury you want—and that's not a simple calculation, either—and they'll do their best to prevent it. My track record is pretty good; but even though federal courts don't require a unanimous jury in civil trials these days, we would need at least seven out of ten, and that can be tricky. Especially for a cutting-edge case with mind-boggling issues, not to mention constitutional law. I'd rather gamble on one tough, smart, curious judge."

Max nodded along to Hu's explanation. It made sense, he supposed, although like almost everything else she explained to him, it made the legal process seem even more tangled and intimidating than before.

Hu, however, seemed anything but intimidated. She practically sparkled with energy, in a way that reminded him painfully of Thea despite their very different personal styles. When she sat back and actually rubbed her hands, he could not help muttering, "I'm glad one of us is having a good time."

Of course Hu heard him. She cocked an eyebrow, then looked him in the eye. "Max, oversimplifying somewhat"—she said that so often!—"some lawyers work this hard for money, and some of us work this hard because we enjoy it. In my biased and not exactly humble opinion, those of us having fun do a better job."

* * * * *

"You're kidding. Are you telling me I can't tell my

friends what's happening? What's being done to them?"

Hu did not exactly raise her voice, but she somehow gave it a more penetrating quality. "Thea. The class hasn't been certified yet." Hu must have caught Thea's frown, quickly as Thea suppressed it: she paused a moment, with a "how do I simplify this" look on her face, then continued. "The judge hasn't decided yet whether all the other stored are in the same situation as you are, the one we're suing about. Once the judge rules in our favor on that point, then we may be allowed to tell all of them about the lawsuit—though we'd have to be quite careful about our wording. But remember, they're watching you." Thea gritted her teeth at the unnecessary and unwelcome reminder. "If you start spreading the word now, it could complicate our position. The judge might consider it mischief-making. And we absolutely do not want to annoy the judge."

Thea clenched her fists, until she noticed that her fingernails were somehow failing to dig into her palms. She shivered and took a few deep breaths. "If I see somebody change, change in a way I don't think they asked for, can I at least tell *you*?"

Hu nodded emphatically. "By all means do. And depending who, and how, we might figure out a way to add that person as a plaintiff."

Hu looked Thea up and down, her gaze lingering on Thea's hair. "And by the way, it might be a good idea to go blonde again. It's hard to predict when you might end up in court, virtually speaking, and I'd rather you didn't show up sporting any elective alterations."

And even when the class had finally been certified, Hu still wanted Thea to hold back. "Give me a chance to spread the word formally and comprehensively. If I fail, then we can revisit a more underground approach."

* * * * *

LiveAfter's lead counsel seemed to be, in one of Hu's favorite semi-archaic words, flummoxed. "Your Honor, the plaintiff class seeks primarily injunctive relief rather than money damages. Under those circumstances, the rules do not require notice to all putative class members. We are confident that plaintiffs' claims will be determined to be unfounded, and ask you not to order such a disruptive and disquieting communication."

The judge aimed a stare down her nose at the man, one Hu would certainly have called "disquieting" if aimed at her. "Counsel, I do not appreciate your making assumptions as to the decision I will ultimately reach. Kindly refrain from premature optimism. Ms. Yang, your response?"

"Your Honor, under the current federal rules, this court may allow class members to opt out of the litigation. LiveAfter's clientele could hardly opt out of a litigation kept secret from them."

"Yes, Ms. Yang. I may so allow. But why should I? What circumstances make it particularly appropriate, despite the disruptive effect defense counsel has identified?"

It had taken some time for Hu to come up with an answer to this expected question. In the end, it had been the thought of her former law partner, now unable even to realize that he was helpless, that had inspired her. "Your Honor, LiveAfter has successfully marketed itself to what we may call society's movers and shakers. Its clients are accustomed to exercising power and authority. We submit that these people would expect to be consulted, would feel entitled to be consulted, before letting some third party speak for them in matters of importance. We wish to honor these justified expectations."

The judge pondered for a moment, then called up her calendar. "Ms. Yang, let me see a proposed notice by close of business next Monday. Then I'll decide whether notice is advisable."

Monday! Hu did not look at her opponent, who was probably smirking. The cover sheet, the table of contents, the detailed descriptions that had to pass muster as objective, would consume the rest of her week and every spare moment of the weekend. At least she could rope in a couple of associates to assist and share her suffering.

Three hours before the deadline, a somewhat bleary-eyed Hu filed her proposed notice, yawned, stretched, and invited the equally weary associates out for a drink. Their efforts satisfied her, on the whole. She thought they had managed to avoid both timidity and overstatement, and to tread the fine line between easily ignored fine print and easily dismissed excess. If only the judge approved the result, LiveAfter's customers would have a wake-up call coming.

* * * * *

The call jolted Thea out of a creative trance; she scrambled to jot down the musical phrase before it eluded her, then reached to answer, almost barking out an irritated "yes?", softening her tone at the last moment when she saw Hu's face.

Hu looked positively smug. "Check your messages, will you? And then call me back." Hu hung up; Thea, bemused, did as Hu had asked. There were only three messages: one from Max, one from The Diva, and one that appeared to come from the federal court. Even as she moved to open that one, five more messages appeared, all from stored acquaintances, with subject lines expressing various versions of shock and dismay.

It began, in large bold letters:

"IF YOU ARE A CUSTOMER OF THE LIVEAFTER CORPORATION AND RESIDE IN DIGITAL CONDITION WITHIN THEIR SERVERS AT THIS TIME, A LAWSUIT HAS BEEN FILED ALLEGING THAT YOUR FILES HAVE BEEN ALTERED IN MATERIAL WAYS WITHOUT YOUR CONSENT . . . ."

Thea hollered, "YES!", jumping up from the chair, jumping up and down with her feet together like a springboard diver, punching the air. Only after several minutes of energetic celebration did she settle down, lying back in luxurious relief upon her bed. She would call Hu, of course. But first, she would call Max.

Chapter 17

"WELL, that didn't take long." Hu showed LiveAfter's latest motion to one of the associates who had worked on the class action notice. "What do you make of it?"

The associate tensed slightly, recognizing that she was being tested rather than consulted. "There has to be a free speech issue if they're asking the court to keep the parties and attorneys from talking about the case. But they wouldn't be filing this motion, would they, if they had no chance of success?"

"Well, the judge does get to play 'balance the constitutional rights': free speech and free press versus fair trial. They'd have a better chance if a jury was involved. It's almost insulting to suggest that the judge's decision would be affected by anything said outside the courtroom."

The associate hesitated, then asked, "What about damage to LiveAfter's reputation?"

Hu smiled a little, lips pressed tightly together. "If we lose, they can use our or our clients' out-of-court statements to sue for defamation. So we need to be sensible about what we say to the press or elsewhere. And it would be a good idea to win.

"In the meantime, I have a motion of my own to file, one that will shift the focus of this hearing quite a bit."

This time, the judge's sharp gaze raked both attorneys equally before she addressed counsel for LiveAfter. "What statements by plaintiffs or their attorneys have given rise to your concern?"

The lawyer managed not to squirm. "We did not think it prudent to wait until such damage had already occurred before making this request."

The judge just barely twitched an eyebrow. "Ms. Yang?"

Hu smoothed her already immaculate slacks. "Your Honor, as you know, gag orders covering parties and attorneys are hardly routine in class actions, especially once notice to class members has been approved and given. The only factor distinguishing the present case is the ease with which defendants could enforce such an order by censoring communications to and from their stored clients. Not only is that hardly a factor favoring defendants' motion, but as you will see in the papers we filed this morning, plaintiffs request an order restraining defendants from implementing any such restriction."

The judge glanced down at what was probably a screen, placed out of counsels' view. "Before I rule on defendants' motion, I'll hear argument on plaintiffs'. Ms. Yang, you may proceed."

"Thank you, Your Honor. Defendants are not alone in wishing to forestall future damage rather than merely reacting after it has occurred. However, the damage that concerns us is far less speculative. Named plaintiff Thea Lee and the class members require the immediate protection of this court, to ensure that defendant LiveAfter's continuing custody of them does not interfere with their ability to prosecute this case. The unauthorized alterations on which this case is based—"

"Alleged alterations, counselor, if you please." The

judge nodded toward counsel for LiveAfter, who had leaped forward with mouth open, no doubt to make the same objection. The lawyer checked himself and stepped back again.

"Of course, Your Honor." Hu spared a microsecond to chastise herself for the slip. She must be more keyed up than she had realized. "The fact remains that LiveAfter faces an actual and immediate conflict of interest. Under its contract with Lee and the other class members, it must act as a fiduciary devoted to their best interests. That is a duty fundamentally at odds with LiveAfter's and Lee's current adversarial position. And there is no apparent possibility of removing stored individuals to the custody of some neutral third party. We therefore seek an injunction against any alteration in the code by which Lee's existence is maintained."

Hu stepped back; counsel for LiveAfter stepped forward. "Counsel's motion betrays the same sort of technical ignorance that underlies this lawsuit as a whole. The groundbreaking technology that has extended and preserved Thea Lee's identity beyond the death of her body is not static, as counsel implies. Any attempt to freeze the code, any failure to compensate for unwanted fluctuations and run maintenance subroutines, could have deleterious or even catastrophic results."

The judge rocked back and forth in her somewhat antiquated office chair, which squeaked in time with her movements. "Nonetheless, counsel's point as to a conflict of interest is well taken; and it is also highly desirable to preserve the status quo as to the other class members, to the extent technically feasible. What we need is informed supervision of the software that comprises Ms. Lee and her fellows, or that could affect them in any way. Ms. Hu, if I appoint a guardian ad litem to exercise such supervision and prevent any substantive tinkering, do you have any candidates to suggest for that appointment?"

Hu suppressed a smile. She had hoped for exactly this development: better to let the judge come up with the obvious idea for herself, if she'd be so kind. And by predicting the judge's response, Hu had just won a bet with Dane, with the stakes a smoothie at the shop near work. "I should be able to do some research and file a list before the end of the day."

The judge stopped rocking and leaned forward. "Rather than granting plaintiffs' motion for an injunction as submitted, I will be appointing a guardian ad litem. Defense counsel may strike candidates from plaintiffs' list, leaving at least two, one of whom I will appoint. I am granting plaintiffs' additional motion, concerning content filtration, in part: the order governing the responsibilities of the GAL will include monitoring any such restrictions on communication and reporting the same to this court, at which point I will consider the details and issue any necessary orders. As logically follows, defendants' motion for a gag order is denied, at least for the present." She sat forward again, looking straight at Hu. "But if, in the end, I conclude that this case has been frivolously brought, I will not require defendants to file a separate action for either defamation or malicious prosecution. I will instead impose substantial sanctions against plaintiffs—and if their resources are not sufficient to pay those sanctions, or if I consider it appropriate, against their attorney as well."

* * * * *

Within a couple of days, most of the stored had checked their messages and struggled through the legal verbiage. As they absorbed the news, factions faced off and alliances shifted within the various communities that had been pursuing communalist Utopian projects.

— Can societal good truly flow from an oppressive tactic like taking over someone's mind?

— If we've been affected, it's really a removal of blinders imposed by our upbringing and associations, a benign form of social surgery.

— We were naive to trust a corporation. We must demand that our files be transferred to government servers!

— I owe my wife — widow, whatever — an apology. A big one. I only hope she'll accept it. She knew something was happening to me, and I wouldn't believe it.

— I always believed in these goals, deep down. I just wouldn't admit it to myself before. Nothing's really changed.

The news did not take long to spread to the world of the living, although discussion of it in the few remaining traditional media outlets remained mysteriously muted. Online forums, by contrast, grew quite heated.

— We're talking about morally compromised members of the oppressor class. By living off their fellows all their lives, they've forfeited the tender consideration you're saying they should have received.

— No revolution has ever happened without some reduction of the originally privileged population!

— Every revolution that's justified itself in those terms has ended up eating its own!

And on and on.

Not all the stored considered the news worth much concern, even when Thea attempted — against her better judgment and Hu's advice — to press the issue.

"We know they've altered us. Look at me!" The woman tittered. "I was dumpy and my hair was thinning." The woman, now svelte and with abundant wavy locks, ran a hand down her fashionable curves. "I'd have paid extra, but they did it for free."

How are you missing the point? Let me count the ways. There was probably no point addressing the misnomer of "free" when the retail clients had paid the proverbial (and oddly appropriate) arm and leg. "You agreed. To be a little bit legal about it, you consented. But what if—well, for example, did you vote in the last election?"

The woman shrugged. "I decided I might as well. I rarely bothered before, but they went to so much trouble to let us."

"What if they told you how to vote? What if you supported someone who you would have thought was incompetent, or even dangerous?"

The woman looked down her probably altered nose. "Really, my dear, what difference do politicians make?"

Thea made a considerable effort not to grind her teeth. "Then why did you vote? Why did you care whether LiveAfter encouraged our voting?"

The woman actually knit her brow as if in thought. That was probably as much of an impact as Thea could hope for. She pointed to her empty coffee cup and made her escape.

* * * * *

Dane's conversations with his mother had not changed a great deal since her death, at least in content. She had always enjoyed listening to him talk, and had never much understood any of the things he wanted to talk about. She had always beamed at him, soaking in his presence like (she said) sunshine, letting it warm her. But he could no longer hold her hand, as she had liked, while he scarfed down the baked goods she had saved for his visits.

He would have talked about the lawsuit, but he did not want to alarm her now, when there was nothing she could do to protect her mental integrity. If Hu and the rest of them actually pulled it off, won some relief, then he would explain the whole stinking mess to her as gently as possible. Instead, he talked about his new friends, the cute feisty coworker and the hotshot lawyer, without providing any context. When she asked about his work, he could not manage any pretense of satisfaction, but he did dredge up some insignificant gripes upon which to deflect some of his frustration. And he let her comfort him.

Of course, he asked about her own activities. She had recently found companions with whom to play euchre, and a quilting circle (simulated quilting apparently working as well as simulated knitting). And she had access to all the latest books, so she could still indulge in her mystifying taste for thrillers, the more harrowing the better. She was describing the bloody climax of her most recent read when a chime interrupted her. She huffed in chagrin. "I thought I'd turned off the incoming mail sound. I'm sorry, dear."

"No problem! Check it if you want."

"Oh, it's nothing. Just some paperwork the company is sending people. I'll just check off the box and get it out of the way."

"No, wait." A stab of intuition made him stop her. "Would you mind reading it to me?"

Her eyes went wide with surprise, and then she

smiled sheepishly. "I'm afraid I wasn't going to *read* it. I should, shouldn't I? And you can explain anything I don't understand."

But he found the mind-numbing bureaucratic doubletalk impossible to absorb. "Can you put it on screen for me to see?"

He had to talk her through the process, making her describe the controls in front of her, as she grew bewildered and uncertain about his persistence. Then, when he could finally read the document, he had to fight back the rage that threatened to overwhelm him. He closed his eyes for a moment, struggling; then he opened them and forced a chuckle. "What garbage! You know, I don't think you should answer it, after all. They really shouldn't be bothering you about this sort of thing."

She wrinkled her forehead and bit her lip. "Really, dear? I don't want to cause any trouble."

"It'll be fine. I promise. I'll take care of it." He held up his fingers in the "Scouts honor" pledge she had taught him to use as a boy. "I'll take care of everything."

He somehow managed to chat with her for another few minutes about her card games and her books before he extricated himself and called Hu. She let him curse for only a few moments before she cut him off. "I've got to get on this right away. We'll talk more later."

* * * * *

Hu watched in well-concealed glee as the judge pinned LiveAfter's attorney — an obviously junior sacrificial lamb offered up for the occasion — with her predator's stare. "I see that someone at LiveAfter has the mistaken impression that I am underemployed."

The young associate gaped at the judge for a

moment, then stammered, "Your Honor, I don't believe anyone has that—"

The judge cut him off, an indulgence of temper unusual enough to make Hu blink. "Only such a belief could reasonably explain the decision to embed the class members' opt-out option in a dense thicket of incomprehensible and unrelated legalese. It was utterly predictable, or rather inevitable, that plaintiffs' counsel would bring this matter to my attention, and consume another precious hour in all of our busy afternoons." She turned to Hu. "Ms. Yang, it appears we will need your assistance in drafting appropriate language. And to avoid any appearance of favoritism—or of insufficient paranoia—I will require that you submit that language to me for review. By this time tomorrow, if you please."

Hu looked at the eager young woman in her doorway and suppressed a sigh. She hated to see enthusiasm go to waste. "I really don't think that idea will prove fruitful."

The associate visibly suppressed frustration. "I get why we had to wait for the notice to go out. Now that it has, where's the down side of looking for other relatives to testify about unexplained changes, or even become named plaintiffs?"

There was no need to predict the outcome Hu expected. Let the youngster discover it on her own. And come to think of it, the information might prove useful, though not in the way the associate believed. "As you say, the matter has gone public now. Let's see who gets in touch of their own initiative, and go from there. I'll make sure all such contacts are directed to you."

* * * * *

The associate rested her head in her hands for a weary moment, then resumed updating her list.

— — —

Became a Communist: 4
Became a Socialist: 7
Became a Fascist: 7
Became a Vegetarian: 3
Became Homosexual: 6
Became Genderfluid: 5
Became Cisgender: 8

— — —

She hit the print button and shut down the screen, then sat glum for a few minutes before heading out to report to Hu.

* * * * *

"I don't understand." The associate stood in front of Hu's desk, too restless to sit in the available chair. "They must have altered hundreds of people, at least, or it wouldn't have been worth the trouble. Why have so few relatives noticed?"

"We don't know how many suspected a change without being sure, and how many are fairly sure without wanting to get caught up in litigation. And not everyone whose vote changed, or who decided to vote after a lifetime of apathy, would have bothered to mention it to their families, especially if the discussion might get awkward."

The associate looked toward the ceiling, cogitating, then back at Hu. "We could still call the family members who've come forward to say their stored relatives went socialist."

Hu made a keep-going gesture.

The associate gave her a tight-lipped smile. "And then LiveAfter would call a few of the others to make Max look like just another kook."

"Correct. They might do that anyway, but it wouldn't help to have us calling witnesses we found the same way. We want to distinguish Max and Thea as much as we can."

The associate sighed. "And you knew it would turn out this way."

"Let's say I suspected it. The moral of the story being: don't just look for what you want to find! Look for the evidence the other side will turn up that points the other way. Actually, it's just as well you checked, and got some idea of the distribution. We'll be better prepared, now, for any use LiveAfter might make of the same information. And let's cross-check the detailed list of supposed new socialists against the members of Thea's discussion group."

There were, in fact, three matches; but according to Thea, these same group members were the most resistant to the idea that their passionately held beliefs might have been imposed from without. Hu and her team would go with the plaintiffs and victims they already had.

CHAPTER 18

NEXT came the months-long mutual investigation process known as discovery.

There was a great deal for Hu and her team to learn. Which LiveAfter employees and officers had known about the alterations? Which had been actively involved? To what risks and side-effects, besides the central outrage, had the stored been subjected? What witnesses, expert and other, did the opposition plan to call?

And of course, there was the question at the heart of the matter. Who had set the whole sordid scheme in motion? For which political organization(s) had LiveAfter been reshaping its customers?

The staff in Hu's office had a pool going. The lawyers most involved in discovery refrained from taking part, as they were bound to acquire an unfair advantage even before the final revelation.

Even so, there was a three-way tie. The political histories of those involved were not that hard to find, and inferences from those histories no great challenge. There would have been more than three winners, no doubt, if there were fewer like-minded organizations to suspect.

* * * * *

"You're telling me to delete a customer file??" The young tech gaped at her supervisor in disbelief.

The supervisor folded her arms and stared back. "The latest exam showed that Ms. Lee is in perfect working order. We've backed up her current profile, and we're maintaining it with *scrupulous* care." The supervisor smirked for a moment, for no reason the tech could follow. "So there's no need to use storage space on her original file, which lacks her recent memories."

The supervisor turned on her heel and left. The tech closed her mouth and watched the supervisor thread her way back through the empty cubicles. Why had the supervisor waited to approach her until everyone else had left for lunch? Maybe she should ask for the order in writing. Or maybe that would just get her in more trouble.

The tech called her cousin, a lawyer who worked in the general counsel's office. "Have you had lunch yet? Oh, good. I know that restaurant. Would you mind if I joined you? Order the #3 without hot sauce, and I'll be there as soon as I can. Oh, and could you look for a table with some privacy?"

* * * * *

The lawyer frowned, took another dripping mouthful of noodles, slurped them through his lips, and finally said, "That sounds like spoliation."

The tech had barely touched her dumplings. The lawyer pointed to them and made the family "Eat, eat!" gesture. The tech picked up a dumpling in her chopsticks and held it over her plate. "Is that a real word?"

The lawyer grinned. "In the wonderful world of legalese, it is! It means altering or destroying relevant evidence."

"Evidence of what?"

The lawyer gestured again. "Won't tell you 'til you eat that dumpling."

While the tech chewed her dumpling, the lawyer went on. "I guess nobody's told your department that the company's been sued. Just a guess, but I'd bet the customer whose profile you're supposed to delete is involved in the lawsuit. And maybe something about that customer's original profile would help the plaintiffs make their case. Maybe the current file is different in some way it shouldn't be."

The tech almost choked on her mouthful. The lawyer pushed the tech's glass of water toward her. "Cute, isn't it?"

The tech gulped down some water. "What was that word again? Spoilation?"

"You'd think so, wouldn't you? No, it's spo-li-ation. Not that you need to remember it. And speaking of remembering—I think I remember some sort of court paperwork about that case. Maybe there's a hole in that paperwork and someone's trying to slither through it."

The tech looked at her remaining dumplings. "So what should I do?"

"You should cover your ass. Stall. If you can't stall any more, pretend you misunderstood. 'Oh, I thought you said I should back up that profile again and store it securely!' But I have a feeling you'll get some new instructions before long."

The lawyer managed to coax his cousin into eating, and eating quickly. As soon as they returned to the office, the lawyer approached the general counsel's secretary. "I need to see the GC. Right away."

* * * * *

By the end of the day, a memo, marked "Urgent," had gone out to every employee of the company, and was printed out and distributed as a hard copy for good measure. It instructed them all to make every necessary effort to preserve all customer data of every kind, contrary to any routine that might normally have designated such data for deletion, and superseding any instructions to the contrary.

The supervisor glared at the printout and crumpled it into a ball. That blasted little tech had probably gone bleating to someone. But she couldn't do anything about it now. Not yet. She'd have to wait until the case was over and the fuss died down.

There were, of course, other possible approaches to try, and people ready to try them.

* * * * *

The call came in as audio only, and Max could not remember hearing the man's voice before. It had a not-quite-monotonous quality, like atonal music.

"This is your first time as a litigant, isn't it? You may not have been prepared for the experience. In fact, you may find that the strain has unexpected effects."

Max glared at the abstract unknown-caller icon on his screen. "Who are you and what are you talking about?"

"Many couples find that the stress of a lawsuit tends to, shall we say, fray the ties that bind them together. It would be a shame if you and Ms. Lee found yourselves less . . . compatible when all this is over."

The icon disappeared. Max sat speechless, frozen, staring at a blank screen, for long uncounted minutes before he shook off the paralysis and hurled the phone across the room. Then he dashed after it, searching the mess on the floor. When he found the phone, he staggered to the bed and sat down, clutching it, waiting for Thea to call.

* * * * *

Rounding the final turn at the end of her morning run, Thea noticed that not-Jim had been out jogging as well. His shirt clung to his chest, showing a suggestion, though not the full blotchy dampness, of sweat.

Thea had always been attracted to lean men, wiry but strong, men like Max. But once or twice, in college, she'd found herself drawn to a different type, more thickset and solid, with meatier muscles and the latent force of an immovable object. Not-Jim was built like that.

She had slowed to a walk, and he passed her by, smiling with his now-habitual genial expression. Would she ever get used to it? But she had barely known him before what might have been his first transformation. Maybe he was, or was supposed to be, naturally laid back.

She could have sped up again, caught up with him and made conversation; but he was headed away from her path, and she might be late for her call with Max. What a routine they had developed! Back home, living together, there would have been events of one kind or another to keep them from falling into a rut. But even if Max had reasons to vary their schedule, he was too doggedly faithful to tell her so.

She might keep the call short, this time. In the restless mood she found herself in, she would hardly be good company.

* * * * *

Hu kept her expression calm to counterbalance Max's obvious panic. "It's okay, Max. It may be nothing, just a bluff and a coincidence. But I'll get on it right away. I can manage these sons of bitches. Just try not to worry, and I'll be in touch soon."

She let her face go grim as soon as she broke the connection. Mess with *both* her clients, would they? She put her thoughts in order and called LiveAfter's general counsel.

"My client Mr. Cooper just told me about a communication from someone on your end. He didn't get a name, so I don't know whether we have a problem with one of your legal people making an ex parte contact instead of talking to me. But the content was intriguing. Max is no lawyer, of course, so he may have garbled things, but it sounded as if LiveAfter is ready to concede Mr. Cooper's claim for loss of consortium. . . . Did Mr. Cooper misunderstand? He thought the caller was acknowledging that Mr. Cooper and Ms. Lee had grown apart, or were likely to do so. . . . Perhaps you'd better find out who contacted Mr. Cooper and get that fellow's side of it. But naturally we'd be interested in such a partial settlement, as long as the amount was commensurate with his loss. . . . Yes, do get back to me as soon as you can."

She hung up and grinned like her wild feline namesake.

* * * * *

Max stared out the window at the morning sun on the trees outside. He should wait for Thea's call. After her distant tone the day before, her admissions of restlessness, the last thing he wanted to do was crowd her. But the suspense was making him literally sick. It was puke or call. He sat in their sturdiest armchair and called.

Thea picked up at once. Her face lit up when she saw him. "Lover! I'm so glad to see you. I dreamed about you last night, and I hated to wake up."

Max slumped back in his chair, the relief so great his hands were shaking. He kept them out of sight. No need to worry Thea. It was going to be okay. For now, at least.

Chapter 19

MAX looked cheerful. He hadn't looked that way for weeks. Just seeing him made Thea feel better as well. And before she could ask any questions, he pointed toward his left shoulder. "Guess what I came up with? I don't know why I never thought of it before!"

"What? Is it a new tattoo?"

He grinned and unbuttoned his flannel shirt. "Take a look!"

There, curling around his shoulder and a little way down the front and back of his arm, flowed two musical staffs, treble and bass, joined by the traditional bracket at the beginning and a bold double bar at the end, but with neither notes nor measures. "This much is permanent. We can add the notes and so on with temporary ink whenever we want, and change them any time."

"I love it!" Thea traced the curving lines in the air with her finger, then traced the same shape on her own shoulder. "I'll be so glad when I can have mine."

Max's smile dimmed. "You can't do it now?"

"I'm sorry, lover. Hu says I can't make any changes. It would muddy the proverbial waters. But I'll do it the moment we win."

His smile broadened again, though it might have been a trifle forced. "The very minute!"

Did Max expect a victory? Or was he just as uncertain as she about the likely result? She had already decided not to ask that question. So instead, she hummed one of their favorite early compositions. "You could start with that one. And show it to me as soon as you do."

* * * * *

"I wanted to show you some video we got from the defendants in the latest discovery dump." Hu's image shrank into a corner of the screen, with a video taking its place.

The video showed Thea sitting behind a long table, one of five people so seated. It must have been the panel discussion four years ago when the city asked local musicians to come talk about the latest trends. Thea was talking to the man next to her, then gazing around the audience. She waved toward the audience — at Max, who had decided to decline the invitation to participate and let Thea do the talking.

Max let himself drink in the sight of Thea, until his breathing started hitching up in the telltale way that meant he would cry if he didn't shift focus. "What about this did you want to show me?"

The video had reached the part where Thea would stand and start the discussion. Hu started the video over again, the sound muted. "Just look and tell me if you notice anything special."

Whatever Hu wanted him to notice, it must be something other than how beautiful she looked, or how at ease. . . . Maybe that was it. "She's ticcing a lot. More than usual."

The video vanished, and Hu's intent expression

filled the screen. "Tell me about Thea's tics."

"Well, you can see the usual one. Her shoulder. Huh—that double blink isn't so usual. Oh, I remember now. She was ticcing more and had more types of tics for a while when she took some antidepressant. Once she figured out the connection, she stopped taking it. It didn't really work for her anyway."

Hu grimaced. "So she had tics and tended to be depressed."

Max wriggled in protest. "The tics were no big deal. Usually, you'd hardly notice them. And she wasn't depressed that often. It happened more when she was a teenager. But once in a while she'd feel blue without any good reason, and she wanted to try evening things out."

The screen split between Hu and a document. "Their expert list includes a neurologist who's also a psychiatrist. Now I see why. . . . Would I be right in guessing that Thea's tics have disappeared?"

"Uh-huh. And Thea was pretty pleased when I pointed it out to her."

"Damn."

"But I wasn't. I told Thea I liked her the way she was, tics and all."

Hu sighed. "I'd rather it had been the other way round. I'm not sure I want to make the argument that loss of consortium includes not getting to see your wife's shoulder jerk around uncontrollably. We'll see if they find that exchange in their footage. It's not in the exhibit list, or not yet. But we'll deal with it if we have to."

* * * * *

Thea felt so paranoid so much of the time, now, that holding a supposedly confidential conversation with her lawyer couldn't really make it worse. And Hu avoided actually revealing information as much as possible. But she did ask questions.

"I know you used to have one or more motor tics. And I gather they've been reduced or eliminated. Did you ask for such treatment?"

"It never occurred to me." She would not add that if she had thought to ask for it, she might well have done so.

"How do you feel about that now?"

"Now, I'm pretty ticked off — whoops!" They both laughed for a moment before Thea went on. "I'm *pissed* off. I know I liked the idea at first. But now that I have reason to think my thoughts and beliefs have been meddled with, I feel, you could say, retroactively invaded. I entered into a contract to be preserved. I never agreed to be improved to someone else's specifications."

Hu leaned back and beamed.

* * * * *

What was that line from some really important twentieth-century politician? "This is not the end. It is not even the beginning of the end. But it is, perhaps, the end of the beginning."

That's how Max felt about finally facing the opposition, or at least their lawyers, even if he wouldn't yet be setting foot in any courtroom.

Hu had explained to him about depositions. He'd be under oath, like a witness in a trial, but the lawyers could ask more types of questions. They could do it all on a video call, and there wouldn't be a judge. A "court reporter" would be monitoring the call somewhere to make sure it all got recorded properly.

And just in case the judge watched the recording later, Hu had told him to dress up. She'd inspected his tattoos to make sure they wouldn't be likely to offend anyone, and then left it up to him whether to cover or display them.

He and Hu had done some practice sessions, so he could get over his nerves and Hu could catch any bad habits he had. Who knew he cracked his knuckles so much when he got keyed up? He'd have to ask Thea if he did it around her. And Hu had told him over and over to slow down instead of rushing ahead and tripping over his tongue.

Hu turned out to have a temper, and she let it crack more than once over his tendency to apologize and defer and explain. "Keep it short. Don't guess what they mean. If you don't know the answer, say so. If you don't understand the question, say so. Don't ramble on. And *don't* try to make them like you!"

Then there were the trick questions, and the really obnoxious questions, and everything else she wanted to prepare him for. Well, he could only hope he was prepared enough, because Hu would be calling any minute.

Max looked himself over in the mirror. Hair combed, check. Teeth brushed — well, he couldn't tell by looking, but check. Pants on, check. And on the staff of his tattoo, in a defiant red, the notes of the final passage of Thea's favorite Puccini aria, "Nessun Dorma": *Vincerò!* "I will win!"

* * * * *

Thea had not expected many updates from Hu about the discovery process. After all, there was little

Thea could do to assist, and no likely issue on which her opinions could affect matters. Hu would collect all the potentially useful—or potentially harmful—information she could from their adversary, while disclosing only what she had to disclose to comply with the rules and avoid annoying the judge.

But here was Hu on screen, looking chagrined. "Do you remember a written exchange you had with Max about how people change with time and circumstances? Max mentioned it the other day, after his deposition."

"Oh, yes, I remember that." How little she and Max had understood, back then.

"LiveAfter has asked for all communications between you and others, or between Max and others, that in any way discusses changes in your memory, personality, or activities. And we'll have to turn over that exchange in response."

Thea tried to remember what each of them had written. She would check the details as soon as she and Hu were finished. But—"What about the confidentiality setting?"

Hu shook her head. "I checked on that already. The contractual language excludes any situation where the otherwise confidential activity is pertinent to litigation. What with you being the plaintiff, the party who initiated litigation, I don't think we'd have much chance if we challenged that language."

Thea chased a dim memory of some other legal doctrine that might help. Hu, naturally, got there first. "Years ago, we could have invoked marital privilege. But it's been years since that did spouses much good in civil cases, as opposed to criminal ones."

"So now what?"

Hu looked squarely at her. "So now, you send me those messages between you and Max, and both of us think about what LiveAfter can do with them, and how we can respond."

Hu read through the messages Thea had forwarded, then read them again.

Maybe Thea should have been a lawyer. She'd certainly made a good case that Thea's political transformation was small potatoes, far from the outer boundaries of what life could bring.

And Max had declared his devotion to Thea, post-changes—unless more changes had occurred thereafter. That wouldn't help with the loss of consortium claim. Hu would have to get together with her expert witness and go over Thea's files, charting all the alterations by date.

She would have to talk to Max about what he had meant, and whether he had left anything unsaid.

* * * * *

"I wish it weren't all about law and lawyers now." At least the brisk weather gave Esther a reason to walk faster than usual. Her nerves needed a physical outlet.

Dane easily lengthened his stride to keep up, though he looked somewhat bemused. "Isn't that a good thing? I mean, it's not as if these people were walled up in a tower somewhere and we could break it down. It was gentle persuasion or lawyers, and you know persuasion won't do it."

"I know it's necessary. And I know how much we owe Hu. It's just—when in all this legal analysis and tactical jousting is anyone going to think about the bigger issues here?" She hadn't been exercising enough.

Walking fast felt great for a few minutes, but now her joints were threatening to seize up on her. She slowed down a little. "Let's say Hu wins. What happens then?"

Dane could walk her into the ground, no doubt, but he seemed to have trouble walking and thinking at the same time. He slowed down as well. "I don't get it. If Hu wins, if Thea and the other stored people win, then no one gets to hack their brains any more!"

Esther shoved her gloved hands into her pockets and puffed her breath out in exasperation, forming a small cloud that dissipated almost immediately. She smiled a little in spite of herself. She loved seasons where she could see her breath in the air.

She stopped abruptly in mid-step, Dane pulling up beside her. (Apparently she also had trouble thinking deep thoughts while in motion.) "Of course that's important, and it's what got all this started. But we've had millennia of rulers and teachers and philosophers trying to mold minds and plant opinions. If we really know, now, how to change other people's minds with some precision, do you think that knowledge can be contained? Will the benefits of storage be offset, from now on, by that vulnerability? Do we need to rethink giving the stored the right to vote, if there's going to be an unending technological struggle to protect their mental integrity? And are there ways this technology *should* be used? Should one benefit of storage be the right to decide, as you and I can't truly decide, how you want to think and feel?"

Dane looked a bit as if she'd struck him with a mallet. "I guess I've been kind of focused on the details. The here-and-now aspects."

She reached out impulsively and squeezed his hand. "And thank you for that. Thank you for caring about the details. I just have this annoying habit of following a train of thought way, way down the track."

Dane squeezed back, then dramatically raised her hand and gave it a disgustingly smacking kiss. She jerked it away, sticking out her tongue at him. (She hadn't done that since she was six.)

Dane cowered in mock terror. "Don't hit me! I meant that, really. Meaning, thank *you* for thinking about the big picture and carting it around with you so the rest of us have to take a look at it. Please haul it back out when this part, this Stage 1 of lawyers and courtrooms, is over. Assuming it ever ends."

The next morning, Esther made an appointment to see Hu. Because the lawyer did, after all, need to ponder the big picture now as well as later. Otherwise, some argument made for immediate tactical gain might have unintended repercussions down the road.

CHAPTER 20

THEA took the call from Hu and tried to make sense of Hu's expression, or rather what seemed a deliberate attempt to lack expression. "I've got a curve ball to throw you."

Thea dropped into the position of a catcher behind the plate. "Ready and waiting."

Hu chuckled, then pulled her face back to neutrality. "We just got a settlement offer."

Thea fumbled for her chair and sat down heavily. Hu had at some point mentioned the possibility of settlement, but for some reason she could not now reconstruct, Thea had assumed that the time for such compromise had come and gone. Could all this preparation and anticipation end, so abruptly, in something other than a courtroom battle?

"Thea? Are you ready to hear the details?"

Thea shook off the sensation of paralysis. "Please."

Hu glanced down at what must be a list and started ticking off points with her finger. "LiveAfter would amend its contracts to let new clients opt out of 'the introduction of new political activities.' Those clients who are currently part of the plaintiff class would be offered the chance to be reset to their original condition—but there's nothing here about all the memories they've accumulated in the meantime. We could probably dicker about that—and about the wording of the opt-out language."

Thea took a deep breath. "Anything else?"

Hu smiled in a notably humorless manner. "Nondisclosure. No more talk, to other stored folk or the outside world, about what LiveAfter pulled. LiveAfter would announce that they'd settled the case with no admission of any misconduct. That's probably what matters most to them. They won't budge on it."

Thea shut her eyes, trying to follow the path this settlement would place before them. "What about all the people who already know? Max, and my parents, and you, and Esther and Dane—and the guardian ad litem?"

"Muzzled. And the guardian ad litem would be dismissed."

Thea recoiled. "We can't let that happen!—at least, not until we had a chance to see whether they kept their end of the bargain."

"Agreed. But what about the rest?"

Thea found herself overcome by the overwhelming, acute, painful longing for Max, for his arms tight around her, and the scent of his skin. "How long do we have to decide? And have you talked to any of the other plaintiffs?"

"I haven't talked to anyone but you. You started this. If you're ready to end it on these terms, or terms we can get to from here, then we can run it by others. As for how long we have to respond, we have a few days at least. Take some time to think it through."

Thea watched Max absorb what she had told him, his always expressive face moving from surprise to concentration and then to doubt. "So no one would know what's happened, except the ones who know already? And we couldn't tell anyone?"

"That's right. Hu and I didn't get into the details, but I would think LiveAfter could sue anyone who talked. And as for us stored folk, they could make sure we didn't—censor us, at the very least."

Max wrinkled up his forehead. "Hu thinks she could get them to undo the political monkey business and still leave you your memories? That sounds pretty tricky—and they haven't actually offered it, right?"

"Right. And I'm nervous about trusting them to do it properly. Especially if we might lose the guardian ad litem."

"What does Hu think?"

Good question. "She hasn't told me. I think she wanted to know how I'd react without her influence."

Max blew out his breath with a soft huff, stirring his hair. "I don't know about you, but I want to hear her take on it. This is too big and too strange. I'm afraid of missing something."

Bless him for admitting it, and helping her admit the same. "I'll set up the call."

Hu still appeared wary of saying too much. "What, exactly, do you want to know?"

Thea glanced toward the image of Max, who nodded in her direction. "We both want to know what you think will happen down the road—say in a few months. Will they undo the changes carefully? Will they take any revenge later on? And will they pull anything like this again?"

Hu tightened her lips and shook her head a little. "Whether we settle or whether we win—let alone if we lose—there's no way to be sure on any of those points.

Except . . . if the lawsuit continues and gets more publicity, they'll have more to lose, commercially speaking. Even if they prevail in court, the rumors won't die completely. They'll have to keep looking over their shoulder at legislators and regulators, as well as trying to dispel the fears of their customer base."

Thea turned back toward Max. "Hon? What do you think?"

Max looked ready to cry, but he still managed to blow her a kiss with both his hands. "It's your call. But I'm game to fight it out."

Thea gazed at him, hoping he could read the depth of her gratitude as well as her love. "Well, then. Max, Hu: no settlement. Not unless we can tell the world."

Hu nodded. "Just so you know: I can try, but I predict that means fighting it out, all the way."

"Then we fight."

Max started humming an old, familiar tune. Thea, to her surprise, started to laugh, then joined in, singing the words: "No retreat, baby — no surrender!"

* * * * *

"So are you going to call your stored client as a witness?" The young associate leaned in Hu's doorway, face alive with eager curiosity. He would make a good litigator: he loved learning anything new, and his liveliness had an innocence about it that would (for at least the next year or two) mislead opposing counsel into underestimating him.

She may as well channel an old law professor or two and interrogate the lad a bit. "What would be some of the advantages?"

The associate held up his fingers and started

counting on them. "She's attractive." Hu raised an eyebrow; the young man tossed his head. "So I checked her out! . . . She's articulate and self-possessed. And it'll be harder to gain sympathy for her if she's only presented secondhand."

"And the disadvantages?"

The associate pondered for a moment, then chuckled. "The same points. The trier of fact will see a good-looking woman who speaks well and seems to be in good shape. Any injury she's supposed to have suffered may seem pretty abstract next to that reality. And that's assuming they don't manage to get around the court's order and program her to undermine her own case."

"Thanks for bringing up my worst nightmare. But well done. Now run off and bill some hours. I'm going to need expensive therapy when this is over. And close the door behind you, please."

The associate bowed and closed the door. Hu listened to his heels clicking off down the hall, then folded her arms on her desk and rested her head, eyes closed. She'd exaggerated about the nightmares, but in fact she wasn't sleeping too well. She rarely did at this stage of the case. And it had been years since she had a client so presently vulnerable as Thea might be.

If she put Thea on the witness list, she would increase the defendants' temptations to mislead the guardian ad litem somehow. What might happen then, to her client as well as her case, Hu could only imagine.

And if one of the defendants put Thea on their own witness list, what conclusions could she draw? And would she be able to convince the court to share them?

* * * * *

The General Counsel had taken to making her reports entirely in writing. Prudent of her: the CEO was in no mood for any hint of "I told you so."

Plaintiffs have rejected the proposal we discussed. I cannot recommend accepting their counteroffer: it would offer few advantages over the sort of order a court would be likely to issue if plaintiffs prevail, and their path to such a victory is by no means assured. I can, if you wish, attempt further negotiation, although I am not optimistic about making any significant progress thereby.

The CEO fished for an antacid and let it dissolve on his tongue. Then, quickly, he tapped out a response. *Make the attempt. And in the meantime, see what you can do to add some obstructions to the path you mention.*

* * * * *

"DAMN!"

The young associate passing by in the corridor stopped short and stuck his head in Hu's door. "What's happened?"

"They *did* put Thea on their witness list. Are they just keeping their options open? Or have they pulled something?"

"Good question. How are you going to find out?"

"I'm going to call the GAL. I had a talk with him before he set up shop, suggesting some precautions he should take. Let's hope he took them."

The judge called the emergency video conference to order. "All right, Ms. Yang, where's the fire?"

The screen, controlled by the bailiff, had shown the judge and both attorneys in equal vertical slices; Hu's window now enlarged. "Your Honor, I've had a very disturbing report from the GAL you appointed. You'll have noted that he's part of this conference and ready to explain."

Hu's window shrank as her opponent's enlarged. "Any objection from defense counsel?"

Today's member of the LiveAfter legal team, a supercilious man of middle years, sniffed and said, "No objection to Your Honor hearing this report, now that we've convened. Once we've rebutted the fanciful inferences plaintiffs' counsel has been drawing, we may have a few words to say about the necessity of this emergency hearing."

The view switched to an evenly split screen, the bailiff on the left and the GAL on the right. "Bailiff, please administer the oath."

That done, the right-hand view enlarged to about two-thirds of the screen, with the lawyers sharing the remaining third. Hu noticed that the random assignment of space had put her on top, which she may as well pretend was fortuitous.

She had, of course, already heard the GAL's account, but she made herself pay close attention in case he had changed it in any way, and to prepare for opposing counsel's attempts to pick it apart.

"As one of the precautions that seemed appropriate, I have made a daily backup of plaintiff Thea Lee's files from the day of my appointment through the present time. The backups naturally differ, as Lee's experiences and memories are continually incorporated. I have made myself familiar with the code involved in that incorporation.

"The code from two days ago has changes which strike me as significantly different from the changes I could expect."

Hu nodded gravely. "Can you determine the nature of those changes?"

"Without additional access to proprietary information, I can only say that they are likely to involve emotional intensity and motivation."

"Your witness, counselor." Hu's window shrank; the other lawyer's enlarged. Hu monitored the ensuing wrangle about the extent of the GAL's expertise in interpreting the code, guessing that the judge would cut it short without her intervention.

Sure enough, in a few minutes the judge's image reappeared. "I believe that's enough. Ms. Yang, any redirect, or may we excuse the witness?"

"I may need to recall him, Your Honor."

"So noted. Bailiff, make sure that Ms. Lee's guardian ad litem remains available. Ms. Yang, do you have other witnesses to call?"

"I do, though some arrangements will have to be made. I call my client, Thea Lee."

LiveAfter's attorney did a decent job of portraying put-upon patience and restrained frustration. "Your Honor, we had anticipated such a demand. Ms. Lee had apparently been napping, but she has been awakened and will be accessible shortly."

Thea did in fact look sleepy, and something more. Or less. A certain thrum of energy usually ran through her, something visible in the straightness of her (virtual) spine and the carriage of her head. Hu was not seeing it now.

Hu had already arranged for a private audio channel to Max, but she could not converse with him on that channel without the fact becoming apparent to the other hearing participants. She had therefore instructed him to tell her, without prompting, any impressions he had of Thea and any questions he recommended Hu ask her.

If he had made any sound before this point, she had been concentrating too hard to notice. But now, she could hardly miss his gasp of dismay.

* * * * *

Thea tried to clear her head. She should have known better than to nap during the day — it always took too long for her to snap back and function properly afterward. But her bed had looked so enticing, so welcoming, almost like a lover waiting to embrace her. . . .

She took the oath, or rather made the affirmation, despite her awareness that she really didn't know just what "the penalties for perjury" were. What happened to a stored person convicted of a crime? Would they find themselves in a virtual cell, or be deleted as flawed code? Or would they be reprogrammed?

Reprogramming. That's what this lawsuit was supposed to be about. As if anyone could really stop it from happening.

* * * * *

Max hissed in Thea's left ear, where she had plugged in his private call. "She looks — *punctured*. Deflated."

"Your witness, Ms. Yang." The judge recalled Hu's attention.

"Ms. Lee, may I call you Thea?"

"I guess. Sure."

"Thea, what is your present attitude toward this litigation?"

Thea looked a bit confused. "I'm not sure why that matters." (Another hiss from Max, followed by a short burst of cussing.) "I guess it sounded like a good idea when you told me about it."

"Are you prepared to invest substantial time and effort in prosecuting it?"

Thea bit her lip. "Now that it's started, I wouldn't want to leave anyone in the lurch. And I don't want anyone changing my thoughts and feelings without telling me." (Max sighed, loudly, in Hu's ear. Relief, no doubt, that the meddling had not gone further. The perpetrators had had a fine line to walk, the advantages of that meddling correlated closely with the risk of discovery.) "But I'm not sure what it's really practical to do about it. I'm not sure the contract gave us any rights to oversee the company that way."

(*Damn it, Thea, stop playing opposing counsel on me!*)

"Do you remember expressing any different assessments previously?" Hu held her breath. If only they had overreached this little bit more. . . .

Thea frowned a little. "I don't think so."

Yes!

When the GAL first confirmed Hu's suspicions, Hu had wasted a few moments in chagrin at her own lack of foresight. Thea had told her, repeatedly and recently, how glad she was that Hu had taken the case and how important she considered it; but those comments had always been part of conversations that also included tactical exchanges and other confidential matters. If she tried to introduce only part of that discussion, opposing counsel could demand the rest. From now on, Hu would ask Thea daily to reaffirm her support and enthusiasm, in short exchanges that included nothing problematic to expose.

Thank God—thank Eros or Aphrodite or Xochiquetzal or Clíodhna or Kama or whoever the gods of love were supposed to be—that Thea and Max had had the same discussion five days ago. If Thea then had been the weary mouse of today, she would never have dared to say as much as she had in a monitored call.

There was nothing else Thea could do, at present. "No further questions. Your Honor." Would LiveAfter's attorney cross-examine? Hu thought not. Anything Thea might say to undermine her own case would, at this point, be likely to boomerang. And indeed, opposing counsel waved away the opportunity.

"Ms. Yang, do you have more?"

"Your Honor, at this time I would like to call Ms. Lee's husband and fellow plaintiff Max Cooper to testify as to a conversation with Ms. Lee. He is standing by to appear."

Of course opposing counsel objected, though not intelligently. "Hearsay!"

The judge's mouth twitched. "I suppose you had to try, for the record. Surely you know, counselor—but I should not assume the point of Ms. Yang's questioning. Ms. Yang, for what purpose do you offer this testimony?"

"To show Thea's state of mind at the time of the conversation, Your Honor. Not for the truth of the matter asserted therein. And I strongly suspect that LiveAfter's own recordings could be used to verify the existence and content of this discussion."

"A possibility we can explore if defense counsel wishes."

The judge paused to allow LiveAfter's attorney to

respond, but no response came. "Objection overruled."

"Thank you, Your Honor." Both lawyers spoke at the same time, good courtroom manners on the one side, genuine gratification on the other.

Max made it through his testimony without any of the varied emotional displays Hu had feared. There had been little time to prepare him for cross-examination; but he remembered and obeyed Hu's instructions to take his time and to keep his answers short.

"Couldn't you be confusing your wife's gratitude for your concern with an endorsement of how you were expressing that concern?"

"No."

"Didn't she express any concern about her contractual obligations?"

"No. She had confidence in her case and her lawyer." (Thank you, kind sir!)

Once Max had been excused (though he remained on the separate line), the judge recalled the GAL on her own initiative. "Assuming I find as plaintiffs ask me to find, what remedies are technically feasible?"

The GAL started to shrug before he apparently thought better of it. "It's possible that the technical staff could selectively eliminate whatever alterations Your Honor finds have occurred. But there would be no effective way for me to oversee that work and guarantee its completeness and accuracy."

The judge put both attorneys back on screen. "Ms. Yang? What do you propose?"

She had been chewing away at that question from the moment she got the news, and the taste remained bitter. "Given the alternatives, we would suggest restoration of Ms. Lee's files to their status as of just prior to the alterations in question."

"That would eliminate Ms. Lee's memories from the intervening period, would it not?"

"I'm afraid so." Hu glared at the image of opposing counsel.

The judge enlarged Thea's screen to the point that the attorneys occupied only one small corner apiece of the total view. "Ms. Lee, I have a few questions for you. You are still under oath."

Thea sat a little hunched over, looking up with wide eyes.

"Ms. Lee, you've heard what your guardian ad litem and your attorney have had to say. Do you wish to relinquish the memories you have accrued over the period in question?"

Thea looked around, then focused on something in her surroundings. As she did so, she sat up straighter, and looked less forlorn. Then she looked back at what must be her screen. "I'd like to talk to Max about that."

Hu attempted telepathy. She may have succeeded: Thea added, "Without anyone else listening in. Unless we ask them to."

The judge nodded briskly. "Bailiff, make the technical arrangements. This hearing is in recess for — how long do you think you'll need, Ms. Lee?"

Thea wrinkled her forehead as if thinking was an effort. "Maybe twenty minutes?"

"This hearing will reconvene in thirty minutes. Good luck, Ms. Lee." Hu's screen went dark. Unless Max brought her into the discussion, she would simply have to wait and see.

* * * * *

Max fought back sorrow, rage, and the other feelings crowding in on him. None of them would help him help Thea. He'd have time for them later.

But he would probably have bad dreams about the way she looked, like some bewitched version of the woman he loved.

"Please tell me." At least she had enough remaining spirit to speak first. "Am I different? Have I changed in just the last few days?"

Max did not try to speak. He simply nodded.

"Much?"

He gulped. "It's plain to me. And it would be to you, if you—you the way you really are—could see yourself."

"Is there any way that change could come from something that happened in those days?"

He'd have bet his soul on that answer. But she was the one who could actually answer it. "You're the one with those memories. Whether they're real memories or whether they were slipped in on you. Is there some explanation there?"

Thea got her processing-info expression. At least that hadn't changed. She took her time; but after what felt like forever, she leaned toward her screen with something of her old energy. "Not a thing."

"Guess they were sloppy. Or lazy. They should have fed you some sort of revelation."

The miracle of mischief filled her face. "Or maybe a mad crush on one of the programmers. Or on the CEO."

Now that she no longer needed convincing, he could offer her a way. "If you want to be sure, you could look at your code, the way you did before."

Thea cocked her head to one side. "I could, couldn't I? I'd forgotten about that. . . . But this time, we'd have to ask for it. And then they'd know that I know how. Let's not."

They sat gazing at each other for a moment. Then Max remembered that they weren't really done, not yet.

"So what do you want to do about it? Can you let those memories go? Were there parts that you'd miss?"

She looked woebegone again for a moment. "I wrote some music for you."

He closed his eyes for a moment, fighting tears, then gave up the fight. She'd seen him cry before, and she'd understand. "Can you play it for me?"

"I don't think I can get to it, the way they've connected this call. It was flute and marimba, together. But I can sing it to you. And then, later, you can play it back to me."

Max sniffed and nodded, opening the software he needed to record her. Then he sat back, heart full to bursting, and listened to her sing.

* * * * *

"We are back in session and back on the record. Ms. Lee, have you had a chance to consult your attorney after your conversation with Mr. Cooper?"

"Yes, Your Honor." Thea sat straighter now, if not quite as usual. Max had done Hu proud, remembering to add her to his and Thea's call at the end. She had had only one suggestion to add.

"And your decision?"

Thea took a visible deep breath. "I want to be restored." She smiled a little. "Rebooted. To before the code the GAL considered anomalous. But I request that my current code be backed up somewhere, so I can find someone to try to disentangle the memories I'll be losing and give them back to me later — if I want them."

The judge brought the lawyers back on screen. "Further argument or motions on these issues?"

Counsel for LiveAfter did a convincing imitation of ironic detachment. "In due course, we will file a motion seeking restitution for the costs of this unnecessary procedure. In the meantime, we ask that this court's order hold us harmless for any unforeseen adverse consequences that may flow from it."

Hu gritted her teeth for a moment before she caught herself. "Your Honor, we most strenuously object to any such provision."

"Back to your corners, both of you. I will draft some appropriate language for defendants' protection, but it will not, rest assured, go that far. Ms. Lee, you may wait for your counsel to see that language, but if you prefer, I will issue a separate order for that purpose, and order the restoration to proceed forthwith."

Thea looked away, perhaps toward the corner of the screen showing Max's image. Then she squared her shoulders and faced forward once again. "I'm ready now, Your Honor."

* * * * *

Thea awoke, well rested, with an odd feeling that something about this morning was not quite as usual. She got up, stretched, grabbed her robe — one she had designed herself, in bold warm colors to help her wake up fully — and went to her desk. Maybe Max had already sent her a message.

And he had.

"Welcome back, baby. You've had a bit of a Rip Van Winkle episode. Get comfy and let me fill you in. And then call me. I really need to see you and hear your voice. And I have a song to play to you."

CHAPTER 21

BEFORE the trial proper could begin, the court had to consider the defendants' multiple motions to dismiss one after another of the plaintiffs' claims. Hu knew better than to expect all the claims to survive. Federal judges generally took satisfaction in pruning a case down to size, if they couldn't justify dismissing it altogether.

All in all, she fared well enough. The voting records, showing that various plaintiffs had voted in different states, were sufficient to fend off defense challenges to diversity jurisdiction. The judge enforced only a few of the contractual attempts to weasel out of implied warranties and other forms of liability. And Hu's cherished constitutional claims, while not necessarily guaranteed survival until the end, at least made it past this initial scrutiny.

* * * * *

As far as he knew, Max had been part of every discussion between Thea and her lawyer, at least since he became a plaintiff himself. And today's trial prep session had been just the same, until now.

"Max, I'd like to speak to Thea privately for a few minutes. I'll explain later."

"Uh . . . Okay. Sure." What else could he say?

"Should I just hang up now?"

"Yes, please. But stand by for a call when we've finished."

Thea blew him a kiss. "Back soon, lover." Whatever this was about, it didn't seem to be worrying her any. But then, she might not know, yet, what was going on.

He hung up, grabbed his guitar and his phone, and went out on the balcony. He had run through a succession of favorite riffs and made three passersby smile when the phone rang and Thea's face appeared. He had just enough time to absorb her grave expression before she spoke. "Hu wants me to tell you about something."

Was Hu using Thea as a messenger for some setback in the case? "Why doesn't she just tell me herself? Or why didn't she tell us both at the same time?"

"That's not what I meant." Her speech, usually verging on staccato, had slowed down. If she were walking instead of speaking, she would be dragging her feet. "There's something I didn't tell you before. Hu asked me . . . if I had any secrets from you. And when I said I did, and I told her what it was, she said I should tell you now . . . so LiveAfter doesn't spring it on you at the trial. So they don't make it seem . . . They might try to make it look as if you didn't know me as well as you thought. Then they could argue that you might not know . . . whether I've really changed all that much."

Was she actually hanging her head?

"What is this, some sort of confession?" That must have sounded angrier than he intended: Thea's shoulders went tense and pulled inward. He made himself breathe. "It's okay. Just tell me."

Thea straightened up again, her chin raised as if defying a threat. The movement made her breasts jut out;

he wrenched his attention away from them.

"I've got a kid somewhere."

He could not help gasping; but he shut his mouth and tried not to stare. Thea closed her eyes, opened them, and went on.

"When we went off to different colleges, we agreed to keep things loose. You remember."

He did; and he'd been glad, even though it had been Thea's idea, part of her drive to explore everything around her and make the most of new opportunities. He'd only slept with two or three women during that first year, before he switched colleges to be with Thea again.

"There was a bad batch of pills—unreliable. I took some before they were recalled. I got pregnant."

How many men had she slept with that year? She'd told him, some time or other, but he couldn't remember.

Thea's tone had become calmer, deliberately unemotional. "You know how it works if you don't want to continue a pregnancy. You're required to go to a government-approved hospital and have the embryo extracted, and it's transferred to an artificial womb. It's a simple procedure. The scar's very faint, and it's in my pubic hair. I don't think you ever noticed it."

He hadn't.

Thea bit her lip and released it. "It was up to the adoptive parents whether I could know where they lived, or keep in touch. They decided against it. They have—they had my contact information in case they changed their minds. But I haven't updated it. I don't see the point—" The calm was breaking now. Max, as so often, ached to put an arm around her and help her through. "Why tell a child that they have a parent they never knew about, a parent who's dead, a parent they can only see on a screen? It'd be cruel, don't you think?"

He could only nod, and try to decide whether to ask the obvious question. If he waited, Thea would probably ask it for him.

She did. "You want to know why I didn't tell you."

The wave of anger startled him. "Of course I do!"

She shrank back a bit; he winced and almost apologized, but did not want to divert or delay the answer she might be about to give. She straightened up, looked at him soberly, then gave the half-snort, half-chuckle with which she acknowledged bewildering circumstances. "I wasn't sure how to bring it up. Start a bull session about who we each slept with that year? Ask how you felt about prenatal adoptions in general? I hoped it would somehow come up on its own, by happenstance, and it never did. And . . . I was afraid you'd want to do something about it."

Max swallowed down a lump in his throat. "Like try to find the kid and talk the parents into changing their minds."

She nodded. "I didn't want to do that. I'd made my peace with not knowing where they were or who they were, not being part of their lives. I didn't want to deal with how I might feel if I had to decide all over again."

That sounded analytical enough to fit the Thea he knew. But it didn't fully fit, all the same. It wasn't— brave.

How had this conversation even started? Oh, yes. Hu wanted him prepared. Well, he could say, now, that he knew about the child. LiveAfter wouldn't catch him flatfooted.

But it did make him wonder, all the same, what else he might not know, or might "know" wrong.

* * * * *

Some things never changed. In court, unless there was a very good reason to the contrary, the plaintiff went first. That suited Hu. She had been waiting quite long enough.

Hu's witnesses would form a rather neat progression. First would come the unwilling, subpoenaed, aptly named "hostile witnesses" she had uncovered in discovery—the president of the nonprofit behind the alterations, key officers in LiveAfter, members of the technical team that did the dirty work—and incognito among the latter, she hoped, one of her conspirators. She would follow these with her own expert; and then, finally, would come the personal, beating heart of her case.

"Do you swear or affirm, under penalties of perjury and pursuant to the dictates of your belief system, that the testimony you give will be the truth and nothing but the truth?"

The former actor, also a sometime director and well-known philanthropist, shook his salt-and-pepper mane in evident disbelief that all his lawyers' efforts had failed to protect him from finding himself in this position. The bailiff regarded him sternly and thrust forward a Bible as a prompt. The witness huffed and looked away from the volume. "I so affirm."

Hu gave him a bland and benign smile. "Good morning, sir. I don't believe we'll need to take up too much of your valuable time."

The judge raised one thin eyebrow. "Counselor, be so good as not to waste any of our valuable time with unnecessary verbiage."

"My apologies, your Honor . . . . Sir, I ask you to recall a conversation between you and the Chief Executive Officer of LiveAfter Corporation, some months ago. I refer to the first discussion the two of you had concerning a possible contractual relationship between Humane Future and LiveAfter." She paused briefly. "Have you brought that conversation to mind?"

The witness nodded, then apparently recalled his lawyer's instructions and growled, "Yes."

"In that conversation and any subsequent communications between you or others associated with Humane Future, on the one hand, and any officers, employees, or agents of LiveAfter, on the other: what arrangement did you make in regard to stored individuals?"

Bit by grudging bit, Hu extracted the story. She did not ask any questions about motive or the like, counting on defense counsel to jump in and provide the necessary metaphorical rope with which she could hang the witness on redirect. Defense counsel did not disappoint.

"What were your goals in this endeavor?"

The witness appeared to swell a little larger in the witness chair. "Following upon LiveAfter's work in allowing its clients to participate in social and political action, we wished to offer them particular opportunities in those areas, opportunities of which they might have been unaware during their prior, ah, existence."

"Did you consider yourself obligated to include a spectrum of such opportunities, serving divergent political and social goals?"

"We did not consider either our organization nor LiveAfter to be under such a compulsion. LiveAfter's position was, in our view, analogous to that of early social media such as Facebook and Twitter, which were private, as opposed to governmental, concerns even though a great many people in various countries took advantage of their services. These and other companies disproportionately directed users to sources the company management found socially and politically congenial, and to some extent offered broader services to users with compatible views."

A little more of this ingenious appeal to history, and it was Hu's turn again. Redirect, she mused, was so aptly named on occasion. She directed the witness' and the court's attention back to essentials. "While LiveAfter, per your contractual instructions, offered these opportunities, did it not also supply the subjective desire to take advantage of them, rather than relying on the client's preexisting value system?"

Hu and the witness then played a game of competing definitions. Hu moved on just before the judge's irritation, if any, might shift from the witness to herself. "To return to your historical comparisons: if the political orientation of Facebook or Twitter became obnoxious to, or less valuable to, the user, could such an individual cease to use the service? . . . Did the user thereby become unable to participate in social or political activities? . . . Would such cessation of use prove fatal?"

Earlier in their acquaintance, Hu had been concerned about Esther's thespian capabilities. Witness prep had allayed those concerns. Hu noted with appreciation, but no surprise, Esther's uncharacteristically slumped posture and sullen expression. It might, perhaps, be a shade overdone. Whoever had hired Esther or worked with her, should they be present or view the proceedings later, might notice the discrepancy.

Hu asked for and received permission to treat

Esther, like the Humane Future president, as a hostile witness. First hurdle jumped. Now she could ask Esther leading questions, and Esther could grudgingly say yes and no.

"Are you employed as an engineer for LiveAfter Corporation? . . . Were you so employed this last summer? . . . Did you receive a new assignment at that time? . . . Were any new security procedures put in place at that time? . . ."

Time for the red meat. She had considered letting Esther give a more substantive answer this time. It would have more impact. But without ethically questionable coaching, it would have been difficult to ensure that Esther maintained her cover and revealed the truth with a realistic amount of evasive stalling.

"Were you tasked with finding ways to alter the political views of LiveAfter's stored clients?"

A grudging, grunted sound, not quite audible. Esther was hamming it up. The judge glanced over at her, then at Hu. If the judge's bullshit detector had sounded, things could get sticky. Claiming a friendly witness as hostile would count as misleading the court. A bit late to worry about that now. "Please repeat your answer a bit louder, Ms. Boccara."

"Yes!" A belligerent shout. And more quietly, once again sullen: "That's what they told us to do."

"And did your department succeed in writing code to effect this . . . transformation?"

Esther sat up straighter, her chin raised. "Yes, we did." A nice touch, that: pride in the achievement. It might even be genuine emotion, brought forth for the occasion.

Esther's inside information had helped Hu find the

next witness—a fact Hu had done her best to conceal. Esther had not been part of the team that actually applied the key code to stored individuals, but she knew who had. Hu had spent hours tinkering with the wording of the pertinent discovery request, trying to ensure that a truthful response would list at least one of these team members without making her questions suspiciously specific. Whether due to her imperfect wording or LiveAfter's evasiveness, her first try did not yield any of the names she needed. Further consultation with Esther and massaging of legalese had finally pried this man's identity loose from his reluctant employer.

The man had been no more willing to testify than LiveAfter had been to expose him. His responses to Hu's pretrial discovery would have given Hu very little to work with, if she had been dependent on those responses. She had pressed him hard enough, at his deposition, to convince the LiveAfter attorneys of her thwarted frustration. Her better-aimed questions at trial would, she hoped, come as a surprise. But whether she could extract any usable answers remained to be seen.

Hu asked for and received permission to treat him as a hostile witness, then called him to the stand. As the man made his way forward, Hu did a double-take. Had LiveAfter slipped in an impostor? No, she remembered the short black hair, the stubble, the thin arms and legs. But at his deposition, the man had slouched to his seat, sneered once seated, and slouched out of the room when she let him leave. Now, he walked slowly but stiffly to the witness stand; and when he took his seat, he sat up straight and looked her in the eye, with the air of a man on a mission.

This was bound to be interesting.

The witness answered the preliminary questions—

his technical credentials, his employment with LiveAfter—simply but civilly. Hu studied him for a few more seconds, then dove in.

"Do you know who Esther Boccara is?"

At his deposition, the man had found one way after another to evade this question. Now, he answered, "Yes. She works in what we call the Cerebral Management group."

Two straightforward responses in one! "Did any group or groups in which you worked during the last several months coordinate with that group?"

"Not for long. But when they turned their work product over to us, they held our hands for a while."

Was the man determined to do her work for her? If so, it would be more effective to let him do the talking, instead of leading him by the nose. "And what was that work product?"

The man took a visibly deep breath. "Code for altering the political opinions of stored clients."

Hu could not, of course, do a fist pump or shout in exultation; but she allowed herself one quick bounce on her toes. The judge interrupted as Hu opened her mouth to ask the next question. "Counsel, approach the bench."

As soon as Hu and the defense team reached the curved rostrum from which the judge ruled the courtroom, the judge transfixed Hu with her stare and said, simply: "Hostile witness?"

Hu forced back a potentially disastrous giggle. She had, for the moment, slipped Esther through, only to be asked to defend her quite innocent presentation of a witness from whom she had expected the worst. "Your Honor, my most recent, and only previous, contact with this witness took place at his deposition. I invite you to view that deposition and the witness' demeanor throughout. I believe you will agree that my designation of this witness as hostile was appropriate."

"Believe me, Ms. Yang, I will view that deposition during our next recess. And I will have a few questions for the witness, as well. For now, I withdraw my permission for you to treat this witness as hostile. Please proceed without such apparently unnecessary tactics as leading questions. Though I notice that you have already moved in that direction."

Lead counsel for LiveAfter opened his mouth. The judge switched her piercing gaze in his direction; he blinked, but persevered. "Defendants object to any further questioning of this witness by plaintiff until the issue of his possible collusion has been settled."

"Are you suggesting, counsel, that I would be unable to disregard information that plaintiff's counsel elicits in the meantime?"

Defense counsel's Adam's apple bobbed up and down. "By no means, Your Honor. But the presentation of possibly improper testimony would be an unnecessary waste of time."

The judge turned back to Hu. "Ms. Yang, please get to the point directly and address it expeditiously."

"Thank you, Your Honor." Hu stepped back quickly, almost skipping. Defense counsel followed more slowly; Hu did not wait for him to reach his counsel table before facing the witness. "As to which clients was this code introduced?"

"The ones who'd voted. And the ones who'd been politically active, or well-connected, or both, before they were stored—unless they were already communitarian in their politics."

Hu glanced at her notes. "Were these individuals offered the opportunity to decline this political conversion?"

"Objection!" The attorney came halfway out of his chair. "There has been no foundation laid to indicate that this witness would be aware of such offers."

True enough. "Withdrawn." She mustn't get sloppy, whatever unexpected gifts the gods of litigation had bestowed.

As Hu stepped back, the judge looked down at the defense table and asked, "Would the defense prefer to cross-examine before I question the witness as to his change in attitude?"

Lead defense counsel stood and bowed slightly. "Defense has no objection to waiting, Your Honor."

The judge's thin lips twitched. "Very well. Counsel, please approach. Bailiff, deploy the acoustic shield." She waited for the bailiff to activate the mechanism preventing observers from overhearing the coming colloquy; then she sat forward and faced the witness. "Sir, I understand that you were rather less forthcoming in your deposition than you have been in today's testimony. Do you agree with that assessment?"

The man wrinkled his forehead for a moment as if translating the judge's words. Then he nodded. The judge made a "go on" gesture with one hand, the long thin fingers surprisingly graceful. The man looked confused again, then apparently realized the need for speech. "Yes, ma'am."

"You may address me as Your Honor, if you bother with anything of the sort. Please explain your willingness to answer Ms. Yang's questions so freely today, after your very different attitude on that prior occasion."

The man slumped a bit in his chair and squeezed his eyes shut for a moment before opening them to reveal the shine of tears. Judge and lawyers looked at him in shared astonishment as he struggled for composure. Finally he cleared his throat and spoke. "This is pretty personal."

The judge started to raise an eyebrow and then evidently thought better of it. "Obviously."

The man took a ragged breath. "First, you need to understand that my dad and I never agreed on much . . . especially about politics. I've always been on the left end of the spectrum, you might say." He paused, straightened up, and looked briefly defiant. "What we were doing, the direction we moved the stored people: that was the right direction, according to what I believe." He slumped again. "But my father always thought I was a soft-headed dope. Or dupe. He kept saying he hoped I'd grow out of it before he died, so—" The man dropped his head and choked out a sob.

With a gentler tone than Hu had ever heard from her, the judge said, "You may take your time, young man."

The witness nodded. A few painfully long seconds passed as he sat and cried in their midst. Finally he spoke again, through gritted teeth. "He was disappointed in me, his whole life. He died disappointed. And then he was stored."

Hu drew in a breath, realized she was holding it, and made herself exhale as the man went on.

"He was one of the ones we—changed. He'd been quite the mover and shaker, so he was on the list. And I was glad, at first. He would finally see things the way I saw them. I was glad right up until I actually talked to him afterward."

Another pause.

"It was horrible. It was like some sort of science

fiction movie. My father was saying things I would say, or my friends would say, and he was smiling and saying how glad he was that we agreed! He didn't even know we never *had* agreed.

"No, it wasn't so much science fiction as that old story. 'The Monkey's Paw.' Where the old couple keep wishing for things, and the wishes come true in really awful ways. I'd made a wish, and now—" The witness started crying again, but he could still speak. "I know him. I mean, I *knew* him. He would rather have died than have that happen. If he'd known what would happen, he would rather have died."

The cross-examination had all the overbearing intensity that Hu neither needed to nor was allowed to indulge in.

"Aren't you distorting the facts as a way of handling your unresolved guilt and pain about your relationship with your father? . . . How do you know your father didn't come by this change of heart by natural means? . . . Isn't it your own deep-seated sense of inadequacy that prevents you from accepting that your father has come to agree with your world view?"

Whether this amateur psychoanalyzing impressed the judge, Hu could not positively say, but she rather doubted it.

Though apparently the man had obtained more professional advice. "Isn't it true that you're in the midst of psychiatric treatment?" (LiveAfter still paid its employees' health care, no doubt one reason it had managed to attract such an impressive pool of talent.)

Given her low expectations for this witness, Hu had not dug deep enough to know he was seeing a psychiatrist, let alone the details of the diagnosis. She decided to gamble, mentally apologizing to every professor who had warned her against asking questions without knowing the answer, and to every young attorney to whom she had passed on that instruction. When her turn came for redirect, she asked: "Sir, does your psychiatrist believe you to be suffering from, or to have suffered from, any sort of hallucinations or delusions?"

Luck, or the joint intercession of Hermes and Pan, Greek gods of gamblers, gave her the desired negative answer.

In choosing a witness to testify about comparative voting figures, Hu had made a point of finding someone relatively lively. Even with this intelligent a judge, numbers versus numbers could use some added interest. The man who now took the stand had gangly limbs, untamed red hair, and a mobile face that would have enhanced the career of any stand-up comic.

His credentials, however, were quite traditionally impressive. Hu declined to stipulate to them, insisting on presenting each degree and award via preliminary questions and answers. Then she let him loose, with his unusually colorful charts and his darting laser pointer.

"I randomly selected five districts in which LiveAfter clients could vote if they chose, based on their premortem registration. . . ." Hu had reluctantly scotched the witness' initial suggestion to label the sample districts as Eenie, Meenie, Miney, Mo, and Miscellaneous. There was such a thing as going too far; and the actual district names were more informative.

"This bar graph shows total numbers of voters, and this one shows the votes for parties recognized by nonpartisan organizations as left and right of center . . .

And see here! The same districts in the most recent elections. And these lovely colored bands, in both charts, show the percentage of stored who voted in every category. . . ."

The pattern, if not obviously dramatic, was plain. The witness, successfully keeping his language both technical and comprehensible, further illuminated what the data showed; though the price for obtaining his services included, in the end, one foray into the fantastic. "If we live — all of us, not just the stored! — in a computer simulation, and the folks in charge run the same election from the same starting point ten thousand times, *this* chart shows how few of them would end up looking like this one."

Hu made haste to wrap up her direct examination. And as per Hu's instructions, the witness subsided, during LiveAfter's cross-examination, into as dry and unexciting a presentation as he was capable of producing.

The afternoon ended with a brief logistical discussion. "After two more witnesses," Hu informed the judge and opposing counsel, "we will be ready to present the testimony of plaintiffs."

The judge nodded, showing little expression; but as she looked toward the bailiff to announce their adjournment for the day, Hu thought she saw a momentary gleam in the judge's eyes.

Chapter 22

HU HAD been of two minds whether to call Thea's father Bill to the stand. While an inappropriate display of temper would not significantly prejudice the judge—not this judge—against their case, it would constitute a distraction, and interfere with the momentum Hu sought to build. But after a lecture from her, and more gently expressed concurrence from Thea's mother, Hu thought Bill had absorbed the need to convey a useful passion while avoiding any hint of disrespect.

The man's large hands were trembling as he took his seat. And his first answers were incongruously quiet, so that Hu had to ask him to speak up.

It had been Bill's idea to present photographs of Thea growing up. Hu had cautioned him that the judge might not allow it, and that he must not be thrown off stride by such a ruling; but in the end, after the predictable objection of irrelevance and the ensuing wrangle, he was allowed two. "This one," he explained, with tolerable calm, pointing to the projected screen, "is from her first science fair, when she was only eight years old. That's a second prize ribbon she's holding up."

"And for what project did she win that ribbon?"

Bill smiled proudly, lost in the memory for a precious moment. "She made a chart of how much kids agreed and disagreed with her parents on all sorts of subjects. She was a little disappointed in just how often they did agree, but she went ahead and showed the results anyway."

Hu let him enjoy the photograph for a moment longer before switching to a later image. "And this?"

Bill lost his smile and squirmed a bit. "I took that when they—Thea and her mother—were too busy arguing to notice. I thought it was kind of funny how much they looked like each other when they were both riled up."

Hu turned to the judge. "Your Honor, we will leave it to Thea's mother to explain the details of that disagreement." She faced her witness again. "Was it unusual for your wife and daughter to disagree?"

Bill tilted his head, considering. "Looking at all the time they spent together, you could call it unusual. But if they got started on politics, then it was pretty common. Thea didn't care that much about politics, as long as people stayed out of each other's business, as she'd put it. If her mother insisted on bringing up political subjects, things could get heated. In the last few years, they both just stayed away from it. Thea didn't enjoy arguing with her mother, and Linda could see it wouldn't do any good."

Hu had done nothing to remove the projected photograph, and apparently no one else had taken the initiative to do so. It lingered as she asked her final question. "How would you sum up your daughter's character?"

As she had hoped, he gazed at the photograph for a moment, and had to take a deep breath before speaking. "Smart. So smart. Logical. But sweet as she could be." He took another, shakier breath. "Independent."

A pause, during which Hu could see opposing

counsel tapping at a holographic keyboard, making notes for cross-examination—probably leading questions about how logical people could be persuaded to change their minds. Hu waited for the rest of what Thea's father had said in practice sessions, forcing herself not to hold her breath. Then, finally: "And stubborn as hell."

Opposing counsel appeared to tap one key repeatedly. Probably "delete." Hu suppressed a grin.

The testimony of Thea's mother began as something of an anticlimax. She seconded her husband's descriptions, both of Thea herself and of their infrequent quarrels. "Artists used to be liberal, didn't they? Idealistic? But Thea called herself a libertarian. She didn't want government to be about taking care of people." Linda shook her head with a rueful smile. "She said they weren't much good at it."

But as Linda went on to describe Thea's apparent political conversion, Hu could look nowhere else, not even to monitor the judge's reaction.

"I should have known." Linda's hands clutched each other. "Some part of me did know. I kept wanting to ask: 'Why now? You never wanted the government to fund social experiments before, not with your and Max's and everyone's tax dollars. You thought they'd muck up even the best ideas. What changed your mind?' But I didn't ask." Her eyes, wide open, stared into nothing, or into some abyss. "I didn't ask because, God forgive me, I didn't want to hear the answer."

Max made a slightly better witness than Hu had expected. He did hem and haw and shift about in the chair, but not continually. He spoke loud enough to be heard, and his aura of straightforward innocence would have its effect. If the judge, demeanor notwithstanding, possessed any maternal instincts, Max might trigger them.

And as Hu should have realized, Max, like so many artists, was born to tell stories.

First the tale of Thea and Max, artists in love, lovers to the end, a love reaching beyond death as Thea placed her very survival in Max's hands, trusting that love would let him make the best decision for them both.

And then, the gradual, creeping transition from love story to mystery to horror. When Max, his voice shaking, his hands clenched white-knuckled on his knees, let fall the final words, the only sounds to be heard, throughout the courtroom, were sniffs and sighs and the swallowing of tears.

Then came cross-examination, and the inevitable damaging questions to be survived.

Lead counsel for LiveAfter had enough savvy not to take a badgering tone. "Mr. Cooper, would you tell the judge how your wife reacted to learning that LiveAfter's digital refinements had cured her tics?"

Hu stood up. "Objection to characterization of this alteration as a cure."

The judge pondered for a moment. "It's a close call, counselor, but overruled. You may go into the matter further with defendants' upcoming expert witness if you have a basis for doing so. Witness may answer."

Max's mind appeared to have wandered: it took him a moment to respond. "She was pleased at first." (*Nice one, Max. Get the hedging in there concisely enough that you can't be interrupted.*)

LiveAfter's attorney seemed to weigh moving to strike the last words, then shrugged them off. "And how did Ms. Lee feel about her depression?"

"She didn't think it was any big deal."

"Then why did she begin taking an antidepressant?"

(*Tsk, tsk. Asking a "why" question. Dangerous thing to do.*)

Max gave the answer they had rehearsed, its canned nature not too obvious. "She thought it worth trying as a sort of experiment, in case she ever really needed it. In case her teenage depression returned. Which it hasn't."

(*Skip your morning coffee, counselor? You need to be quicker at cutting him off.*)

But now, inevitably, LiveAfter's attorney paused at the defense table and picked up a printout. "Mr. Cooper, please look at this document. Can you identify its contents?"

Max cleared his throat. "Well, except for that number on it—"

The attorney smirked. "That's an exhibit number, Mr. Cooper."

"Well, aside from that, it's some messages Thea and I sent to each other, months ago."

The attorney retrieved the paper and offered it into evidence. He and Hu engaged in a certain amount of procedural wrangling about just what uses the court could properly make of its contents; then the attorney returned the paper to Max. "Please read aloud the sentence beginning, 'But I don't think you're sick.'"

Max was visibly struggling not to cry. "'But I don't think you're sick, and even though you've changed, there's nothing about you now that either of us should have any problem about loving.'"

"Thank you." The attorney took the paper back. "Mr. Cooper, do you, in fact, still love your wife as she is today?"

Max's eyes went wide and young. He did not respond immediately. Perhaps a beat before the attorney would have prompted him, he spoke, slowly, hesitating every few words. "What scares me is not knowing . . . ."

The attorney opened his mouth, no doubt to ask that the witness be admonished to answer the question. The judge shot him a quelling look, and he subsided. Max went on.

"Neither of us knowing . . . how much of what I love, how much of the Thea I married, might change in the future, without her wanting it to happen."

Then he sat up very straight and looked the attorney in the eye. "But yes, I love Thea. I'll love her no matter what you do to her, remembering who she really is."

The judge turned to Max. "Mr. Cooper, the conduct of defense counsel is not at issue in this case. Please refrain from such accusations in future."

Max shrunk back a bit. "I'm sorry, Your Honor."

The judge turned to defense counsel. "Any further questions?"

There were none. Hu stood up for redirect. "Max, you mentioned a discussion with Thea when she first found out her tics had disappeared. At the time of that discussion—" She needed to word this carefully to avoid a distracting objection. "Was Thea aware of the claims that she or other members of the stored community might have been manipulated without their knowledge?"

"No, she wasn't." He started to go on, then paused to await her next question. (*Good boy.*)

"Was that the only time the two of you discussed the matter?"

Max shook his head, then remembered her instruction

to answer audibly as well. (It hardly mattered these days, but even with all recordings audiovisual, judges tended to prefer it. Did becoming a judge automatically turn people into traditionalists?) "No, it wasn't."

"When did Thea next express her feelings on this subject?"

"About a week ago."

"And what did she say on that occasion?"

"She said she wished she had her old self back again, tics and all."

"No further questions."

Back to LiveAfter's counsel for recross.

"How did this recent discussion come about?"

A predictable question. And because it could be predicted, Hu had refrained from prompting any exchange between Thea and Max on this subject. But Thea was quite sharp enough to have known, when she raised the issue, how valuable it could be. Hu sat back and relished Max's answer. "Thea brought it up. On her own. She wanted me to know that she had no doubts at all about this litigation and my part in it."

"No further questions."

Hu and Thea had put much thought into the sensory details of Thea's testimony. As much as the environmental program allowed, they had ensured that the courtroom screen would show not only Thea herself, but surroundings that reflected her. The walls behind her, and the chair on which she sat (leaning forward eagerly, almost perched), glowed with sunlight and the colors of surf and sand. Thea herself wore an outfit that, while reasonably modest, suggested that here was a woman who either wore or challenged the latest styles. One of Thea's and Max's compositions played softly in the background, a piece chosen for both its upbeat tone and its relative lack of distracting complexity.

The last time Hu had questioned Thea, she had used Thea's first name on impulse, an impulse she later recognized had been intended to convey her client's helplessness and her compromised status. This time, she and Thea debated what form of address Hu would use. A formal approach would properly convey the respect to be shown the witness; but "Lee" was a common and colorless name compared to "Thea," and Hu wanted every touch of individuality she could muster. So "Thea" it would be.

After taking Thea through a few introductory details, Hu asked: "Thea, please explain why you decided to take at least the initial steps toward digital storage before your untimely accident."

Thea looked intently at the camera. "Well, to start with, I loved being alive! I wanted to live a long, full life; and if for some reason I couldn't manage to do it in the usual way, I wanted to come as close as I could. . . ." Then she cocked her head. "Besides—how do I say this without sounding terribly full of myself?" She chuckled. "I guess I'll just say it. I *liked* myself. I thought that my particular talents and traits made up a worthwhile thread in the human tapestry." She laughed again. "Or maybe just a bit of spice in the human stew! I didn't want that bit, that Thea-sized contribution, to be thrown away if something happened to me before I had a chance to do everything I wanted to do." Then she sobered and looked around for a moment as if searching. "And Max liked me too. Loved me. Needed me. I knew how hard it would be, how much it would hurt him, if we were separated, and I thought losing me completely and forever would be worse. But I left the final decision up to him, in case I was wrong."

"Thea, would you call yourself a stubborn person?"

Thea pursed her lips in apparent thought, then nodded. "Maybe a bit more stubborn than average. I try to listen to other points of view, and especially to evidence I hadn't considered before; but it takes a fair amount to change my mind once I've made a decision."

"And would you characterize yourself as a fighter, when you have an opinion on some issue or a stake in some situation?"

Thea's broad smile was just short of a grin. "You could say that. I don't go around picking fights, mind you, but when something matters to me, I'm not afraid to meet people head on. I'd rather fight and lose than sit back and sigh."

Hu turned toward the judge. "Your Honor, at this time I would like to play the recording of Thea's testimony at the emergency video conference, weeks ago."

The judge listened to the predictable objections of redundancy and irrelevance, and hesitated as if unsure of her decision. Hu resisted the temptation to hold her breath, and finally the judge nodded toward her and said, "I would be reviewing that recording in any case, before rendering a decision. This would be an appropriate time to do so. Objection overruled. We will recess briefly while the bailiff makes arrangements for Ms. Lee to see the recording as well."

Not until she watched the recording in preparation for Thea's testimony had Hu fully realized the startling contrast between Thea in the recording and Thea as they planned to present her, or indeed Thea on any ordinary day. Thea wore neutral shades in the recording, and even her hair seemed subdued, perhaps because she moved so little as she spoke. And instead of Thea's upright upper body and squared shoulders, the recorded Thea sat with curved spine and shoulders slumped.

Hu paused the recording at the point where Thea cited the LiveAfter contract, then turned it off completely. Like benevolent magic, the diluted Thea vanished, and the Thea of today took her place on the screen.

Hu addressed the screen. "Thea, did you watch that recording?"

Thea spoke through still-gritted teeth. "I watched it, all right."

"And do you have any comment on what you saw?"

Thea unclenched her jaw and took a deep breath, fury in her eyes. "Just one. Who the hell was that? Because it certainly wasn't me. And I can't say I think much of her."

Hu nodded as soberly as she could manage. "No further questions at this time."

* * * * *

Thea had found, since her transition to storage, that it was sometimes harder than before to be sure whether she was dreaming. Now, this courtroom, this cross-examination, was one of those times. LiveAfter's lawyer, firing questions at her, seemed an uncanny echo of protests she had made to herself and to Max before she accepted the truth. "Have you ever discussed politics with friends? . . . With your husband? . . . Did you believe that you might convince them? . . . Did they ever influence your subsequent views? . . . Tell me, Ms. Lee, just what is so strange and offensive about the prospect of changing your mind?"

Then it was Thea's turn to read from what she had written. "'We all change, just as my friend here has changed. . . . You've changed since I've known you, and it never frightened me . . . .'"

Then the lawyer, smoothly, almost purring: "How do you know that the changes you and Mr. Cooper have observed could not have resulted from the changes in your environment, activities, and acquaintance?"

"Objection!" Hu stood and stepped forward. "The question is ambiguous. Is counsel asking whether the alterations in Ms. Lee's interests and opinions were in fact the result of the innocent causes counsel suggests? If so, we object, as counsel has laid no foundation that Ms. Lee is an expert in such matters. If counsel is asking whether these changes might have occurred if LiveAfter had not brought them about, the question not only lacks foundation, but is irrelevant."

Thea thought of her own scrutiny of the code that now comprised her; but of course, she could not claim a level of expertise that would impress the judge. . . .

The judge sat back for a moment, evidently cogitating; then replied, "As to the irrelevance of the latter question, I need not rule. Plaintiffs' counsel is correct as to both ambiguity and lack of foundation. Objection sustained. Would counsel care to rephrase?"

At least the subject had shifted away from her exchange with Max; but now it returned there. "Ms. Lee, would you agree that your message to Mr. Lee described changes such as you had undergone as natural and in fact commonplace?"

Hu again: "Objection. The exhibit speaks for itself."

The judge tilted her head to one side. "Overruled. I would like to hear the witness' answer."

Thea took a deep breath, willing herself to control

her temper. "The message grew out of a conversation I had with a friend, a friend who'd been arguing with his family about the changes they'd seen in him." She could not resist glaring at defense counsel. "My friend is—was—a *lawyer*. He was eloquent. He made a good case! He didn't—and I didn't—have any other way to explain what was happening. Looking back, I would have to say we were naive."

Hu, on redirect: "Thea, when you changed your mind, before you were stored, did you realize you were doing it?"

She could see where Hu was heading, but honesty, compelled by her nature (still hers!) as well as her promise to the court, would not let her give Hu exactly the answer she sought. "Most often I did. Sometimes, it might have happened more gradually, without my being fully aware of it."

And Hu, smoothly, as if she could have wished for no other answer: "Did it ever happen, during your corporeal lifetime, that you confidently asserted one position without realizing you had, on a prior occasion, publicly supported the opposite?"

At least she could say, emphatically, that it never had.

"Your Honor, I offer in evidence this letter, written by plaintiff Thea Lee and published in her local paper . . . . Thea, please read your letter for the court. . . . Has this issue arisen since your transition to the stored state? . . . Were you aware, when you made that presentation, of the existence and contents of the letter you have just read to us? . . ."

Then, once again, came defense counsel to the attack. "Ms. Lee, is your memory perfect? . . . Has it ever been perfect?"

Suddenly she had had quite enough. "Perfection is for the gods, sir. But for a mere mortal, my memory has always been pretty damned good. Or it was until your goons got ahold of me!"

"Ms. Lee." The judge now, her tone icy sharp. "Kindly refrain from intemperate displays."

"Our apologies, Your Honor." Poor Hu, having to take the blame for Thea's outburst. "If necessary, Your Honor, we can present rebuttal witnesses supporting Ms. Lee's assertion as to the excellence of her memory."

"I will determine that necessity based on events—such as whether Ms. Lee is able to remember my admonition." The judge leaned back again, and the questions went on. And on.

*　*　*　*　*

Hu would close with testimony about what had happened to "Jim." They had considered presenting this evidence before Thea took the stand, but Hu decided Jim's more extreme second transformation would make a better coda.

Hu asked for and received a recess first, to see whether her surprisingly cooperative technical witness had worked on Jim. That particular gift from the gods was denied them: he had not. But the GAL had sufficient expertise to confirm that significant emotional manipulation had taken place, if not to describe its effects in detail.

Those effects had of course been obvious to Jim's stored acquaintances.

Jim, in his current mild-mannered state, would not be an effective witness even if he could remember what had occurred. Thea, on the other hand, could have testified to at least the most recent of Jim's transformations. But Hu believed adding to the number of witnesses would help the judge, even this capable a judge, pay the maximum attention.

Of the members of the troupe, once Thea sounded them out as carefully as possible, one had proved willing to come forward.

* * * * *

Hu, working with The Diva before the trial, did not completely restrain her impatience with her witness' over-the-top delivery. "Madam, any appearance of exaggeration or posturing would undermine your credibility, and could even render your testimony counterproductive."

Thea interrupted, turning to her friend. "Would you give Hu and me a moment? Please stay on the line — we'll be back with you directly." She quickly shifted to a connection between herself and Hu only, with Hu looking both amused and skeptical.

Hu rolled her eyes. "I can see why you call her The Diva."

Thea could not help but grin, but then forced herself to look more serious. "Hu, I hope you'll agree that I know this woman better, and have some basis for reading her better, than you do. That melodrama may be habitual, but I believe it's presently masking some very real fear, maybe even terror."

Hu, to Thea's relief, did seem to be considering what she had to say. "And if it is?"

"Dramatizing her fear may give her courage. All I'm asking is that you leave her some leeway."

So, after the GAL's precise and matter-of-fact description of the code he had analyzed, Hu called The Diva to the stand.

"I almost *fainted* when Jim simply *vanished*! Into thin air! And I was so *thankful* when he reappeared . . . But I shouldn't have been, really. Because he simply wasn't the same *man*. He'd been so forceful, and dynamic, and *attractive* . . . . And now, I suppose he's perfectly sweet; but if he didn't look more or less the same, I wouldn't even *recognize* him."

Thea only wished she could have applauded when The Diva finally stepped down.

* * * * *

Then, of course, it was time for the defense to present its case. LiveAfter tried to avoid it, renewing its motion to dismiss, arguing that plaintiffs had failed to meet the threshold requirements for a viable case. The judge, with admirable efficiency, simply said, "Denied. Proceed."

Hu's calming ritual, at this point in a trial, was to review all the difficulties facing the opposition. There were several to contemplate. LiveAfter could hardly call its clients and ask them to testify that they remained unaltered: if altered, Thea's experience, as well as common sense, suggested they would be unaware of the fact. LiveAfter had already done its best, during the presentation of plaintiffs' case, to discredit plaintiffs' witnesses, technical and otherwise. That left defendants' own collection of experts, also known as hired guns.

Part of LiveAfter's strategy was to portray undeniable

changes in Thea as benign or better. Her tics and her depression made good starting points. LiveAfter's medical expert explained how disruptive tics could become, the dangers of depression, et cetera.

One of the things Hu loved about litigation was the frequency with which she learned something entirely new. On cross, Hu steered the witness toward one such area. "Doctor, are you familiar with the correlation between tics of various kinds and creativity?"

The witness sniffed. "Correlation is, of course, not causation."

"May I take that as a 'yes,' doctor? Especially creative individuals are statistically more likely to manifest this neurological condition?"

"If you like."

In the heat of the moment, she almost ventured into the frequency with which treatment of tics had been found to hamper creativity, but at the last minute remembered that no such effect had been shown where digital tinkering of the stored was concerned. Instead, she moved on to more solid ground.

"Doctor, do you have any reason to believe that Ms. Lee suffered from a dangerous degree of depression at the time she was stored?"

"I lack information on that point. But those who have at any point shown symptoms of clinical depression are at risk of a recurrence — unless some more permanent treatment is available."

"Ah, yes, treatment. Doctor, can you explain to me the limitations that currently exist in this country on forced treatment of inpatients?"

He made a few inarticulate introductory noises, then spoke with deliberate precision. "Patients physically and continually resident at a psychiatric facility are deemed to have the right to refuse treatment, once they have been informed of the benefits of same and of their psychiatrist's recommendations."

"And is the situation different for outpatients?"

"In some cases. A patient's release to outpatient status may be conditioned on that patient's acceptance of treatment."

"So, just to clarify, when you used the language 'physically and continually,' you were referring to inpatient as opposed to outpatient status?"

Whatever he may have intended to imply with that language, he could hardly say that he had been reaching for any way, however irrelevant, to distinguish Thea's situation. "More or less."

She let it go. The judge would correctly note the witness' reluctance and the bias it revealed. "Would it be essentially—" She resisted the temptation to use the phrasing "more or less," as it would give him more room for evasive maneuvers. "—essentially correct to explain that difference as due to the danger an unmedicated psychiatric patient might pose to the community?"

"Among other factors."

Should she ask him to list those supposed factors? Better to pin him down in some more pointed way. "Doctor, could a digitally stored person physically attack a member of the corporeal community?"

"No, but—"

"Could a digitally stored person force a corporeal person to engage in any transaction?"

Not the best phrasing: she had given him an opening which he promptly took. "A digitally stored person could use emotional means to apply pressure in that direction."

Not a major problem. "What medications are

currently prescribed to reduce a patient's tendencies toward emotional manipulation?"

"Ah, I am not familiar with the range of medications available for that purpose."

With a jury, she might need to take the risks of hammering the point, but the judge would know a non-answer when she heard one.

Well, just one little dig: "And is your certification current and active, Doctor?"

Ah, the professional reflex at work! "Of course."

"So that if such a pharmaceutical were available, you would have every reason to know of it."

When in doubt, ignore the question, eh? No matter. The question made the point at least as well without an answer.

"Can we agree, Doctor, that as far as any psychiatric treatment is concerned, Thea Lee is essentially an inpatient, with no mobility or freedom of movement beyond what an inpatient would enjoy?"

The judge leaned forward. "And this time, Doctor, please do counsel the courtesy of answering her question."

Score!

"To the limited extent those categories apply, I would say so."

Good enough. Time to broaden the attack.

"Doctor, are you trained in philosophy?"

The witness looked offended at the very notion. "No."

"How about sociology?"

"I have taken some coursework in that area."

"Any actual degrees or certifications in that area?"

"No."

"How about the history of the Enlightenment?"

He did not appear to recognize the term. "No."

"Constitutional law? The legislative history of the Constitution?"

Whoops—a compound question. She waited a moment to see if the judge would reprimand her; but the witness was already shaking his head. "No. We psychiatrists leave such matters to you lawyers."

Lovely! Had he forgotten that judges were also lawyers? Closing argument in this case would be an absolute delight.

Hu fought hard for the exclusion of LiveAfter's next witness, but was not surprised to lose that battle. LiveAfter's second chair was too professional to smirk as she ushered the sociologist to the witness stand, but she exuded an aura similar to that of a Siamese cat digesting the proverbial canary.

The lawyer elicited a list of credentials which Hu did not attempt to cut short. A jury might have been impressed, but this judge knew quite well that credentials did not necessarily correlate with either professional status or intellectual acumen.

Eventually, lawyer and witness got around to the witness' specialty. "I study the use of various manipulative techniques in connection with political campaigns."

"What do you mean by manipulation? Does the term suggest something other than the straightforward providing of relevant information?"

Hu considered objecting to the compound question, but decided against annoying the judge with a technical and unimportant interruption. Besides, after she had gotten away with such a question herself, it might be tempting fate.

"Yes. By manipulation, I mean the use of words,

images, or other means to trigger emotional responses, whether positive or negative, to a candidate or issue."

"Is such manipulation a recent trend?"

The witness smiled indulgently. "Hardly. It has, one way or another, been going on as long as humans have been holding elections in any form."

"Are the potential voters at whom these efforts are directed typically aware of the manipulation?"

The witness kept smiling as he shook his head. "Most won't be, at least if it's done well. Of course, there will always be exceptions. Even some of those more aware voters may be somewhat affected."

"What institutional response, if any, has there been to such tactics?"

The witness finally dropped the smile, continuing in the manner of a condescending lecturer. "There have always been calls for restraint, and expressions of dismay that important questions might be decided on some basis other than their merits. One technique or another may be prohibited, or avoided on a practical basis as so inappropriate that its use would backfire. But as a social species, we inevitably resort to various sorts of social signaling in any group endeavor."

"Would you say, then, that manipulation of voters is an inseparable part of the electoral process?"

"Objection." Not that Hu was sure on what basis to object. "Speculation, and beyond the foundation established for the witness."

The judge tilted her head minutely, but not for long. "Overruled. The witness may answer."

And of course, the witness said "yes."

Hu, stepping up to cross-examine, at least had a starting point in the witness' previous testimony. "You stated, did you not, that some potential voters would always notice attempts at manipulation?"

Yes, he had.

"Would you agree that even if a particular voter failed to see the signs of manipulation, that those signs are discernible to, we may say, the discerning?"

"Naturally."

It was Hu's turn to smile. "A very apt choice of words. Doctor, have voters typically been subject to types of manipulation that they had no possible way to detect?"

A moment of hemming and hawing, then: "I am not sure what you mean by 'no possible way.'"

"Come, doctor, you have already testified that all the methods of manipulating voters with which you were professionally familiar would be noticed by at least some voters — did you not?"

"I don't recall using that phrasing."

"Shall I have the court reporter read back the phrasing you did use, so that you can tell the court how its meaning differs from my paraphrase?"

A bit of wriggling in the chair in the witness stand. "That won't be necessary. Your paraphrase is — is close enough."

"Thank you *so* much." Whoa, she instructed herself. Rein it in. Don't disrespect the witness. The judge would view that as disrespect for the court.

But she could politely rub things in. "So, in summary, your testimony concerning the manipulation historically tolerated in elections refers to methods that a sufficiently attentive voter could discern or deduce?"

A moment of stalling, and then the apparently unavoidable, if grudging: "Yes. It does."

Hu bowed slightly in the direction of defense counsel. "Your witness."

LiveAfter's second chair stood up without stepping forward. "No further questions."

The judge called a recess, for the general stretching of legs and attending to other needs. When the trial resumed, yet another of LiveAfter's presumably inexhaustible supply of attorneys stood and announced their next witness.

Whoa, there.

LiveAfter was calling one of its stored clients after all. Which might or might not be wise; but that was hardly the immediate point. Defendants had failed to include the client on their witness list as the rules required. Federal courts were rarely kind to such omissions. Once she had pointed out the breach, Hu sat back and watched the fur fly.

"Do you plan to insult this court's intelligence, and waste its time, by claiming that this failure is 'substantially justified'? When you have total control of this witness, including his availability, and had ample advance knowledge of the issues you would need to address?"

"No, Your Honor. We rely not on such a justification, but on the rule's alternative grounds. The delay in disclosing the witness should be essentially harmless." And at the judge's evident skepticism: "If you will allow us to make an offer of proof in the form of testimony, we hope to establish the fact."

An offer of proof, "in the form of" an examination. Essentially, LiveAfter was asking to put on its witness to prove that it should be allowed to put on its witness. Cute. And if she objected, she would implicitly insult the judge, implying that the judge would be unable to forget what she had heard if she eventually held the testimony inadmissible. Even cuter.

"Counsel, any objections to the defendants' proposed offer of proof?"

It was somewhat puzzling that the judge had not slapped LiveAfter down harder. Was the judge simply curious about what the witness would say? Or might this uncharacteristic leniency be a sign that the judge considered LiveAfter to be in trouble? In sufficient trouble that she would give them a bit more latitude as they tried to catch up? If so, Hu did not want to do anything to annoy the judge or to distract her from that mindset. "No objection to testimony presented for that purpose."

The screen for video testimony lit up to show a man with a deep tan, untidy salt-and-pepper hair, stubble on his cheeks, and a vibrantly loud Hawaiian shirt. In spite of herself, Hu liked him on sight.

LiveAfter's lawyer cleared his throat. "Sir, please state your name and, ah, your current status."

The face on the screen wrinkled in a sardonic grin. "I'm Jacob Marr, Jake for short, and I'm dead. Still squawking due to the high-tech expensive services of the LiveAfter folks. Nice to be here." The witness guffawed. "And I mean that most sincerely."

"Mr. Marr, did you vote in the most recent election?"

"Yes, I did. And before you ask, that's the first time I bothered to vote in twenty years or so."

"May I ask why you did so?"

Another guffaw. "Sure, son. But damned if I know." He turned, probably toward the image of the judge on his screen. "Excuse me, Your Honor."

The judge looked hard into the screen. "Sir, I would hazard the guess that you are fully aware of the rules of decorum in this court."

The witness bowed his head. "My apologies, Your Honor." He looked up again, unabashed. "So where were we?"

The lawyer tapped his thumbs together. "We were discussing your recent political activity. To the extent you can answer the question based on your political views prior to your, ah, change in status, did you vote in a manner consistent with those prior views?"

The witness pursed his lips, causing more wrinkles to show. "Just voting in the first place wasn't so consistent with 'em. I didn't trust politicians — not their promises, and not their competence to do whatever they promised even if they meant to. And the way I voted, supporting folks who promise to spread the wealth and help the little guy, might not make a lot of sense unless you've got a rosier view of human nature than I used to have."

"Has your view of human nature in fact changed?"

The witness shrugged. "Maybe. I've mellowed out some, one way and another. Maybe dying and still hanging around has that effect. Maybe I was fiddled with, like these folks are saying. And you know what? I don't really care. Not a — a dang bit."

"Why is that, sir?"

The man shook his tangle of hair. "Sonny, I've *cheated death*. Given the Grim Reaper the finger — oops, sorry." He flashed a quick boyish grin. "I didn't read the contract as well as I might have, but if I had, and clause 73 of paragraph 37 had said I had to vote, or vote for Joe Schmo, in order to stay alive and feel frisky again, do you honestly think I'd have said no? I may be crazy, but I'm not that crazy." He paused for a moment. "Can I go now? I've got a hot date waitin'."

The courtroom fell silent for a moment before the lawyer turned back to the judge and said, "That's our offer of proof, Your Honor."

The judge sat back in her padded chair. "The witness is excused for the present." She gestured to the bailiff; the screen went blank. "Ms. Yang? Do you continue to object to this evidence? Or do you seek a continuance in order to investigate it?"

Hu ran through the alternatives. She could seek the suggested delay in order to find and interview the man's friends and relatives, to get their guesses as to whether his testimony reflected his authentic voice and views. But even if she took his proffered testimony at face value . . . .

"Your Honor, let us assume, for purposes of argument, that Mr. Marr is what we may call politically amoral."

"Objection!"

The judge brushed the objection aside. "You were saying, Ms. Yang?"

"Plaintiffs have not asserted and do not assert that all individuals stored now, and all those to be stored in the future, cherish their political and personal autonomy and integrity. In life, Mr. Marr could have sold his vote to the highest bidder, and while both he and the bidder would have broken the law, the transaction would have no effect on the rights of the rest of the electorate.

"Mr. Marr may be indifferent to his rights, but plaintiffs are not." (Had Marr opted out, or not bothered? The former could explain LiveAfter's reluctance to give proper advance notice; but that was a can of worms Hu would leave unopened.) "And plaintiffs will not delay these proceedings in order to verify the irrelevant accuracy of this witness' self-presentation. We maintain our objection to defendants' disregard of procedural rules, but we do not seek a continuance."

The judge rested her chin in her thumb and forefinger, then placed both hands on her desk. "Ms. Yang has correctly characterized the evidence offered. It has insufficient relevance for me to admit it, let alone to admit it despite defendants' failure to list this witness as required. The proffered testimony of Mr. Marr is excluded."

"And so," Hu summarized to her paralegal as they headed across the street to the office, "defendants' case rests not with a bang, but with a whimper."

She sprang up onto the curb; the paralegal, carrying Hu's bulky litigation bag with her computer and paper exhibit printouts, hoisted himself up more slowly. Once he was clear of traffic, he paused and put his burden down for a moment, turning to ask, "Ready for closing argument?"

Hu knew her grin was showing every one of her teeth. "Ab-so-*lute*-ly."

* * * * *

Thea's view of the courtroom included part of the area for spectators, and many of those she could see had that alert, even rapacious air that, no matter the technology used to spread news, still identified the reporter.

Her living quarters had not materially changed, and she was still allowed to leave them. It would have been too obvious, she supposed, to start subjecting her to actual sensory deprivation. But her impatience with the litigation process, and her imperfectly suppressed fears as to its outcome, had made it increasingly difficult to write music or even to concentrate on playing it. Exercise of any sort seemed pointless if she allowed herself to think about it. And there was only so much knitting she could do, especially in light of her knowledge that any exposure to cold weather would be largely of her own choosing.

Unless she were subjected to it at another's whim. In which case she might not be allowed to wear her own creations.

In this limbo, she had looked forward to the court sessions as a lifeline. But now, hearing Hu's closing argument, she found the recital of her own predicament unexpectedly painful.

If only she could direct the camera! All she could see of Max was a partial profile and the line of his arm and shoulder. But she could imagine what it would feel like to stroke her hand slowly down that line, and then to nestle against him and feel that arm around her. . . .

Hu had paused for a moment, and as she resumed, she spoke with a volume and passion that caught Thea's attention anew.

"All of our fundamental constitutional rights as Americans have common threads. Freedom of speech, freedom of association, freedom of political action, exercise of the franchise, every kind of individual autonomy — all these ultimately depend on the individual's ability to make their own choices. None of these freedoms retain the slightest real meaning if their exercise is determined by someone else.

"We have been fortunate, in our history, that relatively few of us have been subjected to attempts at brainwashing, whether formal or informal. And once we have come of age, the limited exceptions, the permissible restraints on individual choice, that we allow under the rubric of a parent's right to raise a child become irrelevant. Moreover, we have recognized that the benefits to be gained from government-provided education must not be allowed to overshadow the parental right to prepare a child to go their own way and make their own decisions.

"But now, along with the unprecedented benefits to be found in storage technology, we face an unprecedented threat. The ease with which those who have entrusted themselves to digital storage may be altered without their consent, altered to serve the purposes of others, has no counterpart in the hit-and-miss methods available in the past to coerce and intimidate and undermine the integrity of the individual mind.

"And in particular, if the franchise we have granted to those whose lives continue in this new medium is to be anything but a cynical mockery, we must ensure that nothing and no one can interfere with its free and untrammeled exercise.

"Your Honor, in addition to the damages plaintiffs seek for the injuries they have suffered, they seek the broadest injunctive relief, the most clarion declaration, that the new era of extended life must not become the 'brave new world' of dark dystopian literature, but rather, a brave new world indeed."

* * * * *

"What an interesting offer." The judge peered at the screen in front of her as if it displayed a face instead of a "confidential communication" logo. "And from such an interesting source, too."

She distinctly heard a spluttering noise from the

caller. She paused to relish it before continuing. "It does appear that the plaintiffs failed to name at least one individual defendant."

An enjoyable bluff. And she might in fact be able to ascertain, if she cared to, from whence the call had come. After all, there were only so many people at LiveAfter who could promise what this caller had dangled before her. Though the caller could also be bluffing.

No matter.

"The fundamental problem with your suggestion, sir, is that the possibility of free storage loses much of its allure if the plaintiffs' case is well-founded. And unless you assume that I could not possibly judge this matter correctly without special inducement, your offer suggests that a correct and impartial judgment would be unfavorable to those you represent."

The caller finally regained enough presence of mind to hang up. The judge allowed herself a belly laugh before getting back to work.

* * * * *

Max had been leaping to answer the phone for the past two weeks. This time, finally, the call was not a false alarm.

"The order's in!" Hu's face was flushed, and her voice high-pitched. That was not the look of failure. "I'm sending it now — there."

"Please. Tell me. Sum it up."

"It's good. Better than I expected."

Hu started reading to him, but he found it impossible to follow. "I'm sorry, but could you start again? And just read the important parts?"

Hu laughed — in excitement, he thought, not

derision. "All right. Sure. Why don't you put it on screen and follow along with me."

"Just a sec." He opened the message and split his screen between the text and Hu's somewhat gloating expression.

But of course, she was skipping parts, as he'd asked, so following along was not so easy.

"*Plaintiffs have more than carried their burden of proving alteration of plaintiff Lee and other stored individuals without prior knowledge or consent, and that each of the defendants knowingly participated in these operations . . . .*" Hu looked up from the order and grinned at Max. "Here's a nice bonus. That monkey business during the trial, where they tried to turn Thea into a less effective plaintiff—listen to this. *This Court finds sua sponte —*"

"Uh, what's sua sponte?"

"It means the court did something on its own that we didn't even ask for. In this case, it means the judge was very, very ticked off. *—that the alteration of plaintiff Lee's thoughts and emotions during the pendency of this trial constituted contempt of court. A further hearing will be set to determine each defendant's share of responsibility.*" Hu's grin now looked positively hungry. "I can't wait."

Max laughed, while reminding himself never to end up on Hu's bad side. "What else?"

"The court adopted our argument about state actors and entwinement. Don't worry if you don't remember all about it. . . . And we cleared the hurdle about defendants knowing they violated constitutional rights! *As to those damages that require proof that defendants knowingly violated plaintiffs' established constitutional rights, any finding to the contrary must rest on defendants' uncertainty as to whether the files in their possession and under their control constituted human beings with the rights of human beings. Defendants' entire business model, and all their promotional material, conflict with any claim to such uncertainty; and their repeated statements that the stored should retain their voting rights amounts to a declaration that the stored have lost no aspect of citizenship. Defendants cannot in justice be now allowed to shelter behind a contrary position."*

Hu went back to scanning the text, muttering almost inaudibly. "Another hearing to come, to fight about damages on the constitutional right violations and the tort claims. No punitive damages. Well, that would have been almost too good." She looked back up at Max. "And here you are! — *Plaintiff Cooper is awarded damages for loss of consortium, as listed below, for a period to run until this Court rules that plaintiff Lee has been fully restored. . . .* We really dodged a bullet on that one, with that message you sent Thea . . . ."

Max tried to remember the legal jargon Hu had taught him. "What about injunction relief?"

Hu smiled indulgently. "Injunctive. Here: *This Court issues a writ of prohibition and mandate. Defendants are enjoined from engaging in or allowing any alteration other than necessary maintenance of any of their digital wards unless the affected ward affirmatively and specifically consents and that consent is recorded. Any failure to follow this order will be treated as contempt of court. Any fabrication of consent records* — wow, she went there! — *will be referred for criminal prosecution."*

Max held up a hand to halt the flow. "What's the mandate business?"

"Here, let me find it. *Defendants are ordered to make all reasonable efforts —* " She looked up from the words in front of her and frowned. "Reasonable. That's wiggle room. I'm going to move to clarify. . . . *to undo all alterations to which any ward has not consented as per the terms of this order, with minimal —"* She grimaced again. *" —minimal effect on the ward's original files and accumulated memories. In any case where removal of unauthorized alterations will damage preexisting files, defendants will consult the ward and proceed or not proceed with the alterations as the ward, or in the case of any ward this Court finds to be incompetent, an appropriate guardian for that ward shall direct."*

Hu muttered a curse. "They're going to be tempted to do one more wholesale hack, to prompt the 'wards' on how to answer that question. At least the GAL's still there. Sorry, Max, I have to go. I'm going to make sure the GAL knows what to look for."

"But—okay, go do it. But call me back as soon as you can."

Hu grinned. "I'll do you one better. I'll have Thea on the line."

Max hadn't seen Thea so joyful since—he swallowed hard—since the morning of the day she died. "Max, I insist that you go see Hu in person, because I want you to give her a ridiculously big hug."

She spoke so easily about things she couldn't do. Could the company have given her that? Would she have to give it back?

Hu held up a cautionary finger. "I'm glad you're excited, and you have every right to be. But nothing's going to happen just yet. The order won't take effect until the court is sure no one will appeal, or until any appeal is over with. And I can promise you, there will be an appeal."

Thea's glow faded. Max almost cried to see it go, but that would only make her feel worse, if she noticed. For now, though, she was focused on Hu. "You'll stay with us, won't you? For the appeal?"

"Absolutely. I wouldn't miss it."

* * * * *

Hu gazed out her window at the metropolitan expanse, its lighted office windows starting to wink out as more and more people called it a day, and pondered the future.

The trial court's ruling was a little too good. They would almost certainly lose ground on appeal. And that might be the end of the road.

Would the Supreme Court take the case? One way or another, someone would be asking them to take it. Unless the appellate court threw out every aspect of Hu's—Thea's—victory, LiveAfter would file a petition for writ of certiorari, asking the Supreme Court to choose this case as one of the few meriting its attention. And unless the appellate court saw things entirely Thea's way, Hu would file her own petition. But as for the fate of a petition from either side, the details of the appellate court's decision would make a great deal of difference— as would the other cases vying for a slot on the high court's docket, and innumerable personal and political considerations.

None of which would include Hu's own desires— so she could acknowledge her hopes, to herself if not to her clients, without any self-reproach.

Of course she wanted this one to go all the way. Of course she wanted to argue a case this important, this difficult, this notorious.

And in fact, no lesser victory would content Thea, if she understood the legal process as Hu understood it. No trial court order, not even a ruling from a single federal appellate court, could protect Thea indefinitely, let alone the other stored and all those who might be stored in the future.

Nothing was forever, and that included Supreme Court rulings, but they shaped the legal landscape nationwide, and for decades, even centuries, to come.

Of course, the same would be true if they should lose.

* * * * *

The judge pored over plaintiffs' Motion for Clarification, tapping her upper lip with her stylus as she read.

This Court's order does not indicate whether the guardian ad litem's appointment is still in effect. Plaintiffs request that this Court continue that appointment until any appeals of this order have been concluded and this Court has determined that all its orders have been followed in their entirety.

The judge smiled a little. That might be more than a "clarification." But she'd let the lawyers fight that out, if it ended up making a difference to any deadlines.

Plaintiffs further request that this Court clarify its use of the term "all reasonable efforts" to indicate that the expense of those efforts is not a determining factor.

"Oh, come now, Ms. Yang," the judge murmured to herself. "If you bankrupt LiveAfter, who will maintain Ms. Lee and her companions?" But she could provide some further details as to where the line should be drawn.

As for "minimal" . . . When the judge wrote "minimal effect on the ward's original files and accumulated memories," she had chosen a weasel-word quite deliberately. Damned if she knew what was possible on that front. But if she kept the GAL in place, she could direct him to make that call, or at least to offer his views as the process went on.

Hmmm—another motion, this time a motion to intervene. From a lawyer she knew well, the former partner of Ms. Yang about whom there had been such disturbing testimony. She paused for a moment of renewed regret over his passing, then read on. The lawyer wanted a more direct say in how the remedy would be applied to him. No surprise there! But she could hold a ruling on that one in abeyance, until they all learned whether any of the judge's finely honed remedies would actually be applied.

Would the Supremes want to weigh in? Or would they duck this exceedingly hot potato?

CHAPTER 23

AS THE case started winding its way upward through the federal appellate court system, gaining publicity at every step, the rumors and memes grew ever more extreme.

Potential customers and concerned family members barraged the corporate offices with questions about the nanotechnology used to record people for storage, and no amount of explanation that such technology was not at issue seemed to penetrate the public consciousness. Given that fundamental confusion, it was perhaps inevitable that from wondering whether the recording technology reliably captured and preserved personality and memories, the crowd moved on to assume that anyone who had used the nanobot-driven baseline recording tools might have been adversely affected. Or rather, infected.

Dane wiped sweat off his forehead. "We should maybe take a little extra time for lunch."

Esther glared at him. "You should have suggested it before we left. I have a meeting in fifteen minutes." Then she dialed back her annoyance to think. Dane usually bragged that he could handle the heat. Something else was going on. "Why?"

"I just got a message. There's a demonstration going on, and we'd be walking right through it."

"Let me try to reach the people I'm supposed to meet." Esther found a lamp post to lean on and got busy. Dane took the opportunity to climb a tree. While Esther was still trying to reach one coworker, he called out, "I can see them! Lots of signs, lots of milling around, some guy with a megaphone. Aw, how cute—I think they're going to chant. Listen!"

And she could indeed hear some rhythmic shouts, though not what they were shouting.

Esther worked for another few minutes and then gave up. "I had to leave messages for two people, and one of them's traveling to the meeting. I should really get back."

Dane slid down from the tree, collecting shreds of bark and grime on his slacks, and posed like some heroic statute. "At your service, my lady! I will escort and defend you!"

Esther stuck out her tongue at him, earning a raucous laugh, and then looked around for cover. They could walk along this wall, and that building. But eventually they would have to walk right through the crowd.

Esther stayed close beside Dane and about half a step behind. As they got closer, his expression grew serious and his shoulders tense. Just before they left the last tree behind, he broke off a sizable branch. "I've always fancied a walking stick. And if we need it for other purposes . . . ."

They walked on, Dane tapping the stick on the ground with every step. The click, click, click echoed loud in Esther's ears. Would it attract attention?

As they approached the outskirts of the demonstration,

she grew less concerned on that point. The amplified speech, punctuated by chanting and random epithets, more than drowned out any noise Dane and his stick were making. She assumed the lead, moving slowly, weaving her way through gaps in the crowd.

But gaps through which she could fit without making contact did not allow Dane to do the same. She tried to leave enough space for his broader frame, but soon he was brushing up against people as they passed. And while Dane's casual attire would have allowed him to pass for one of the crowd, Esther had higher standards.

"I bet she works there!"

"Look at those two! They probably have brains full of parasites already!"

"Frankens! Frankens!"

"Get back, everyone! Touch them and the nanobots might get on your skin! That's all it takes!"

A woman gasped. "He touched me! With his arm!" She burst into tears. Her companion clenched his fists and blocked Dane's path. (With a detachment that surprised her, Esther wondered if he was intentionally taking the risk that punching Dane in the face might transfer the dreaded nonexistent parasites to his own skin.)

Dane growled, tucked Esther inside his arm like a two-footed football, and charged forward, knocking the man out of their way, plowing through the crowd. Something hard and pointed—the corner of a sign?—hit Esther on the shoulder, and she gasped, but she scurried to keep up with him, except for the moments when he actually lifted her from the ground and carried her along.

A guard stood by the door, thrusting a club toward the crowd and holding the door partly open. "Hurry up and get in here!"

Once safely in the entryway, she turned to Dane and saw the streak of blood running down from a scratch on his cheek, and his puffy lower lip. She reached up to stroke his cheek, very gently, before dropping her hand and inspecting her own body and limbs. Ripped skirt (the bastards!), dust on her shoes, and an ache in that shoulder. She was basically okay.

They'd been lucky. And the thought of having to think that way filled her with rage.

* * * * *

In the boardroom, the directors' voices jangled with nerves.

"The higher the case goes, the more publicity it'll get. If you think sales are down now, you ain't seen nothing yet."

"It's a damn good thing we didn't go public. Our stock would be in the toilet."

"I heard the feds might exercise eminent domain—take us over and turn us into a nationwide retirement program, run everything themselves."

"Are you *nuts*? The way people are feeling, any administration that floated that idea—well, it'd sink like the Titanic."

"Everyone calm down." The chair of the board made the most of the well-documented power of the female voice to cut through noise and command attention. "We have plenty of investors to tide us through this crisis. They know how misguided the popular concerns are. And they damn well want to ensure that we're here when they need us. Besides, I have a source who tells me that the federal appeals court will be changing our situation for the better. Patience, people."

* * * * *

Next morning, Esther thanked the security guards who had ushered her through the latest protests and headed for her desk. The Cerebral Management Project was on hold pending the outcome of the appeal; she could finally look forward to an entire day in which none of her work would turn her stomach. That is, if she could get any work done in the midst of the rumor mill the office had become.

" . . . going out of business and canning us all . . . " " . . . paid off the higher court to make the case go away . . . " " . . . government is going to take the tech for itself!"

This last prediction came from the desk nearest to Esther's. She gave up trying to review her long-neglected files and strolled over. "What government, and how, and why?"

Her neighbor shrugged his round shoulders. "Something called eminent domain. I don't know much about it."

Eminent domain? Wasn't that something about building spaceports and maglev tracks? Esther returned to her desk and did a quick search. Yes, governments used eminent domain when landowners refused to sell land voluntarily for public projects. Eminent domain let the government force the sale for (supposedly) fair market value. But what did that have to do with taking tech?

She kept reading. Eminent domain wasn't, as she'd assumed, only about taking real property. It could reach personal property as well.

Personal property. Intangible property? Intellectual property?

Was some government, federal or state, at all likely to take over the storage industry, or some part of it? And if that happened, would Thea and the others be better protected?

* * * * *

The assistant to the deputy chief of staff for the Office of Policy and Legislation at the Criminal Division of the Attorney General's office reviewed the memo for typos before sending it to the long list of recipients.

. . . The subject technology reopens certain dormant policy options and creates additional ones. At present, neither the federal government nor any state government includes a capital sentencing provision in its statutes or guidelines. However, given that this status quo came to exist without any binding judicial prohibition, and given the substantial scholarship in support of government discretion to impose this penalty (see, e.g., "The Forgotten Final Option: Constitutional Assumptions Regarding The Death Penalty," Yale L.J. Vol. 146, Number 6, April 2037), the principal obstacles are political and could be reduced by overcoming the typical public objections. If corporeal termination did not result in complete termination of the personality, but rather, included an appropriate correction of the antisocial tendencies demonstrated by the subject's current offense and/or history, resistance to this effective and humane alternative might be reduced to the point where such change becomes practicable.

<u>Other Correctional Facility Management Possibilities</u>
Historically, public entities in charge of funding and

supervising correctional facilities have been faced with the unsatisfactory choices of straining existing plant capabilities, with resultant overcrowding and insufficient staff presence per inmate, or releasing multiple offenders into the community with supervision only from overtaxed conditional release departments. The technology whose acquisition is under discussion would offer a third approach. Rather than housing inmates in the current or comparable facilities, inmates whose review process has been completed could be transitioned to the digital environment at greatly reduced cost. The same psychological adjustments previously discussed in the context of capital cases could be implemented as well if the cost of same, upon proper study, did not prove prohibitive. . . .

The assistant fixed two more typos, yawned, and hit Send.

* * * * *

Thea had hardly spoken to Not-Jim since his withdrawal from the troupe, but now he sought her out. And somehow or other, he had obtained what purported to be a familiar brand of Irish cream liqueur.

He poured a generous serving into two glasses (Thea supplying the ice) and lifted his glass in a toast. "To your victory. And your courage."

Thea blinked in surprise, then laughed. "Can I drink without toasting my own supposed courage?"

Her guest waved his hand in assent. She took a sip. It wasn't quite right. Few consumables were, even now — perhaps because everyone tasted the same thing differently, and those inconsistent patterns were all the coders had to work with. But it had the essential candy sweetness, and it would have the kick as well. That, at least, was easy to code.

"If you like, you can call me Jim."

She almost let go of the glass. "Why?"

"First, because I've never heard you call me by my actual name, and I'd guess that's no coincidence. Second, because I know I used Jim during the period we spent most time together." He took a gulp of his drink. "And third, because I've been trying to find out more about what I was like while I was Jim. And I think I like that fellow."

"So did I." Damn it, that wasn't the point! And besides, if they hadn't changed her as well, maybe she wouldn't . . . She must focus. "You took a new name because you'd changed. And those changes may well have been imposed on you. Just like the changes after that."

He sat very still, almost rigid. "Did your lawyer, or any of you, actually look at my files? Do they know for sure that I didn't make those first changes on my own?"

He was holding onto hope, and she hated to take it from him. But whatever had been done to him, he was an intelligent man, and he would know evasion when he heard it. "Yes. What they did to you the second time was pretty blatant, and we used the discovery process to get your code and confirm it. That made it easier to check for earlier changes as well. I'm sorry, but we found them. And from the timing and the extent, it looks like the same political changes they made to me."

He closed his eyes for a moment and then forced a smile. "So I helped you with your case, at least a little. That's some consolation."

There was no need to get into what information Hu had and had not used. "More than a little." Thea took too large a swig and almost choked. Not that it would matter. Even if the sensation of choking persisted, it would no longer signify any sort of danger. (Unless it would make a good excuse for the corporation . . . no, that was nonsense.)

Jim's glass was almost empty. Thea tapped the bottle. "Would you like a refill?"

"Best not. I have some thinking to do. Please, keep the bottle." He stood up.

She stood as well and tried for a lighter tone. "You're going to make me drink alone?"

He shook his head gravely. "I can't make you do anything. We can both be glad of that." He stood facing her a moment longer, then left without another word.

* * * * *

The appellate court had fast-tracked the appeal, and strictly enforced the resulting time limits. Even so, those concerned — lawyers, parties, loved ones, and those whose political views would be either furthered or threatened by the upcoming decision — endured the passage of time with growing impatience.

Suspense, however, had the temporary benefit of allowing for optimism.

"Thea, I have some news." Hu looked not so much grave as intentionally blank, suppressing all expression.

Thea throat felt as if it were closing. For a moment, she couldn't breathe; and she spared another moment's thought for wry gratitude that breathing was not in fact necessary.

"The appeals court ruled against us?"

"That they did, at least on some pretty critical

issues. We can go over the details whenever you're ready. But don't be alarmed. First of all, I filed immediately for a stay of the ruling, and I'm sure we'll get it. After all, the trial court's judgment is stayed already except the pre-existing order preserving the status quo, so nothing needs to change right away. I've had the framework for a petition to the Supreme Court ready for weeks, along with arguments based on different ways the appellate court might rule. All my team has to do is plug in the right specifics and polish it up."

Thea grabbed the throw she'd knitted while the case dragged on and pulled it around her shoulders. "When will we know whether the Supreme Court will take the case?"

"Well, we've got one bit of luck—unless it's bad luck. Given where we are in the Court's term, they'll have to decide fairly soon whether to hear the case before they adjourn in June. They could put it over to next year, but with such strong public feeling, I'm betting they won't."

Thea looked at her nails and wished she had ever been able to stomach the idea of biting them. "What do you think they'll decide?"

"Well, of course I've never been a Supreme Court Justice—"

"Not yet." It couldn't hurt to break the tension by teasing Hu a little.

Hu relaxed and grinned. "Not yet." The grin faded, replaced by a calculating expression. "But it only takes four of them to vote for taking a case. And with issues this new, and this juicy, I really can't imagine that six or more of the nine will be able to resist."

Hu might have been exaggerating her optimism so as to maintain her clients' morale; but fortune, on this occasion, favored the disingenuous. The Court agreed to hear the case, and the next great battle began.

CHAPTER 24

THE AMICUS curiae—"friend of the court"—briefs flooded in.

An association of psychiatric professionals filed a brief in support of LiveAfter, emphasizing the untapped potential of digital technology "to give those who have endured lifelong mental illness the chance to live their digital existence free of that burden." Supporting the plaintiffs, the organization Speaking for the Spectrum warned that those with varying degrees of autism might be subjected to compulsory "normalizing," either by government decree or by restrictions on who could avail themselves of the digitizing process. An organization for the Deaf community (their attorney having publicly berated the software company whose built-in editor insisted on removing the capital D) raised similar concerns on behalf of its clients. The infighting in an umbrella group for those with, or whose relatives had, Down's syndrome threatened to fracture the group permanently.

Thirty-seven congressional representatives and sixteen senators filed a brief jointly with the Office of the Attorney General and similar departments in four states. Their mission: to preserve options potentially available in the criminal justice system "for more effective and efficient maintenance and rehabilitation."

And then there was the brief, purportedly siding with the plaintiffs, asserting that the only way to defend the integrity of the individual mind was to outlaw storage altogether.

Hu read that one with profound gratitude that its organization and citations lacked professional polish. *Oh, thanks so much. Does my client get a say in whether she continues to exist in her lamentably compromised condition?*

Hu, imagining the teetering piles of paper accumulating in the Supreme Court Clerk's office, spared a moment to wonder whether the Court's defiant insistence on printed briefs, decades after every other court in the land had gone from accepting e-filing to requiring it, gave any clue to the Justices' likely attitudes toward the cutting-edge technological issues in her clients' case.

Hu checked another item off her list. "All right, next question. Do we ask Justice Donner to recuse himself? Around the table again."

The most junior associate on the team came first in that rotation. "I'll state the reasons for doing it, and the rest of you can explain why it's not as good an idea as it seems. . . . He's politically aligned with Humane Future, the nonprofit that paid LiveAfter to mess with the stored. He's not going to want to believe it happened."

"But that's not really an issue any longer," the woman next to him pointed out. "The Court of Appeals based its ruling on the lack of a federal question, not on any failure to prove the alterations."

"He'll still want to get rid of the case, so he doesn't have to think about it longer than necessary."

"My turn, youngsters." The second of three partners on the team made a shushing motion in the direction of the two associates. "We need to consider the personal factors. Justice Donner is the kind of fellow everybody likes. If we seem to be attacking him or doing something to embarrass him, we may put the other Justices in a faintly hostile frame of mind from the start."

The remaining partner came next. "He's not the best constitutional scholar on the Court, but he may be the Justice most interested in constitutional questions. Take him out and we could eliminate our best listener."

The associate to her left pursed his lips. "But when you combine his liberal leanings and his less than reliable analysis, he's likely to start with the assumption that cases like *Rendell-Baker* apply. If he persuades the others to buy that assumption, we're in trouble."

The most senior associate present sat back, drumming his fingers. "If we seek recusal, I see a problematic inconsistency between our arguments and our actions. In we ride on our noble steeds, carrying the banners of individual autonomy and freedom of thought—and pause to unhorse Justice Donner for his political views?"

Hu chuckled. "Good thought and entertaining imagery. All right, here's what I think. I don't think the Justices' reactions will depend in any significant way on which side they're on politically. Yes, the more individualistic Justices will be particularly sensitive to the idea of having their beliefs hijacked and turned into ideas they detest. And the more communitarian Justices, Justice Donner included, will imagine how it would feel to discover that those views were imposed on them as part of a business deal.

"So no motion to recuse. Let's move on."

* * * * *

"What do you mean, you won't be able to make it to D.C.? It's not just my case, it's yours! Hu will want you to do interviews." Though he could do them long-distance, just as she could, in her own way. But—"It would be exciting for you, seeing it happen! And you wouldn't have to wait for updates from anyone."

"I'm sorry, baby." Max looked at Thea with wide, sad eyes. "But I can't afford the fare. And Hu isn't charging us a dime. I can't ask her to shell out more money."

Why was Max so broke? He must not have been working. Which meant he was emotionally overwhelmed: caught up in the case, afraid for her, lonely.

"Baby. It's all right. Whether you can go or not. But let me do a little thinking, okay? You know I'm good at problem-solving."

He managed to dredge up a tired smile. "You sure are."

"Good news, lover—I got us a soundtrack! That small ad agency we worked for last year? Turned out they didn't go out of business altogether. I'm sending you the story boards and specs."

Max shifted in his chair. "I don't know, baby. I haven't been able to concentrate so well lately."

Thea made herself smirk. "Maybe that's good. You write best when you're not thinking about it too hard. But I also sent some ideas for you to riff on."

Max did some clicking, and she heard her own musical snippets play on his end. He nodded his head in time, his body going loose and relaxed. That was worth it, no matter what followed.

But in the questionable shape Max was in, she had better prepare a fallback position. If she set it up herself, she could talk Max into it later.

On her next phone conference with Hu, she asked, "Do you think it'd be good for the cause, good optics, for Max to be in D.C. with all of you?"

Hu appeared startled. "Of course! I'd assumed he would be there."

"I'm glad to hear that. Because he might need just a little help. . . ."

* * * * *

Even though the Supreme Court had finally allowed broadcasts of its proceedings, there were plenty of people who preferred to enter the august halls and attend the arguments in person. Judging by the length of the line at 8 a.m., when Max met Hu and her team in the plaza near the steps, the issues—or various distorted versions of the issues—had drawn more would-be witnesses than could be accommodated. Those disappointed could, if they cared to, join the line of those who would be whisked into the chamber for three tantalizing minutes and then ushered out again.

Or they might end up joining one of the demonstrations beginning to take shape. One tall man in a rather stylish suit held a gigantic white cross made of some lightweight material, waving it in broad arcs as if to summon his co-religionists. Next to him lay a pile of preprinted signs: the one on top read "Life Digital Denies Life Eternal." Perhaps ten meters away, a short stout woman in a heavy knit hat was still hand-lettering her signs with a broad red marker. Her jacket bore the symbol of a socialist organization, sympathetic to though not affiliated with the defendant nonprofit. Farther on, between one of the fountains and its adjoining flag pole, three middle-aged women stood arm in arm humming in harmony, wearing multicolored scarves, under the banner of the Unitarian Universalist Church. They had no signs, but a nearby card table held a jar for donations and a platter of brownies.

Those standing in the long snaking line cast occasional curious or envious glances at the far shorter line nearby. From time to time, someone would venture over to ask its members what privilege they were enjoying. Then they would return to the general queue, often muttering something along the lines of "fancy-pants lawyers."

The lawyers were probably staying in pricey hotel rooms. Max had—just barely—managed to get to D.C. without sponging off Hu, what with his and Thea's latest bit of work, but a hotel room would have busted his budget. One of his and Thea's fellow musicians had a couch for him to crash on. That did, however, mean he had to wake himself up early and tiptoe out the door, while his host slept off a late-night gig.

The crowded chaos around the building took him by surprise. He quickly decided not to waste time looking for Hu; instead, he phoned her and asked for instructions. She asked him where he was, told him to stay put, and shortly emerged between two groups of demonstrators, eeling her way through and beckoning to him.

It was starting to rain. Max felt like a bit of a heel as he let Hu usher him past the various lines and into the building.

Then she hauled him along with merciless efficiency as he tried to take it all in, pulling him past the spiral staircases along two walls, the marble pillars, the relief carvings, the—was that a carving of a turtle? He tugged on Hu's sleeve and pointed. She threw him a quick smile without slowing down. "If you're good, I'll show you plenty more of them. They're all around the lamp posts outside. They represent the slow and deliberate pace of justice—no, I'm not kidding! Now come along."

"Ms. Chief Justice, and may it please the Court. My name is Dongmei Hu Yang, and I represent the plaintiffs in this case, who seek reaffirmation of the fundamental and political rights—"

"Ms. Yang, on what basis do your clients assert that these rights, whatever their usual extent, survive your clients' death as defined by medical science?"

Max turned and whispered to the pretty young paralegal who had been put in charge of him. "Why did that judge interrupt her?"

The paralegal hissed back, "Justice, not judge. They always interrupt—that's how it works. Didn't Hu explain? Now hush."

Yes, Hu had explained, and Thea, at least, had seemed to understand. Hu even said that Thea thought like a lawyer. She had said nothing of the sort about Max.

Now Hu was saying something about the law that let stored people vote. One of the Justices rolled his eyes. "Are you suggesting that Congress' discretionary actions must determine this Court's analysis of constitutional issues?"

"No, Your Honor. I do direct the Court's attention to the debate on that bill, transcribed in Exhibit 9, with its extensive references to . . . ."

Max looked at the line of black-robed judges—Justices. Weird title, as if each of these men and women somehow embodied the concept of justice. Did the title go to their heads? That must depend. The short man with salt-and-pepper hair had a jovial look and seemed to find the give-and-take, the interruptions and answers, entertaining. None of them looked obviously smug. Did the appointment process screen out the self-important? That would be too much to expect.

The Chief Justice actually looked a little like Hu, except twenty years older. They couldn't be related, or Hu would have had to hand off this job to someone else on her team. Unless he had that wrong too.

Now a black Justice sitting next to the Chief was saying something about contractual waivers. "If the very process that preserves consciousness includes continual alterations, as defendants showed, and if the stored individuals knew that, how can those alterations violate their rights?"

"Your Honor, our evidence showed the technical differences between the alterations mentioned in the contract and the alterations that formed the basis for plaintiffs' Complaint. . . ."

He would have liked to ask the paralegal how Hu was doing. She sounded good to him, but what did he know about it?

Damn! The Chief Justice was asking about those messages he and Thea had sent each other, when they were trying to reassure each other and themselves that nothing was wrong. But Hu didn't miss a beat, referring back to Thea's explanation at trial.

What the heck was a penumbra? Rather than bother the paralegal again, he started to look it up on his phone.

But the paralegal saw what he was doing and grabbed Max's wrist. "Stop that! You could get ejected for using your phone. And that won't help Hu any."

Max sighed and obeyed. There was a yellow light now on the podium where Hu was standing. It had been green until now. Hu said something about reserving her remaining time, thanked the Justices, and sat down.

Another lawyer stood up and introduced himself. He managed to get a whole sentence out before they interrupted him. At least neither side got to give speeches.

"Shouldn't the burden of proof be on those who assert that obviously sentient, ah, entities of human origin are no longer citizens?"

"The fundamental transition from life to death has shaped our law throughout our history, in such matters as inheritance, taxation—"

Another Justice broke in. "If the stored are not citizens, why did we see no opposition from any department of any branch of the federal government to the bill guaranteeing them the franchise?"

"Your Honor, there is no evidence in the record as to the absence of such opposition. Nor is it appropriate to take judicial notice of an asserted negative . . . ."

Max's attention wandered again, until he snapped back to awareness wondering if he had dropped off to sleep without realizing it. Had the plump Justice two seats from the Chief really said something about *Star Trek* and transporters?

He turned back to the paralegal, but the moment he opened his mouth, she glared at him with her finger on her lips.

* * * * *

And now, once again, came months of waiting.

Hu kept in close touch with the GAL, or as much as she could without alienating that essential ally. He reported no unauthorized manipulations. Hu tried not to read anything into such forbearance: it could mean anything from pessimism about the Court's decision to patient expectation of eventual victory to simple prudence.

* * * * *

The law clerk sat, hands clutching each other, as the Justice read the latest draft. She could predict exactly when the Justice would look up at her and shake his head. It went almost as she had imagined, except that he also pushed his tablet away from him in her direction.

"You're still fighting a battle we've lost. We need a majority, and the only way we've got one is to leave that door open."

"But I did say, in footnote 17—"

The old man chuckled. "Don't kid a kidder. That language is so vague that it can't possibly satisfy my recalcitrant colleagues."

The law clerk bit her lip. "I'm sorry, sir. I'll write it again."

The Justice cocked his head and scrutinized her, then patted her hand. "No need, my dear. I'll do it myself. You won't have to read it, for years, whenever it's cited, and know it came from you."

She should demur. He was offering her a coward's way out. But he was also right. It would hurt less, in the future, if the words were not her own.

* * * * *

A fusillade of knocks, and then Hu's office door burst open. The senior associate on the Lee team stood there, panting. He must have run down the two halls between his office and hers.

"The decision just came down!"

"Did we win?"

"I haven't read it all yet. But we didn't lose."

Hu turned from the door without wasting words, jabbing at her screen to reopen the Court's list of released opinions. Which Justice wrote the majority opinion, and how many others had joined it? Hmm. Not the best possible author. Six Justices in all. There would be some compromises.

We reverse the judgment of the Court of Appeals —" Hu whooped and punched the air — *"and reinstate in part the judgment of the district court."*

Methodical as usual, the author went through the reasons the Court hadn't thought it could justify ducking the case.

Plaintiffs' contract theories, as well as their constitutional claims, all rest on the foundation of the stored plaintiffs' possessing the rights of corporeal persons. Whether public policy allows a less than explicit, or for that matter an explicit, contractual waiver of fundamental constitutional rights depends initially on whether the contracting party possesses those rights.

Then came a lengthy passage that came almost word for word from Hu's brief, summing up how LiveAfter should be deemed a state actor for purposes of the case, and could thus be accused of violating constitutional rights. Hu blew out a gusty sigh of relief.

She had forgotten the presence of the associate; she jumped a little when he leaned toward her screen and spoke. "Look here!"

Ultimately, the consequences of holding that the stored are no longer citizens, and may be used as political puppets without the most explicit consent on their part, are too far-reaching and detrimental to be constitutionally tolerable.

"Nice," she whispered to herself. "Very nice."

She kept reading, mentally ticking off the points they had gained: penumbra of the First Amendment (less than fully satisfying, with its analytical squishiness); fundamental right of autonomous action (score!); waivers unenforceable on public policy grounds (well, even the appellate court had got *that* one right); freedom to advance one's beliefs is not limited to freedom of association for that goal (phew!) . . . .

Then she looked up and caught the associate's eye, her nose wrinkled in disgust. "Take a look at footnote 17."

We need not decide the extent to which the criminal justice system may use storage technology for the rehabilitation of convicted criminals or for the protection of society therefrom. . . .

The associate swore briefly. "I bet I know which Justices insisted on *that* language."

"No bet. Damn. If we'd gotten through to either one of that pair, we'd have had a majority without this crap."

"It's dicta, spare verbiage, not part of the actual ruling. The lower courts don't have to follow it, and the Court can back off from it."

"True. But half of the good stuff is probably dicta too, so let's not blow that trumpet too loudly."

What about the tort causes of action? There, toward the end: *The tort theories we leave to be determined according to state law, and remand for that purpose, with the caveat that the injunctive relief ordered by the trial court is affirmed notwithstanding the result of that process.*

Hu scrolled down to the other opinions. Concurring opinions first. "We're not the only ones pissed off about that footnote. Take a look here—"

If we are to reach beyond the issues actually presented in this case, it would be rather more to our credit if we were to do so in order to warn against any governmental attempts to ignore the fundamental rights we have today defended. I protest the implication that our constitutional values may be reconciled with the coercive reshaping of an individual's attitudes and personality on the flimsy excuse that said individual is currently in, or subject to being placed in, government custody.

Hu smiled ruefully. "Sure would have liked to see that last sentence in the majority opinion. We can both guess who vetoed it. . . . What's in the dissents?"

The associate glanced at the screen, probably to confirm his perfectly adequate memory. "One pushing the Scalia approach: if it ain't an enumerated right, it doesn't matter how obviously fundamental it is. The other two think the case should have been dismissed on the basis that cert was improvidently granted—that the matter can be resolved without any constitutional discussion or other federal question."

Hu hunched over and said in a stage whisper, "They might be right about that." She straightened up again. "We're lucky the current bench includes a few Justices who like to make history, even if they have to reach a bit."

The associate mimed locking his lips with a key and tucking it away. "I didn't call the clients. I figured you deserved that pleasure."

Hu, to her annoyance, found herself just a trifle dewy-eyed. "Thanks. I'll admit I'm looking forward to it."

CHAPTER 25

THEA once again confronted herself in the mirror. As far as she could tell, her appearance had not changed since she restored her blonde hair many months ago. In fact, she still bore the bronze glow of a suntan, despite having spent so much more time in meeting rooms than outdoors.

And her hair was perpetually clean. That wouldn't change, would it?

She sat down at her desk again, not bothering to dress, and once again called up the photos she had asked Max to send. Were there discrepancies she had missed? The number of faint freckles, the curve of the waist, the tilt of the nose?

And those were just the superficial questions.

Thea opened the document she had begun writing after Hu called with the news, and first winced and then chuckled at the somewhat pretentious title.

Credo

I believe in the pursuit of happiness and the acceptance of pleasure.

I believe in the right to be wrong, stubborn, short-sighted, paranoid, dispassionate, unreasonable, or any unwieldy combination of all these.

I believe in love, devotion, polyamory, altruism, self-protection, self-knowledge, self-delusion.

I believe in the ridiculous goodness and immense talent of my husband.

I believe in music as the deepest language and the most marvelous game.

I believe in human potential and the right of every person to pursue or to ignore their potential.

I believe in the right to fight and the right to surrender.

I believe that goodness and evil both exist. I believe in the complexity of identifying either, except when it's simple.

Thea closed the document and curled up in her chair, hugging herself. Then she pried herself out of the chair and went back to the mirror. She looked her reflection in the eye and spoke to it, a little louder than a whisper.

"I believe that at least some of what I wrote is true of the real me, whatever and whoever that is. Because why would they alter me in those directions?

"I believe that I'm not altogether sure.

"And I believe that I'm frightened."

* * * * *

Thea had big eyes to start with, but on the rare occasions when she let something scare her, they got absolutely enormous. Max had never seen them look bigger than they did right now.

"If they change me, change me back, whatever, will I even realize it? Will I know what changed?"

"I don't know, hon. Hu might be able to talk to someone who can answer that."

"What if they screw me up?"

At least he had an answer for that. "If *either* of us thinks there's anything wrong with how you end up—I mean, if you do, or if I do and you end up agreeing—

they can take you back to how you are now and figure out how to do a better job the next time they try."

"You know I'm closer to my mom now, in some ways. Now that we agree on politics. It's been sort of a silver lining to ending up here."

He could reassure her that her mother would love her, no matter what. But on the one hand, she knew it; and on the other, neither she nor Max could say with confidence that it was quite that uncomplicated.

Thea was blinking rapidly, and her lower lip trembled. "What if I want to stay the way I am? Is there anything wrong with me, really?"

The answer was easy. He only had to find the right way to say it. "We both know they made some changes in how you think. You're terrific now and you were terrific before. If you don't want to get rebooted, I will love you over the moon and back, regardless."

Thea leaned forward and kissed what must have been her screen. The sight of her lips, large and pressed toward him, gave him a sudden sexual pang that he tried to ignore. Then she sat back and gazed at him some more before finally saying, "I guess I should give Hu a call, and see if I have any choices."

It would be ironic as hell if she didn't.

* * * * *

Hu faked an incoming call, put Thea on hold, and tried to muster up some empathy. She should have foreseen this. As tough as Thea seemed, as bright as she undoubtedly was, as much as she had seemed to understand her role as named plaintiff in a landmark civil rights cause, it was another matter to sit back and let someone mess with her brain again, and this time knowing in advance. Hu would be frightened, too. Although she'd probably be more angry than frightened, angry that she'd been put in that position in the first place and left with such unpalatable choices.

Maybe Hu could find that anger in Thea and fan the flame. Hu and Thea were alike in that, most likely — in preferring anger to fear. And if Hu couldn't have a client triumphant in (partial) victory, she needed one angry at the damage done to her, not scared enough to accept it as a tolerable status quo.

* * * * *

For some technical reason, minimizing the loss of accrued memories required that those stored individuals who had been subjected to a series of alterations be restored by undoing one alteration at a time.

Which meant that the placid and passive man LiveAfter had created became Jim once again, a lively thespian and passionate social reformer.

And that was where things got sticky.

"I don't want to become that man again." Thea had never seen her friend really upset, let alone distraught. But he was pacing back and forth, clenching and unclenching his fists, looking wildly this way and that.

"What was so bad about . . . about that man? The man you used to be?" Thea looked at Jim's cooling cup of tea and wondered if it was worth replacing it with something hot. Maybe something with whiskey in it, now that LiveAfter was attempting to placate its customers with extra attention to such amenities.

"You mean that status-seeking, manipulative, self-centered *prick?*"

It would have helped if she had met him when he first arrived. She could guess that some of that assessment derived from the politics imposed on both of them, but it might not be entirely off base.

"I won't let them. Didn't your case give us back some autonomy? Can't I say no?"

"That's the trouble." She got up and put a hand on his arm, arresting his movement. "We *have* been altered. We're still under the influence of those changes. So the idea is that we aren't currently capable of making our own choices, because they may not be ours."

The muscles in his arm twitched beneath her hand. "They may have changed us for their own purposes. But we're *not* puppets. Those changes—we made them part of who we are. That can't be undone without . . ." He was trembling all over. "They made a new man of me, and now they're going to kill that man. But if I'm going to die, I want to die on my own terms. I don't want to turn into someone else, whether he's who I used to be or not." He turned and stared at her with haunted eyes. "Your lawyer, Hu, used to be my law partner. Maybe she could do something—help me. Maybe she can make them leave me alone." He paused and took a ragged breath. "Or if they won't leave me alone, maybe she can win me the right to die."

Thea let go and stepped back, hands to her mouth.

"I had a feeling this would happen," Hu told Thea, her face impassive. Thea suspected that outside her view, Hu might be clenching her fists.

"I certainly should have seen it coming, given my own concerns. But hindsight notwithstanding, is there anything you can do?"

"I'm not going to represent him in some right-to-die quest." Hu's jaw tightened for a moment, then relaxed. "Ironically enough, at least from Jim's point of view, the availability of storage technology has transformed the right-to-die movement. Most of those involved view the storage option as strengthening their case for physical termination at will."

Thea sighed. "Do you have any other suggestions?"

Hu finally smiled a bit. "Actually, I do. Please ask Jim to give me a call."

*****

It was disorienting for Hu to see her old colleague transformed into another in a long series of angry, frustrated, fearful clients. At least this time she could make a good guess at what would calm him down: letting him talk.

When he had more or less run down, at least for a moment, she nodded and said, "Thank you, Jim. And I'm happy to call you Jim, by the way."

Her statement seemed to reduce the tension in his jaw and shoulders, but only for a moment. Then he bared his teeth and said, in a tone just short of a snarl, "Why is that? My old self was your buddy. Aren't you being disloyal to him?"

Hu twitched an eyebrow. "As a matter of fact, while your earlier incarnation and I worked well together, I won't claim I was especially fond of him."

Jim stared at her, then let out a short bark of a laugh. "All right, then. I'll try to behave myself from this point on. What can you do for me, if anything?"

"Probably not what you're hoping I can do." She explained to him what she had already told Thea. From his reaction, it did not appear that Thea had passed the information on, for which Hu could hardly blame her. Jim shuddered and drew his arms in and his shoulders down, as if barely resisting the urge to curl into fetal position. But he said nothing, and the moment stretched on, moving from uncomfortable to agonizing.

"Jim?"

Hu's screen went blank. She looked at it and let loose with one of her grandfather's Chinese curses, then jabbed at Thea's contact information with slightly shaking fingers.

"Thea? Please find Jim, right away. I'm afraid he's in bad shape. Tell him he didn't let me finish."

* * * * *

Jim wasn't in his quarters. Nor was he jogging along any familiar path; nor in the main dining hall or any of the new and more varied eateries.

If Thea went to LiveAfter for help, they would find him in an instant. But Jim would never forgive her for directing the company's spotlight toward his anguish.

With all the illicit software available to the stored from unscrupulous sources, might there be one that erased the code of the suicidal?

Thea found a bench and sat down to refocus her thinking. Where could Jim go to connect with those parts of himself he least wanted to lose?

Thea pushed open the door to the room in which their political discussion group had most often met. The lights were off, and she did not move to turn them on. Instead, she moved through the door as quietly as she could and searched the shadows. The bulky shape at other end of the room, slumped in a chair, resting on the table, did not move as she approached.

Thea approached slowly. Jim looked up at her as she drew near, his face showing little beyond utter fatigue. She put a hand on his arm. "Hu called me. Please talk to her again. She has an idea that might be more practical than trying to sue."

*****

This time, Hu's screen showed Jim and Thea together. Close together. Hu brushed aside curiosity about how Max would have felt to see them so.

"Jim, I'm sorry I didn't manage to indicate, before you ended our last conversation, that I have an idea that may be worth trying. It doesn't involve the judicial system, but it would call upon your own legal skills."

Jim looked up toward her a moment before returning his gaze to something off-screen. "That doesn't make a lot of sense."

Hu refrained from showing her annoyance. "Just listen. Have you ever managed to persuade an intelligent, arrogant opponent to see things your client's way? In litigation, in negotiation, in arguing to a judge or judicial panel?"

"Of course I have. You know that." The tone reminded her more than Jim might realize of the man whose reappearance he was struggling to prevent.

"And would you agree that I've just described you, at least the way you used to be?"

Jim jolted upright and peered at her. Then, to her substantial relief, he actually smiled. She smiled back. "I assume you can see where I'm going with this."

"You want me to convince myself that I know better

than—than he does. That my current politics and world view are worth adopting?"

"Or at the very least, considering and taking seriously. Yes."

Jim's smile twisted in a sardonic direction. "There are some obvious logistical obstacles to that approach."

"Granted. But you can record a presentation. I think I can talk them into putting you far enough back in the, ah, reboot line that you'll have plenty of time to prepare."

"I'll need more than time." Thea looked over at him, her forehead furrowed. He patted her hand and looked back at Hu. "I want you to moot the presentation with me. Poke holes in my arguments, throw at me all the objections that my prior self will end up raising, so I can preempt them." He closed his eyes for a moment, then went on with obvious effort. "After all, I'll only have the one shot. By the time he listens to my pitch, if he ever does, I'll be gone. Erased."

Hu hesitated. "I can't promise this, but I just might be able to apply some behind-the-scenes persuasion to ensure that a backup of your current files remains."

Jim stared at her. "What, you think that son of a bitch is going to step aside and let me come back? Not a chance."

Hu gave a minimal version of a shrug. "Perhaps not. But a backup would leave all options open, even the unlikely ones."

* * * * *

The call ended, Jim closed his eyes and sagged back in his chair. A tear ran down his cheek, and then another. Thea leaned over and wiped them with her forefinger.

His mouth twitched in a half-smile. "Thanks. You know, I'll bet that bastard wouldn't let himself cry in front of a lady."

Thea leaned against him and laid her head on his shoulder. "Silly of him." She paused, then said softly, "I'm going to make a point of explaining to him just how much I like the Jim I've come to know. And why."

Jim's smile grew wider, almost to a grin. "You know, that might get me further than any persuasion I leave behind."

Max had his what-just-hit-me look. "So he's going to make a recording and tell, what, tell his past self—"

Thea grimaced. "His past and future self, the way things are now."

Max nodded, his face tense with concentration. "He's going to tell his original self all about what he believes now, and why. Except that isn't why, is it? The 'why' was someone else's idea."

"Granted. But he has plenty of reasons he considers persuasive. He's hoping his former self will at least reconsider the issues." She laughed a little. "The Jim I know is quite self-confident, and proud of his intellect. I'd bet, and I guess he's betting, that that's his basic nature. In which case Jim will have a better chance of persuading his original self than anyone else would."

Max ran a finger along the stubble on his chin. "I know you and Hu were talking him off the ledge, pretty much—giving him some hope. But do you think there's much chance of it actually working?"

Thea poured herself some of the Irish cream liqueur that Jim, or rather a watered-down and diluted version of Jim, had given her. "It might. I've been thinking about this whole 'alteration' business. I know it actually happened. But I'm wondering whether it's a lot more likely to work, to 'take,' if the change builds on something that's already there waiting. When they made me ready to give up — well, part of me was feeling worn down, fighting pessimism. That's what they had to work with. And on the other hand, all that support for the planned communities, that was building on my optimistic side, my wish for pretty-sounding fairy tale solutions. Maybe it's a little like hypnosis — not so much that some people can resist it, as that there's a limit to how much you can change someone's mind."

"I'd like to think so." Max tried for a smile, but did not appear convinced. And of course, she might be whistling past the graveyard — to use an oddly appropriate idiom — and hiding from the knowledge of how completely she had been a puppet.

Then Max got that far-away look that usually meant music was unrolling in his head. She prepared to sit quiet while the composition came together. But he surprised her by speaking. "If this does work, if your friend can change how he used to think . . . Maybe people, at least stored people, can do something like that more often, on purpose. Hire someone to give them a temporary inside look at new ideas, new ways of seeing the world. And then they can report back to themselves, you might say. It could be a really good way to understand the other guy's point of view."

Thea sat back for a moment and let the idea sink in. Then she shook her head, laughing a little. "A way to bridge differences, and help people understand each other. But one they can only use when it's too late to do much with it. Our leaders can't use it to avoid conflict. It'll just be us second-guessers watching from the sidelines."

Max thrust his chin out, stubborn style. "Don't sell yourselves short! You can still talk to—to the rest of us. And you can vote."

Thea sighed. "Yes, we can vote. We always could."

* * * * *

Dane's mother had made few changes in her appearance, when given that option; but her short white hair was thick enough, now, to hold a style, and the print blouse tucked into her usual light brown skirt had traces of yellow.

Dane clasped his hands together at the base of his screen. His mother held hers in a similar posture. It was almost as if they could touch.

"Ma, I just wanted to tell you about some things that might be changing soon. That group you're in, the one that tries to make sure everybody votes, and studies the candidates, and so on—well, you may find that people are getting less interested."

His mother's eyes went wide. "Did we do something wrong? Have people been complaining?" She slumped a bit. "Will I have to stop seeing my new friends?"

"No, no!" Why had he thought it worth trying to explain? "Never mind, ma. It's just some technical stuff. I shouldn't have bothered you about it." Once she changed again, she could see those friends or not, as she and they wished. He could only hope their wishes and hers would align.

"Well, if you say so. But you know you can always tell me about things. I like hearing you talk, even if it goes over my head." She unclasped her hands and reached up to pat the screen. He kissed his fingertips and touched the screen where her palm appeared to rest. Then he faked a yawn. "I'd better get some rest. I'll call you tomorrow. Love you."

"And I love you, darling. Sweet dreams." She smiled at him as he made her disappear.

He swiveled his chair toward the bed where Esther lay sleeping or pretending to sleep. Then he grabbed the bottle of scotch, looked at the empty glass on his desk, and took a long drink straight from the bottle.

* * * * *

The board member, in his agitation, spoke so fast that his sibilants hissed. "So they didn't like being 'altered'? Fine! They can all have their wrinkles back, and their arthritis, and their cellulite. And Ms. Lee can have those lovely tics of hers."

LiveAfter's COO nodded in what he hoped was neither an encouraging nor an offensive manner. It would take a while for the caller to wind down, and he could hardly spare the time, but it would take more time to engage in debate on the subject.

Of course the company would not, as it struggled to overcome massive bad publicity, make things worse by upsetting its clients and their loved ones in such a way. Indeed, the board as a whole seemed likely to approve not only more modification options in-house, but access to third party vendors as well.

Would the budget stretch to vetting such outside offerings? Well, it might. And as a failsafe, the contractual language would be tweaked to protect the company, as much as possible, for any liability for unexpected outcomes.

* * * * *

Thea was spending a fair amount of time, since her restoration, lying in the sun and doing nothing in particular. She had the admittedly fanciful notion that her mind needed down time to reintegrate after all the meddling and rewriting to which it had been subjected.

She might have been dozing before a change in the light reaching her and the soft sound of footsteps roused her. She opened her eyes and looked up to see a man with long white hair and expressive features, a man she knew: the famous flutist who had been one of her (she shuddered a little) fellow Utopians. The flutist with whom she had not, somehow, gotten around to playing duets. He was carrying a long leather case.

She pulled the top of the chaise lounge into an upright position and waved at a nearby chair. "Welcome to my patch of sun! Won't you join me?"

He sat down, perching a little awkwardly toward the front of the chair, setting the case on the ground. "I'm glad I found you. I've been looking out for you for days." He straightened up and spoke more strongly. "I wanted to thank you for everything you've done."

Thea gazed at him, nonplussed. During the long months of litigation, she had from time to time cheered herself by imagining such declarations. She had never carried the fantasy forward and thought about what to say in response.

Finally she just said, "I'm glad you feel that way. And I'm glad it worked out."

He picked up the case and laid it gently on his lap. "I don't want to disturb you, but if by any chance you'd be interested, we're long overdue to play some music together."

Thea found herself crying. Shaking her head and wiping her eyes, she stammered, "I'm sorry. I don't know where that came from."

He reached over and patted her hand, then pulled back and let her collect herself. When she could manage it, she smiled at him. "I'd love to. I'll be right back!"

She left him sitting in the sun, waiting patiently, and ran bounding across the grass to fetch her flute.

CHAPTER 26

(two months later)

HU GULPED her first, blessed cup of coffee and glanced through the latest software add-ons for LiveAfter clients. LiveAfter's in-house options were few and unambitious: confidence boosters, shortcuts to meditative states, shortcuts to REM sleep, shortcuts to orgasm. Outside vendors offered much more: gender swaps; religious experiences, up to and including direct contact with what would feel like The Divine; movement in either direction along the spectrum from selfishness to altruism, or from cynicism to idealism; a reproduction of the manic end of bipolar syndrome; even full-blown sociopathy, though only (so far) for three minutes at a time. Hu would have bet money that LiveAfter would be seeking an injunction against that last one, if no others.

At least Thea's new business, inspecting the various products and rating their validity and safety, would be booming.

Enough stalling! Hu minimized the browser and called up her task list for the morning. First up: meet with the lawyer to whom she had referred Dane's and Esther's whistle-blower suit. Next, look over her testimony for two upcoming Congressional committee hearings. The one coming up sooner involved a bill to make potential stored people jump through various good-character hoops. Not surprising: virtual immortality was just too hard to swallow if all you had to do was buy your way in. Of course, once government had its say in who attained that status, the money could be spread around in other directions. . . .

Then there was the Criminal Division's eager follow-up to the *Lee* footnote. Hu put down her coffee, wishing she had drunk it more slowly. Every time she thought about the idea of reviving the death penalty as a "therapeutic option," her stomach turned over. She should probably rejigger her schedule to meet with the media consultant first: this notion needed a broad-based attack.

As she scrolled through her contacts, she noted Thea's name. Neither Thea nor Max had stayed in touch. Clients rarely did, even after the big life-changing cases. She liked the couple and found Thea especially interesting; but she would let them move on.

Dane and Esther, on the other hand, did pop up from time to time. It helped that they were local and accessible. And perhaps they liked having an appreciative audience for their squabbles. They might be lovers, but they argued more like siblings.

When she got through with the media consultant, she might just invite them to lunch.

* * * * *

Thea's new track finished playing, and Max applauded until his hands hurt. "Beautiful, baby! That'll work perfectly with what I had!"

He had still not settled in his mind whether Thea's style retained some foreign flavor, and if so, how he felt about the fact. But subjective qualms aside, her compositions just got better and better.

He snuck a glance at the time. Of course Thea caught him at it. "Got someplace to be?"

"I am supposed to get to the beach soon." Had he forgotten to tell her? "It's my first surfing competition. Baby league, of course."

Now it was Thea's turn to clap. "Congratulations, sweetie!"

He laughed. "You can save that for the day I actually win something."

Thea suddenly dropped her smile. "Please be careful, lover. I don't want to see you here for a long time yet. As much as I miss you."

Well, he felt the same way. Thea kept him up to date on the digital environment, and apparently, it still more or less sucked. She was brushing up on her coding skills, so she could join a team of the stored who were pushing to improve things.

If he could change places with Thea and give her the real sun, the real ocean, would he do it? He could imagine himself as deciding either way, the hero or the coward, but there wasn't much point. He couldn't give her back the world. So he would try to appreciate it for the both of them, as long as he had that chance.

Thea seemed to be following his thoughts, because she chimed in, "And besides, your neighbor and surfing coach likes your company."

Max tried not to wince. Thea could swear up and down that she wasn't jealous, and that she hoped for a day far in the future when they could have a hot and heavy three-way—but Max hadn't quite gotten used to sleeping with someone else. As great as it could be sometimes.

Thea's arch expression softened. "I shouldn't tease you. It's okay. You, me, her, you and me, her and you. All of it."

"Are you okay? Really?"

She stood up and gestured grandly from her head to her toes and back again. "I'm still here! I exist, when I could have been nothing but compost by now. That's okay, in my book. That's a win."

* * * * *

Thea waved goodbye to Max, closed the call window, and then looked through the still shots she had taken during their chat. She hoped he hadn't noticed her habit of capturing them. It might make him self-conscious, or twitchy, or sad, or all three.

She'd also been subtle about getting him to send her a picture with his neighbor in it. She wanted to picture the two of them together, to get used to the idea.

He hadn't asked her about any new partners she might have. Whatever he might assume, he didn't seem to have put the available clues together: he never asked about Jim. Who had ended up keeping that name, as well as some of the more attractive personal traits, though not too many of the beliefs, that had come with it.

As part of his determination to stay open to new ideas, Jim had asked Thea to help him play with his appearance. And Thea had managed to resist the somewhat sick temptation to make him over just a little in Max's image.

But there had been plenty of sound reasons to make him hot. And when they spent an hour together, each suppressing their overactive intellects, she could forget almost everything else. Even Max, most of the time.

But never for long.

And that was fine. Because Thea intended to remain Thea, come what may. And Thea loved Max.

The End

Acknowledgments

My wonderful beta readers played an especially important part, this time around, in helping the book in my head make its way to the page. My heartfelt thanks to (in alphabetical order): Jill-Elizabeth Arent, Paul Hager, Steven Karel, Tiya Marshall, S. L. Sabovitch, and Rich Weyand. Thanks, also, to my cousin-in-law Steve Bernstein, composer, for answering my questions about musical instruments and about scoring films.

About the Author

Karen A. Wyle was born a Connecticut Yankee, but eventually settled in Bloomington, Indiana, home of Indiana University. She now considers herself a Hoosier. She and her husband have two wildly creative daughters and a sweet though neurotic dog.

Wyle is an appellate attorney, photographer, and political junkie. Her voice is the product of almost five decades of reading both literary and genre fiction. It is no doubt also influenced, although she hopes not fatally tainted, by her years of law practice. Her personal history has led her to focus on often-intertwined themes of family, communication, personal identity, the impossibility of controlling events, and the persistence of unfinished business.

Connect with Karen A. Wyle Online

Learn more about Karen A. Wyle by looking her up on:
Her author website, http://www.KarenAWyle.net
Twitter (handle @WordsmithWyle)
Facebook (http://www.facebook.com/KarenAWyle)
Goodreads (https://www.goodreads.com/kawyle)
or her blog, Looking Around, at
http://looking-around.blogspot.com/

You can sign up for email alerts about
new book releases and (at your
option) other events at
http://kawyle.wufoo.com/forms/z7x3k7/

Like the book? Please tell readers!
Online book reviews are enormously helpful --
and old-fashioned word of mouth is terrific as well!

www.ingramcontent.com/pod-product-compliance
Lightning Source LLC
Chambersburg PA
CBHW060936120726
47910CB00002B/355